MeMORABLe

MEMORABLE

Written by
Laurisa White Reyes

Santa Clarita, CA

Skyrocket Press
28020 Newbird Drive
Santa Clarita, CA 91350
www.SkyrocketPress.com

Cover design by Blue Water Books
Interior design by Laurisa Reyes

ISBN: 978-1-947394-80-3

ALSO BY LAURISA WHITE REYES

For my mother
Cynthia Ball White

RYAN

ONE

THREE PILLS.

Three stupid little pills, and now my entire future is screwed.

"We have a no-tolerance policy here at Middleton," says Commander Norton, tapping the eraser end of a pencil against his desk. "You knew that coming in, Ryan. You signed the agreement like everyone else, didn't you?"

"Yes," I mumble.

"Speak up, son."

Norton is big. Like weight-lifter big. I keep my eyes down because I don't want to look at him, and I sure as hell don't want him looking at me. Still, I do my best to say something that sounds compliant.

"Yes, sir!"

I've never been in Norton's office before. It's smaller than I expected, with a wooden desk and floor-to-ceiling shelves filled with books that look like they've never been read. Only troublemakers end up in here, losers who don't give a damn how much money their parents shell out for private school tuition.

I am *not* one of those. At least I wasn't before today.

Norton claims he won't bring in the cops if I answer some questions "in light of the situation." I see the *situation* through the office window—paramedics wheeling Cadet Jenn Bonner out on a gurney, an oxygen mask strapped to her face.

My buzz is starting to wear off, but the room wobbles, and is the heat cranked up in here?

The window blinds rattle as the office door opens and someone else enters the room. I hear the labored limp of my dad's prosthetic leg. Of course *he'd* come instead of Mom. I slump lower in my chair. Dad shoots me a hard look before fixing his gaze on Norton, who acts like he's consoling a funeral-goer instead of a concerned parent.

"Thanks for coming, Major Rojas." Norton stands. They salute, then shake hands. "Sorry I had to call you under these circumstances."

He offers Dad a chair. Dad lowers himself into it and crosses his arms. Dad is big too, with muscles sculpted from sixteen years in the Marines. Despite losing his left leg in Afghanistan, he still works out every day.

"What happened?" Dad asks.

Commander Norton leans back in his chair, that pencil of his still tapping away. "Go ahead, cadet."

Me? He wants *me* to tell him? I'm not afraid of my dad, but he's always trusted me. I've never given him a reason not to. How do I tell him things have changed? That I'm not the perfect son he thinks I am—that I should be?

"I, uh, I took some pills. A girl took some, too."

What else am I supposed to say? With quarter-terms coming up, I needed to get my mind off the stress. So, I took half a bar. A bunch of us did. Wasn't the first time. But Jenn took a full one and blacked out in chemistry class, hit her head on a desk on the way down.

Part of me wants to tell Dad everything, about the pressure I've been under trying to keep up at school, about not wanting to let him and Mom down. But another part of me wants to deny all of it, to say what happened to Jenn was a mistake and that I had nothing to do with it.

I can't bring myself to do either.

Norton drops a plastic baggie with a few bars of Xanax onto the table. An hour ago, that baggie was in my pocket.

"Alprazolam. Anxiety meds," says Norton. "Students take them for their sedative effects. Xanax is one of the most abused drugs on high school campuses because it's so easy to acquire. They get them from friends or even parents who have prescriptions."

Dad fingers the tablets through the plastic. His eyes narrow, peering into mine. I'm having a hard time keeping my eyes open, but I force myself to meet his gaze.

"We don't have these at home," he says. "Where did you get them?"

"I bought them," I answer, and that much is true, though not from any store. But I can't say that with Dad's eyes drilling a hole through me. He's probably thinking what a disappointment I am, that's he's literally given everything to make things good for me—and this is how I repay him. I wish I could melt into the floor and disappear.

"How long has this been going on, Ryan?" Dad asks.

How long has *what* been going on? Popping pills at school? Off and on for a couple weeks. But the booze and the weed? Since Dad came home in pieces almost two years ago.

It's not like I do it every day, but sometimes I just need to escape. Maybe I should just get this over with, confess everything. Tell Norton to call in the cops and slam on the cuffs. That's what someone brave would do, someone like my dad. But I'm not like my dad. I'm a coward.

I shrug limply. "I dunno."

Norton rests his elbows on the desk. The fabric of his uniform rustles stiffly. "This is very serious," he says. "A cadet is on her way to the hospital with a head injury, though that's not our biggest concern right now." He pauses to rub his hand across his mouth. "You do realize that mixing Xanax and other drugs can potentially cause brain damage or even death, and we don't know what other substances the girl took."

"Christ," Dad mutters.

Death? No—no, I'm okay. I'm okay. At least I didn't drink today. I'm already straightening up, though it still feels hot as hell in here. But Jenn. Jenn can't die—can she? I think of her crumpled on the classroom floor, the gash on her forehead leaking blood onto the carpet.

God, I'm going to be sick.

"You've been a good student here, Ryan," continues Norton. "You've maintained a 4.0 since freshman year, and I hear the music department is still trying to convince you to come back."

I wince. Music is the last thing I want to hear about right now.

"In any case, I hate to see something like what's happened today damage your chances of getting into Kings Point. That is where you're planning to apply next year, isn't it?"

Kings Point, the U.S. Merchant Marine Academy, Dad's alma mater. My parents' dream is for me to follow in his footsteps.

"The fact is," continues Norton, "one of your fellow cadets claims he saw you give the girl those pills."

I look up sharply. "What?"

Norton picks up his pencil and starts tapping his desk again. "Someone's been bringing prescription meds to school and selling them."

It takes me a second to realize what he's saying. He thinks *I'm* behind all this.

"I never sold anything to Jenn or anyone else," I tell him. "I swear it."

"Then who did?"

That's when it hits me. Why I'm really in Commander Norton's office. He doesn't believe I'm responsible, but I know who is.

A sudden shriek from outside makes me jump. I look out the office window and see the ambulance speeding away—with Jenn Bonner inside. Even when I can't see it anymore, I still hear the fading siren, like a bad dream that sticks with you long after waking up.

The only way out of this mess is to snitch on my friends. If I give Norton what he wants, I won't have any friends at all. Ryan the Rat. That's who I'll be. But if I say nothing, and Jenn ends up dead...

I'll lie, tell Norton I don't know where Jenn got the stuff and that I got mine from her. Her word against mine, right? But this is Jenn Bonner—straight 'A', nice to everyone Jenn. She deserves for me to tell the truth, that she's a good kid who just veered off course a little. It's not like we're close or anything, but from what I hear, she's got a good shot at getting into West Point. Now she's on her way to the hospital—and she might not make it home again. I just can't betray her like that, but no way am I taking the fall for this. Like I said, I'm a coward.

"We both got our stuff from Chris Segarra," I say, clutching at the ache in my stomach. "And he's been dealing a lot more than Xanax." Unlike Jenn, Chris isn't the ace student, but we used to be tight a couple years back. After this, he'll be expelled for sure, maybe worse.

Better him than me.

I dare a glance at Dad. His jaw is clenched tight.

"Thank you, Ryan," says Commander Norton.

I stand on shaky legs and wipe my sweaty hands down the front of my pants. "Sure," I say, trying to sound like this was no big deal. "Can I go now? I've missed most of American History, and it's last period."

Norton points his pencil toward my chair. I sit again.

"As I was reminding Ryan before you came in," Norton says to Dad, "our school has a zero-tolerance policy for drugs of any kind on campus. Middleton will not press charges against Ryan since he's been cooperative. However, consequences *are* in order. At this point, Mr. Rojas, you have two options. Either voluntarily withdraw Ryan from the school, or we can expel him."

"Wait. What?"

Did I just hear what I think I heard?

Norton slides a blank withdrawal form across his desk. Then he hands my dad a pen. This can't be happening.

"But I gave you Chris's name."

"Yes, you did," says Norton, smoothing down the front of his uniform. "And I appreciate the courage it took for you to do that. But school policy is firm on this. You've left us no choice, I'm afraid."

"But you can't expel me! I'm one of your best students!"

"I understand what you're saying, but our policy—"

"Screw the policy!"

"Ryan!" Dad's voice shuts me up. I know I've been shouting, but no one's listening to me. I try to pull myself together, to talk calmly.

"This is crazy. I can't leave here. Where else would I go?"

"I'm sure Kennedy High would be happy to take you," says Norton with a placating grin.

"You don't understand," I try again. "I want—I *need* to stay at Middleton. My mom—" I avoid Dad's eyes, ashamed I'm bringing this up. "My mom works really hard to keep me here."

And if you kick me out, my chances of going to Kings Point are shot.

I can't bear to look at Dad, but I have to keep going. "I know I screwed up." I'm begging now, but I don't care.

"I'm sorry. I'll do anything to fix this—anything. I'll do KP duty for a year."

"Ryan—" Norton sighs like he's embarrassed for me.

"I'll clean the bathrooms. Pick up trash!"

"Cadet Rojas—"

"Just please. Please don't expel me."

Silence drops into the room like a delayed-action bomb. Norton leans back in his chair, tents his fingers, and stares at the clock on the wall. He sits like that for a full minute before he finally nods, like he's come to a decision.

"There is one possible alternative." He studies me as if wondering whether what he's about to say is really worth it. Waiting for his final verdict about kills me.

Finally, he opens his file drawer and pulls out another form. "Let's discuss independent study."

PENNY

TWO

LEA PACHERO SLAMS into me like a wrecking ball, hurling me onto the school basketball court. When I hit, pain vibrates through my entire skeleton. That is definitely going to leave a bruise.

"What're you doing, Tate? This's no time for a nap!" Coach Anderson gives her whistle a long, shrill blow. "Get up! This isn't kindy-garden!"

A hand appears in front of my face. I take it, and Tali Akuila yanks me to my feet.

"Thanks," I tell her, rubbing my throbbing shoulder, which took the brunt of my fall. Tali pats my back and jogs off to take her position under the basket.

First-generation Tongan-American, Tali's the tallest girl on the team and the best guard we have, hands down. She's also the closest thing I've got to a friend at Kennedy High.

The whistle blows again. Tali passes me the ball, and I dribble two, three steps toward the basket, raise my hands to shoot, and *wham*! Pachero jabs an elbow into my ribs. My body jerks sideways from the sudden jolt of pain, but not before the ball explodes from my fingertips. And just as it swishes through the net, I crash to the floor—again.

"Foul!" shouts Coach. "*This* time."

In all fairness, I should be given a free throw, but the buzzer on the wire-caged wall clock releases an ear-splitting wail, signaling the end of the period.

"Showers!" shouts Coach. My teammates leap over and dart around me. I pull my knees up and rest my forehead against them, trying to catch my breath.

"You really should ice that, Penny." Tali extends her hand again, but I wave it away.

"Thanks, I've got it." I get to my feet, grimacing from the pain.

"You'll feel better by Saturday," Tali says.

"I hope so," I reply, brushing dust from my shorts. "I plan to cream Eldridge High. But looks like I have to battle my own team first."

Tali and I watch as the last few girls disappear into the locker room. We take our time following. Neither of us relishes socializing with the others, especially in our underwear.

"Don't let Pachero and her gaggle of primpy-haired snobs get to you," says Tali.

"I wouldn't if she'd stop acting like we're playing football. I swear the next time she touches me, I'm going for the throat."

By the time we reach the lockers, most of the girls have dressed and headed out. A few are just finishing their showers. I change out of my clothes and step into a stall, letting the spray of hot water flow across my bare scalp.

Tali, opting to shower at home, changes into her jeans and T-shirt. "Coach must've seen something in you to put you on the court with a bunch of juniors and seniors whose heads are stuck up their butts."

Lea, wrapped in a white towel, darts a sour glance in our direction. I stifle a laugh when Tali crosses her eyes at her.

"What about you?" I ask Tali.

"What about me?"

"You're a senior. How do you like having a fifteen-year-old on your team?"

Tali snaps her locker shut. "Anyone who can make a basket from behind the division line—with three guards on her—a player like that deserves some respect, don't you think? Plus, if it weren't for your help, I'd completely bomb Shaw's Spanish class. So, you could say I owe you."

"Great," I reply. "So, you're my ally out of obligation."

Tali laughs. "I'd call it inspiration."

"Well, then, my inspired friend, hand me my shower gel, will you?"

Tali grabs a travel-sized bottle from my backpack and tosses it to me. I catch it and plop some of the pink gel into my palm.

"What is *this*?" Tali asks.

"What's what?"

"This!" She steps closer to the showers and waves a white letter-sized envelope in front of my face. "It fell out of your bag. Oh, crap! It's from IMG!"

I finish rinsing, turn off the water, and grab my towel. "Don't read that."

"Why not? It's already open."

IMG Academy is a private school in Florida for high school athletes. While I dry off and slip into my clothes, Tali scans the letter. I don't mind. She already knows I've dreamed of going there since I was a kid.

When she's done, she gawks at me. "They're offering you a scholarship!"

"Yeah, so?"

"Are you taking it?"

Am I taking the scholarship?

I want to—with every cell in my goddamn body. I was the brightest star on my middle school team. I had to be. If I was going to stand out because I was bald, then I was going to stand out on the court too. Once I got to Kennedy, I worked my butt off on JV and have had to work even harder since I was recruited to Varsity as a sophomore. I've waited years to get into the best sports school in the nation, but now that my chance is here...

"I don't know, actually."

Tali huffs. "You don't *know*? If you'd taken your dad up on his offer to pay your way, you'd already be there by now instead of this crappy place."

"I don't want my dad's money. Not after what he did to my family."

"I get it," she says, holding up the letter. "But now you don't *need* him."

"I know, but—"

"But what?"

I take back my letter, smoothing out the wrinkles against my thigh. Then I fold it in thirds and slide it into its envelope.

"God," says Tali as I zip it into my backpack. "Is this about Brett?"

I cut Tali a warning look. A few of the girls are still in the locker room, and IMG—and my brother—are none of their business.

Tali lowers her voice. "You are *not* passing on the opportunity of a lifetime because of your crazy older brother."

"He's not crazy. And this isn't about Brett. It's about me. I don't want to go, that's all there is to it."

Tali gives me her *yeah right* smirk. She knows me better than I give her credit for. The truth is Brett's exactly why I'm turning down IMG, but how can I tell her that? I can hardly admit it to myself.

"What does your mom think?"

I sit on the wood bench and tug on my socks. "My bus is leaving in ten minutes, Tali, and aren't you meeting Connor or something?"

"You haven't told her, have you?"

"Not exactly."

"Penny! Why the hell not?"

I pull on my Vans and tie the shredded laces, but I'm tired of Tali's questions, the same ones I've been asking myself all day. "Because if I do," I finally say, "I'll be heading to Florida next semester."

"And that's a bad thing?"

The final bell rings. Tali shrugs on her backpack and heads for the door. "I don't get you, girl. If some posh school offered me a $70,000 scholarship, I'd be outta here faster than you could say bon voyage. Listen, I gotta run, but we're gonna talk about this later. You hear me?"

"Yeah, sure," I call after her, though I have no intention of talking about IMG again with her, or with anyone.

My mind must be in another world because I don't even notice Lea sneaking up on me until the Sharpie makes contact with my scalp. She barely touches me before I spin around and smack her upside the head with my backpack.

Lea stumbles back, stunned by the blow. Unluckily for me, that's just when Coach Anderson walks in. I half expect her to blow her whistle and call "Foul!" Instead, she hollers, "What are you two still doing in here?"

Lea dabs at her split lip. Guess my water bottle in the side pocket got her.

"She hit me, Coach. Didn't you see it?"

"Don't you have somewhere to be, Pachero?" asks Coach.

When Lea doesn't respond, Coach points a rigid finger at the door. Lea grimaces at me as she caps her pen and slinks out of the locker room. Coach grabs a damp towel from the hamper and tosses it to me. "Get a move on, Tate," she says, then gathers up the rest of the dirty towels and walks out.

I make a beeline to the sink and pump some suds on the corner of the towel. I try to scrub off the deformed squiggle behind my left ear, but no matter how much soap I use, the black smudge still remains to remind me how much I hate Lea's guts.

I'm still thinking about how to get even when I climb onto the city bus to head home. In fact, the more I think about how Pachero and some of the other girls have been dissing me on and off the court, the madder I get. By the time Brett boards, I'm fuming. Then, as if things couldn't get crappier, he sits four rows behind me without even acknowledging my presence. Just great. I've had enough of this garbage today. I am *not* putting up with any more.

After the bus lurches forward, belching black exhaust out its back end, I turn in my seat to glare at Brett. He avoids me for a few minutes, but he can't ignore me forever. Finally, he looks up, his dark hair falling across his eyes.

"What?" he asks, half-shouting.

I don't care that there are a bunch of strangers sitting between us. I just peer between their heads.

"You're in a mood," I reply, "and you're taking it out on me. That's what."

An old woman with blue-tinted hair squirms in her seat. She leans to the side, giving me a clearer view of my brother.

"What's going on, Brett?"

"None of your business," he says, turning to the window, but he's not getting off that easy. I stand and step over the person sitting beside me, a middle-aged man in a threadbare suit. "Excuse me," I say, nearly stumbling over his briefcase. I reach the aisle and make my way to Brett's seat, where I plop down beside him. He doesn't scoot over.

"Tell me," I say, trying to sound empathetic. Though I'm definitely not feeling it. Not today.

Brett glances at me, but only briefly. "Leave me alone."

"You know, I've had a pretty fart-filled day so far. Thanks to that hag Lea Pachero, I kissed the court not once, but twice. And then the wench decided to tag my head. I'm not in the mood to take any more crap from anyone, especially you."

Brett doesn't say anything, so I plow ahead, his silence frustrating me even more. "Did I do something wrong? Drink your last Coke? Mess up your Spotify password?"

That's when I notice Brett fingering his class ring, the ring he gave his girlfriend to wear.

"Is this about Celine? Did you two break up?"

Brett crushes the ring into his fist. "Shut up, Penny."

Damn it. So they did split, though I can't imagine why. They've been together forever. I thought maybe they'd even get married after graduation. No wonder he's pissed.

This is bound to get bad. My guts are already in knots just thinking about the rages and despair to come. But maybe I can head things off. Get him to talk. Calm him down.

"What happened?" I ask more sincerely this time.

Brett grips the ring so tight his knuckles are white. He squints out the window, staring hard. I'm losing him, but I've got to try to bring him back, get his mind off Celine.

I turn the side of my head toward him. "Look," I say, stabbing a finger at the mark behind my ear. "Somebody told me they saw the Blessed Virgin in it. Maybe I can sell tickets."

Nothing.

"Brett?" I touch his shoulder, but he shakes me off.

"I said shut the hell up!" he shouts.

By now half the people on the bus are staring at us. I've pushed him too far.

The bus slows down, grinding to a halt at our intersection near the park. When the doors slap open, Brett doesn't even wait for me to get out of my seat before climbing over me and sprinting off the bus. I hurry after him, but by the time my feet hit the sidewalk, he's already gone.

RYAN

THREE

DAD THINKS IT'S best not to call Mom during work with the news about school. I'm not sure telling her in person will be any better. Either way, I'm doomed.

After we leave Middleton, Dad drives across town to pick up my little brother Justin from school. When we pull up, he's sitting on a concrete planter pinching leaves off a bush. He leaps up when he sees us and pulls open the van's side door.

"Why'd you pick up Ryan first?" Justin asks, settling into the backseat. He's a twerp—a shorter, smaller version of me—short brown hair with eyes to match.

Dad doesn't answer, but that only makes Justin more curious.

"Are you sick, Ryan?"

"No," I tell him.

"Did you go to the dentist?"

"No."

I can't see him sitting behind me, but I imagine his freckled ten-year-old face all scrunched up, trying to figure out the mystery.

"Ooooh!" he says, finally getting it. "Ryan's in trouble!"

I reach into my backpack, pull out the Kit Kat I bought from the school vending machine that morning, and toss it over my shoulder. "Shut up."

Justin catches it and tears into the wrapper. "Thanks!"

At home, Dad sends Justin upstairs to do his homework. The next hour waiting for Mom is hell. Dad sits on the edge of the couch watching the afternoon news, flipping the channels at every commercial. I sit next to him, thumbing through stupid Instagram pics on my phone.

The first thing Mom does when she comes through the door is slip off her shoes, kicking them into the corner. Then she pulls the rubber band out of her hair, which is several shades lighter brown than mine, and falls to her shoulders. She's wearing her postal uniform: blue slacks and a jacket.

"Hey guys," she says, dropping her car keys on the entry table. Her shoulders droop, and her eyes are half closed. She looks exhausted. Usually does after a ten-hour shift.

She started working when Dad came back from Afghanistan, to help make ends meet and to keep me in Middleton. She never complains, but she used to say how much she loved being home with us kids. So I know what a sacrifice it is for her. She's the kind of person who does what needs to be done, no matter what. And now I've let her down.

"It's been a long day," she says. "And I'm starving. Did you find the pork chops I defrosted?"

Dad gets up to greet her. Mom moves in, wrapping her arms around him for her customary "Thank-God-I'm-

Finally-Home" kiss, but when she sees his worried expression, she stops short.

"What's wrong?" she asks.

Dad draws a deep breath as if to say, *Here we go*. "Well," he begins, "there was some trouble at school today."

He clicks off the TV, and Mom listens in grim silence as he takes her through the events of the afternoon. When he tells her about Jenn, she presses her hand to her forehead the way she does when she's worried.

"That poor girl," she says. But when Dad gets to the part about me and the pills, anger blooms across her face.

"Xanax?" she says. "He was expelled for getting high on Xanax?"

"Not expelled," Dad explains. "They're letting him do independent study."

"What does that mean?"

"It means Ryan will do his schoolwork at home for a few months."

Mom cuts a look between me and Dad, her fists moving to her hips. "You mean homeschool. Then who's going to teach him? I'm at work all day."

"I will," says Dad.

"But you have doctor appointments and physical therapy. You can't do all that *and* babysit our sixteen-year-old son."

"I'll manage." Dad straightens up, but winces. Though it's been more than two years, his leg still bothers him. Mom notices too. She used to reach for him, help him balance on his prosthetic. He fell a lot those first few weeks, though now he's pretty stable. But I see the almost imperceptible shift in Mom's body, resisting the urge to grab hold of him.

"Where do we get his books?" She's pacing now. "Will he be held responsible for that girl's injury? And what happens after 'a few months'?"

Despite Mom's interrogation, Dad remains calm. "The school will provide all his materials, and the accident wasn't Ryan's fault. As for his future with Middleton, the board meets in February. Commander Norton said he'll arrange a hearing for Ryan. They'll review his case, and if his schoolwork and test scores are good enough, they might let him back in."

"*If* his schoolwork is good enough, they *might* re-enroll him?"

"Well, there is more."

Up until now, I've managed to stay out of the conversation. I've been sitting on the couch this whole time, feeling smaller and smaller. I'm a tiny speck of dust by the time Mom finally looks at me, wanting an explanation. I tell her what Norton told me, that the school board will expect not only top grades but also proof that I'm worthy of their school. He said I have to volunteer somewhere, give back to the community and all that. Twenty hours' worth between now and my hearing. That way, the Middleton Academy school board will know I'm serious.

"And just where do you plan to volunteer?" asks Mom.

"I don't know," I answer.

"What about the community center?" suggests Dad. "It's close, and I'll bet they could use some help."

The community center is a dilapidated building in the middle of the park where kids go after school for art classes and stuff.

With an exasperated huff, Mom marches into the kitchen. Cupboards slam, and I hear the clang of a frying pan on the stove. "You didn't even cook the goddamned chops!"

Dad steps awkwardly to the fireplace and leans against the mantle. We both know Mom's tirade has nothing to do with dinner, and with every noise from the kitchen, the tension in the room gets thicker.

After a few minutes, Mom comes back, a spatula gripped in her hand. "What else are you on, Ryan? Speed? Meth?"

I blink against Mom's accusations. I never do any of the hard stuff, just smoke some weed, drink a little liquor. But right now, admitting even that would be enough to send Mom through the roof.

"Nothing," I tell her.

"Oh, c'mon, Ryan," she scoffs. "Give me a break. I'm not an idiot."

"I'm clean. I swear."

But she ignores me, shaking her head like I'm the biggest disappointment of her life. Then she holds out her hand. "Give me your cell phone."

"What?"

"You heard me. Hand it over."

I guess it was too much to hope that I wouldn't get punished. I look at Dad, searching for some sign that he'll come to my defense. Instead, he makes a small movement with his head, which means—*better do what she says.*

I pull my phone from my pocket and lay it in Mom's palm. She curls her fingers over it and waves it in front of my face.

"No phone. No video games or TV. No car. No hanging out with your friends. You will do your schoolwork and that volunteer crap. Nothing else. Got that?"

It isn't a question. It's a command to remain silent, so I clamp my mouth shut.

"And you'll be drug tested," she continues, "at random—whenever the hell I say so." She looks at Dad. "Juan, run by the pharmacy after dinner and pick up some kits, will you? I'll call ahead with the order." Then she turns back to me, her expression hard as stone. "And if one test strip so much as blushes positive, I will not only cancel your phone account, but your driving privileges will be permanently suspended. Is that clear?"

Her glare pierces right through me. I feel lower than the floor, lower than the moldy earth under our basement. I know my mom. If she threatens to do something, she will do it.

"I said, is that clear?" she repeats.

"Yes," I answer. "Crystal."

Mom hands Dad my phone and the spatula. "I'm going to bed," she says.

As she turns to leave, Dad steps in front of her and takes her gently by the shoulders. He's a good eight inches taller than her and much wider. She's slim and in good shape, a carry-over from her military service where she and

Dad met eighteen years ago. But despite her strong build, Dad still dwarfs her.

"It'll work out, Marissa," he says. "I can handle it. I promise."

He pulls Mom close, and she lets him hold her for a minute. Her eyes are red and watery. One tear escapes before she swipes it away. Then she pulls back from him and looks at me, her lips pressed into a tight line.

"I expected better from you," she says. Then she heads upstairs without another word. A moment later, her bedroom door slams shut.

Dad slips my phone into his pants pocket and taps his thigh with the spatula. "Hungry?" he asks.

Though the effects from the pills have pretty much worn off, I couldn't eat even if I wanted to. Not after seeing my mom cry.

"Not really," I tell Dad.

"Me either." He heads into the kitchen and comes back without the spatula. Then he grabs his car keys from off the table. "Guess I got an errand to run. Why don't you head over to the community center and see what you can arrange? And when you get back, put the pork chops in the oven."

He reaches for the doorknob, but I can't let him go. Not like this.

"Dad?"

He pauses. "Yeah?"

"I'm really sorry. About everything."

Dad clutches his keys, weighing them in his palm. He glances toward the ceiling, like he's looking right through it at Mom.

"Me too," he says. Then he opens the door and walks out.

I know my apology is worthless. Nothing can fix the damage I've done. All I can do now is try to get back into school—and never screw up again.

PENNY

FOUR

I *CANNOT* BELIEVE THIS! But of course I believe it. Brett started acting like a douche a few days ago—hiding in his room, snapping at me and Mom. I should have seen this coming, done something to stop him from spiraling. But how could I have known about him and Celine breaking up?

Now he's taken off, and Mom's going to have my head.

Every bit of me wants to go after Brett, to make sure he's safe. But if I do and he spots me, I'm in for it. He hates being spied on. Talk about a rock and a hard place—the wrath of Brett or the complete freak out of Mom.

I run into the house and chuck my backpack into the corner of the living room. Then I call Brett's cell, but it goes straight to voicemail.

"Brett, I know you're upset, but if you're not here when Mom gets home, she'll be worried sick. Just don't stay out too long. Okay?"

I end the call, and then I send him a text:

PLS COME HOME. MOM'LL BE PISSED.

I glance at the microwave clock. How much time should I give him before I call Mom? She had to cover for someone on the day shift, so she won't be home for another hour.

I should look for him.

I chew my lip, fighting the impulse to run to the rescue. Instead, I fish my math book from my backpack and out spills the letter from IMG. I stare at it as if it might vanish in a puff of smoke, like some genie reneging on his wishes. Then I pick it up. I don't need to read it again. The words are seared into my brain. A scholarship. A *full* scholarship.

My fingertips take in the texture of the crinkled envelope, but I can't be thinking about this right now. And besides, I've already made up my mind—haven't I?

Tucking the letter into my textbook, I sit at the kitchen table, hoping to keep my mind off everything. I open to the practice test Ms. Danner assigned today and start working out the first problem. When I've got the answer, I jot it down in bold, black numbers on a fresh page of lined paper. Ms. Danner hates when I use pen. "Pencil. Only a number '2' Pencil" is her personal mantra. Why? "Because," she always says in that whiny voice of hers, "errors are inevitable. We must always allow room for correction."

Which is why I prefer ink.

I start on the second problem, but my mind flees to the hills behind the park. There's this steep, well-worn trail leading from the baseball diamond to the crest of the first hill. Brett and I discovered it a few years ago, long before we moved to this neighborhood, when we first started hanging out at the community center. Beyond the trail are miles and miles of open land. I'm pretty sure that's where Brett was heading. When he disappears like this, he usually comes back after he's cooled off. But sometimes, like today, he gets so worked up, I worry that he might never come back.

After ten minutes, I've only finished that first stupid math problem. Screw it. I'm going after him whether he likes it or not. He can swear at me all he wants. I don't care. He doesn't even need to know I'm looking for him. Maybe I can keep out of sight. If I can spot him from a distance, at least I can reassure Mom that he's all right.

I send another text to Brett and then slide the phone into my jeans pocket. Maybe he'll answer once he's feeling better. But what if he doesn't feel better? What if—?

No. It *will* be fine. Just like all the times he's run off before, I'll scour the hillsides and shout Brett's name. I'll text him, call him, curse him. He won't respond. After half an hour or so, I'll give up and go home where I'll chew my nails down to stubs until Mom shows up and I have to tell her everything that happened. It's a routine that's all too familiar and way too frequent. And I hate it. I hate it because I can't change it or make it stop.

I hurry out the door and into the winter-barren hills. I spend half an hour roaming around, scanning every inch of horizon, trying not to look too conspicuous. But I don't find Brett, and I have to admit that I'm both worried and relieved, worried because who knows where the heck he is or when he'll be back, and relieved that if he has done something stupid, I'm not the one who'll discover it.

Back at the house, I consider returning to my homework, but there's no way I can concentrate now. Mom will be home soon, and I'll go stir crazy if I wait in here. Besides, if I'm outside, I could spot Brett coming home a mile off in any direction. That's where I want to be, need to be.

I go to my room for my basketball and then head for the front door. But first, I slip the envelope from the pages of my math book. Who am I kidding? I'm not going to IMG. I tear it into a dozen pieces and let them drop like snowflakes into the garbage. Then I tuck the ball under my arm and slam the door shut behind me.

RYAN

FIVE

IT'S A NICE DAY OUT. The sky is a shade of blue California doesn't usually see until summer. Our house is one of a couple dozen nearly identical tract houses bordering both sides of the park, half of which is a sprawling field of green grass dotted with pine trees and picnic benches. The other half has a play gym, tennis and basketball courts, and a baseball field. On the far end is the community center, a brick building with brown doors and barred windows. During the day, the park attracts a lot of moms with strollers. In the afternoon, kids hang out on the field or in the center. Sometimes, at night, teenagers meet behind the building to smoke and stuff.

Right now, the park is pretty empty except for one kid shooting hoops on the basketball court. He looks close to my age, or maybe a little younger, though it's hard to tell from this distance. He's wearing jeans and a sweatshirt with the sleeves pushed up to his elbows.

And he's bald. Not the shaved head, white supremacy kind of bald. I mean totally and completely baby butt bald.

I've seen him a few times before, with other kids at the court. Maybe he knows something about the center?

He makes four shots in a row and misses the fifth. He snatches the rebound and shoots again. *Swish.* I watch him make a few more shots, but something's off about him. I don't know what exactly, maybe the way he holds himself when he dribbles, or how the ball looks so big in his hands. Why hadn't I noticed before? Never looked long enough, I guess.

I'm not much of a sports guy, but I've played basketball in P.E. at school. Maybe this guy would let me shoot a few. Perfect way to break the ice, ask some questions. So, I jog across the grass toward the court.

The kid's got his back to me, and he's intent on his solo game, so when I near the edge of the court, I call out to get his attention.

"Hey!" I shout. He turns to me, his expression startled. I freeze and can actually feel the blood drain from my face as my eyes drop from the guy's bald head to his chest—his very curvy chest. This is no guy.

It's a *girl.*

I stand at the edge of the court like a bonehead, while the girl spares a brief glance in my direction.

"Can I help you?" she asks.

I have to say something, or she'll think I'm an idiot, so I pull myself together, forcing sound through my lips.

"Yeah, I'm—uh, Ryan, from across the street."

Move, feet, I think, willing myself to close the distance between us. "Nice basketball."

Ugh. Could I be any lamer?

She rebounds another shot, then holds the ball between her palms. "What do you want, Ryan from across the street?"

There's something odd about her face. What is it? Then I realize—eyebrows. She doesn't have any. Or lashes either. Without them, her eyes are big blue orbs, nearly the same color as the out-of-season sky.

She holds the ball out to me. I can't just stand here gawking, so I take it and dribble a bit. When I shoot, the ball collides with the rim and veers off to the right. With the grace of a dancer, the girl snatches it midair, spins, and sinks it. She's good. Really good.

"You on a team?" I ask, trying way too hard not to look at her head—or her eyes—or her boobs.

"Yep," she says.

"What position?"

"Point guard." She shoots again, then passes the ball to me. "You go to Kennedy?" She's looking at me with a cautious expression, like she's not quite sure about me, like I could be some perv off the street.

I take a few seconds to line up the shot. This time, I make it. "Middleton," I tell her.

"That private military academy?" She retrieves the ball and passes it to me. She seems distracted, keeps glancing past the court toward the hills.

I take another shot, but I'm finding it hard not to look at her. Her skull is round and smooth, and her skin is the color of brown sugar.

She scoops up the ball and shoots. The ball pushes through the net like it's anxious to get this whole thing over with. The girl lets the ball bounce a few times before grabbing it again. Then she tucks it under her arm, letting it rest against her hip.

"So, what do you want?" she asks, focusing her eyes on me like gun sights. "I mean why'd you decide to come over here? It wasn't to play basketball."

She's right, of course. Might as well be straight about it.

"Actually, I was heading to the community center. I need—I mean, I want to volunteer."

"*You* want to volunteer?"

Her skeptical tone sets me on edge. "Yes," I say, trying to sound sure of myself. "Why? Is there a problem?"

"It's just that we don't see a whole lot of teenage boys show up wanting to help out."

"Well, I guess I'm one of the rare ones."

She dribbles the ball a few times, then holds it again. "Why do you want to volunteer?"

Why? I should tell her it's none of her business or say I'm there out of the goodness of my heart, but instead, what comes out of my mouth is the truth.

"I have to. Because of school."

She smirks, and I know I've made a mistake. She takes another shot, makes another easy basket. I'm about ready to give up and go home when she says, "C'mon."

I follow her off the court to the front of the building. She pulls open the weathered door, its black paint faded and peeling in places, and we step inside. The microscopic lobby holds two worn-out chairs and a glass display case filled with sports trophies, plaques, and ribbons from years gone by. On the wall is a message board with a bunch of fliers and posters thumbtacked to it. Another wall is decorated with dozens of crayon drawings of trees and stuff. There are a couple rooms with narrow windows in the doors. I glance into one of them and see three kids about my age playing music. Some kind of neighborhood band. One of the kids glares at me, a skinny boy with glasses and a guitar. Guess they don't like intruders.

The girl I met outside leans over the front desk. "Fred! Fred, someone's looking for you."

Beyond the desk, I take in the rest of the facility, which isn't much: a ping-pong table, a pool table, a big screen TV with a couch, and some vintage arcade games: *Pac Man* and *Street Fighter*.

A man comes out of the back office, blonde hair pulled back in a ponytail. He's got a clipboard in one hand and a granola bar in the other.

"You working today, Penny?" he asks.

Penny. Her name is Penny.

"Tomorrow," she says. "But this guy wants to sign up."

"Yeah?" he asks, giving me a once-over.

I pull Norton's form from my pocket, unfold it, and hand it to him. Fred reads it, and his expression deflates.

"I see. Well, we can always use another hand around here. When are you available?"

I think of my now wide-open schedule. "Anytime, I guess."

Fred consults his clipboard. "Are you free Tuesday and Thursday afternoons?"

"Fred!" says Penny, her blue eyes widening.

Fred feigns innocence. "What? We got two new kids in your group."

"I can handle it just fine on my own," Penny says, cutting me a sharp look.

"One's in a wheelchair," says Fred. "You're gonna need some help."

Penny huffs but doesn't object further.

Fred signs my form and hands it back to me. "Be here tomorrow at four. Penny'll show you the ropes. Next week is the last before winter break, but then you can pick up again after Christmas."

"Thanks," I tell him. "I'll be here."

As we turn to leave, Penny throws Fred a mock punch, which he blocks with an awkward karate move.

"So, Penny," he says, "BandMasterz starts after the holidays, and we're short a bass player. Tell that brother of yours we could use him this season."

"I'll tell him," Penny answers, and then pushes through the door and heads back to the court. I follow her outside.

"So, what do you do here exactly?"

It occurs to me that I've just committed to twenty hours of doing who knows what. But Penny ignores me and lines up her shot. I guess she's not happy about having an assistant.

I watch her for a second, keeping my eyes away from her scalp and on her hands. She has long, delicate fingers with short, unpainted nails. She grips the ball with the resolve of a mountain climber.

"Okay, well, I, uh, better get back," I say. "I guess I'll see you tomorrow?"

I wait a second longer to see if she'll respond. When she doesn't, I start across the grass toward my house, but I can feel Penny's eyes boring into my back.

"I don't have cancer."

Her words stop me like a cement wall. I turn back. "What?"

"Cancer. That's what you're thinking, right?" Penny takes the shot, makes another perfect basket. "I don't have it," she continues. "Never did, hopefully never will."

She shoots again, and the ball slams against the backboard before spiraling into the net. The collision rattles the entire basketball post, the metal protesting like it's in agony.

Across the street, on the opposite side of the park, a dusty blue sedan pulls into one of the driveways. The house stands out from the others, with its red door and gargantuan cactus on the porch. A woman in medical scrubs gets out of the car and heads inside.

I glance back at Penny and realize she's watching the woman too.

"I gotta go," she says, lining up one more shot. This time she hesitates, the first hint of uncertainty I've seen in her. The ball sails away from her in a fluid arc, but at the last second, it slices off the rim into the bushes.

I don't know why I do it, but as she turns to retrieve the runaway ball, I jog over and step into the bristly shrub. The ball is wedged between two thick, gnarled branches. I pop it free and step back onto the court.

Penny looks at me with a weird expression—part grateful, part confused. I hold out the ball, and as she reaches for it, the tips of her fingers brush against mine. They're much softer than I imagined.

"Thanks," she says, her eyes briefly connecting with mine. "See you tomorrow." Then she runs across the park and disappears behind that red door.

I head home. I should be worried about school, about what the next few months will bring, and I am. But right now, I'm thinking about that girl, the way she looked at me with those saucer blue eyes of hers.

I can't get her face out of my head.

PENNY

SIX

I FIND MOM SITTING at the kitchen table sipping a mug of herbal tea and flipping through today's mail.

"Hi, Sweetie," she says when I come in. "How was school?"

I roll my basketball down the hall into my room and join her at the table.

"Fine, but Brett's disappeared again." No sense postponing the inevitable.

She sets down her mug and rests her fingertips on the rim.

"You know he's been edgy all week," I continue. "He got off the bus and just took off."

"And you didn't go after him?"

"I did, but what would I have done if I'd found him? Begged him to come home? You know how that'd go over."

"Have you texted him?"

"Of course. I called, too, but it went straight to voicemail, as usual."

Mom gets up from the table and pours her tea down the sink. "So, while your brother is God knows where, you decided to go play basketball at the park."

She doesn't mean it. This is what worrying about Brett does to her sometimes.

"Mom, you know that's not fair," I tell her.

She turns from the sink, her arms folded, fingers drumming against her elbow. "I know. I'm sorry. It's just— Did he take his pills this morning?" She checks the shot glass on the windowsill, but the absence of pills is no guarantee he actually swallowed them. A few times in the past, Mom found stashes of them hidden in his room. Why he'd hoard them instead of just washing them down the sink or chucking them in the garbage is beyond me. Guilt, perhaps? Or maybe he was saving them.

"How long has he been gone?" Mom asks.

"An hour."

She studies the clock. Then she moves for the door.

"I need to find him."

"It won't do any good," I tell her. "He'll come home when he's ready. He always does."

Mom knows I'm right. This isn't the first time Brett's run away, and it probably won't be the last. There were times early on when Mom spent hours in the car driving up and down every street calling Brett's name, like searching for a stray dog. But humans are smarter than dogs. If they don't want to be found, they won't be.

"We should be here when he gets home." I lead Mom back to the dining table. "In the meantime, I could use some help with my homework."

She sits but keeps looking at the clock. I know what she's thinking. She's wondering how long she'll give him before taking action. She has a sort of built-in timer, a predetermined number of minutes she'll allow him to make his way home before she calls the police, which she's done twice before. The first time was two years ago, when he was sixteen, just after Dad left. It was almost midnight, and Mom panicked. The sheriff found Brett sitting on a swing at the school playground just four blocks from our house. The second time didn't end quite so well. The call wasn't made until he'd come home and started breaking everything in sight. When he threatened her with his pocketknife, Mom called for help, landing Brett in a seventy-two-hour hold in the psych ward.

I don't think she ever forgave herself for that.

Mom fidgets with the stack of envelopes on the table. I lay my hand over hers. "He'll come home. We just need to wait."

We sit at the table, not speaking, watching the sun set through the kitchen window. My math book sits open next to me, though I don't think either of us really expects me to get much studying done tonight.

We're still sitting there when Brett finally comes through the door at half past seven. Mom weaves her fingers together to hide the fact that they're trembling.

"Hi, Honey," she says as if her son's vanishing act is nothing out of the ordinary. "Where've you been?"

Brett halts, his sneakers squeaking on the kitchen tile. "Nowhere."

He yanks open the refrigerator door, inspecting its internal organs like a surgeon. Then he lugs the half-empty gallon of milk to the counter, pours himself a glass, downs it, and pours another, which he takes, along with a stack of Oreos, to his room. He leaves the milk out, the fridge door open, the cookie package abandoned.

Mom sighs. She gets up from the table and methodically starts putting everything away like one of those assembly line robots programmed to do the same mundane task over and over. Finally, she takes a cookie and pops it into her mouth—the whole thing—and crushes it between her teeth. Her face melts into a look of relief and satisfaction. She takes another, this time biting it in half.

"Want one?" she asks, holding out the package. "Or ten? Honestly, I could eat the entire box right about now. Please eat some, so I won't have to."

Mom binges when she's stressed, and normally, I'm happy to binge along with her. But right now, my stomach feels like it's full of rocks.

She finishes off her cookie with small, measured nibbles. "I'll give him some time to cool off," she says, shoving the cookies into the cupboard, "and then I'll go check on him."

When she turns back to the table, her jaw pops open like a car trunk. "What is *that*?" Three determined strides and she's behind me, squinting at the smeared Sharpie on my scalp. "How didn't I see this earlier?"

"It's nothing, Mom. Really. Some girl at school—she was just messing around."

"Just messing around?" She's livid, the tension about Brett spilling over. If I don't say something to calm her down, she may just stampede into the school tomorrow and embarrass the crap out of me.

"It's no big deal." I try my best to sound indifferent. "It'll wear off in a few days."

She steps away from me and returns to the kitchen. I think maybe she's going for the Oreos again, but instead she just stands there, bracing her hands against the counter. I go to her and wrap my arms around her waist. Mom turns into me, snaking her trembling arms around my body and pressing me close.

"Oh, Penny. Penny." The warmth of her breath coming from deep inside her comforts me a little, and I think, in some way I can never understand, I comfort her too.

RYAN

SEVEN

A SHRILL ALARM JERKS me out of a deep sleep. My heart feels like it just ran ten miles, it's pounding so fast. I fumble for the clock, slapping the *off* button.

Who the heck set my alarm for five freakin' a.m.?

I blink my eyes open against the harsh bedroom light and find my mom glaring at me from the foot of my bed. She drops something onto my blanket. "Fill it, dip it, dump it," she says.

It's a small plastic cup with a test strip and folded instructions tucked inside. A drug test kit. Great.

I drag myself out of bed and head down the hall to the bathroom, Mom following right behind. I try to close the door, but she stops it with her hand.

"Some privacy, please?" I say.

"You've lost your right to privacy," she answers. "You're not getting away with dunking the stick in water. Now pee."

I do what she tells me, grateful she's at least not peering over my shoulder. But she does stand at the door like a sentry. I fill the cup and dip in the strip. I'm pretty sure it's negative because, first of all, the tests Dad bought are cheap at-home weed tests. But I'm not telling her that. And second, it's been more than a month since I got stoned with Andrew, and it was just one joint. It should be out of my system by now.

I glance at the strip, see the pale yellow patch, and breathe out in relief. Then I hold it out to Mom. "Satisfied?"

I drop the wet stick into the trash pail and dump the contents of the cup into the toilet, flushing for emphasis. "I'm going back to bed now."

I spent half the night wrestling with nightmares—kept seeing Jenn smacking her head on that desk and hearing those wailing sirens like the cries of the dead—so I'm still pretty tired.

I wash my hands in the sink and dry them on a towel. Mom straightens it on the rack when I'm through.

"Your dad and I talked about everything last night," she says. "I understand the school's volunteer requirement, but we both agree it isn't enough. So, in the morning, you're to be showered and dressed by 6:30. Eat breakfast. Then you'll have a few hours to do chores before you start your schoolwork."

"What chores?"

"I made a list."

I moan. Mom loves making lists: grocery lists, to-do lists, lists of people to send birthday cards to. She even keeps a detailed, color-coded list of Christmas presents she plans to buy every year. It's disturbing. I can only imagine what she's written on my Punish-Ryan-with-a-Bunch-of-Stupid-Chores list.

"Mom, you don't have to do all this," I tell her. "It wasn't my fault that girl got hurt."

"What about the drugs?"

"*Legal* drugs so I could focus better and keep trying to be the best student possible." I slip in the last part, hoping for a shred of sympathy, but instead she just frowns.

"Ryan, you messed up—big time. You got kicked out of the only decent school in town."

"Almost kicked out," I correct her.

"If you think you can get off without any consequences—"

"Consequences I don't deserve!" I say it louder than I should. I don't talk back to my parents, but this is too much. "I made one stupid mistake, and I'm willing to make up for it. The homeschool thing. Volunteering at some run-down after-school program. But now on top of all that, I've got chores too? It's not fair."

Mom's face hardens instantly, and she presses a palm against the bathroom wall as if to steady herself.

"You want to know what isn't fair, Ryan?" she says. "Working ten-hour shifts delivering mail when I could be home with my boys. Or sinking every penny I earn into your future, only to have you throw it all away for drugs. Or how about your father getting his leg blown off on a land mine."

Then Mom loses it. A violent sob bursts out of her, but she claps her hand against her mouth and squeezes her eyes shut. The only other time I've seen her like this was when she got the call about Dad. But this time, it's me that makes her cry.

Me.

I watch as she tries to pull herself together. I'm seeing a side of her she normally keeps to herself. She always wants to be strong—for Dad. For Justin. For me. But I know, maybe more than anyone, how hard everything's been on her.

I want to move close to her, to touch her shoulder and promise that everything'll be all right. But it's a promise I can't keep. So, I just stand there and say nothing.

She opens her eyes and dries her face with the corner of the towel. Then she pulls in a sharp breath.

"Just get back into school," she says. "Then we'll talk about what's fair and what's not."

As I walk back to my room, I listen to her footsteps moving down the stairs and out the front door. I pull back my drapes and watch her drive away for work.

It's barely a quarter to six. I want to go back to bed, but after all that, I'm not sleepy anymore. Mom's words run over and over through my brain: *Just get back into school.*

I grab some clean clothes and head back to the bathroom to shower. The house is quiet when I go downstairs a while later. Justin won't be up until seven, so I pour myself a bowl of cereal and slice a banana on top. Scooping a spoonful of it into my mouth, I spot Dad's old laptop on the kitchen table. He hasn't used it in a year, not since Mom got him a tablet last Christmas. What's it doing down here?

I open it and power it on. A few seconds later, Middleton's name and logo appear across the top of the screen. I grab the mouse, move the cursor over the INDEPENDENT STUDY link, and click. The screen changes, and the words WELCOME RYAN come into view.

"The computer is for school."

I glance up to see Dad coming down the stairs. In a couple weeks, it'll be two years since his accident. He still has a hard time of it, with his leg and all. He has to grip the railing and take it slow. He's wearing his favorite blue sweatpants and a Semper Fi T-shirt. He steps into the kitchen and pushes a brown grocery bag across the table toward me.

"Yesterday, after I dropped by the pharmacy, I went to the school supply store and picked up what I could to get you started," he says. "I probably went a bit overboard."

He starts pulling stuff out of the bag like a magician pulling things out of a top hat: pencils, erasers, a ruler, paper, some books. "Your lessons will be online—science, geometry, German—"

"I'm taking German?"

"It was that or Mandarin Chinese. I can still change it if you want."

"No," I tell him. "German is fine."

"Commander Norton emailed me this morning, said you should take the first few days to acquaint yourself with the program."

Dad stops talking and looks at me, expecting me to say something, like maybe, "Wow. This is amazing. I'm so excited!" Or "Gee, Dad, you went through all this trouble for *me*?" And while I know he did, I'm the exact opposite of excited.

Dad reaches for the mouse and clicks on my name. A list of school subjects appears on the screen, each in its own virtual file. "Your mother installed Web Watcher," he says. "She'll be able to see your history, so don't go looking at porn or anything."

"Dad!" I turn in my chair to gape at him. "I don't do that crap."

"You'll start the morning with chores. Mom told you about that, right?"

"Yeah." I take a bite of stale Cheerios.

"You'll start them at seven. School begins at nine sharp. Lunch is at noon. Did you find out about the volunteering situation?"

"I signed up across the street."

"Doing what?"

"Not sure yet. I'll find out this afternoon." I run a finger over the computer keyboard, thinking about my earlier conversation with Mom. She won't budge, I'm pretty sure of that. Maybe Dad'll be more sympathetic.

"Is all this really necessary?" I ask. "Couldn't you talk to Norton and get him to tone it down a bit?"

"What do you mean?"

"I mean all those hours I could be studying. How am I supposed to stay ahead if I'm wasting all that time *volunteering*?"

Dad raises an eyebrow at me with a knowing smirk. "I'm sure you'll find a way." He shifts the mouse and puts the computer into hibernate. "All right. Let's get you started with those chores."

I grab my shoes and hoodie and follow Dad out the front door. The yard is a jungle of knee-high weeds. It used to look a lot better than this, with trimmed hedges and a green lawn, but once Mom started working, she didn't have time for it anymore, and Dad never had much of a green thumb.

A rectangular section of the yard, maybe ten feet long by five feet wide, has been marked off with a string attached to four wooden stakes stuck in the ground. A shovel leans against the house.

"So, what are we doing?" I ask, pulling on my hoodie.

"*You're* planting a garden." Dad grabs the shovel and pushes it into my hands.

"A garden? It's December."

"Mom wants a garden," he says, "you give her a garden."

"It's like fifty degrees out here."

"Then be glad we live in sunny California. If we were in Montana, you'd be shoveling a butt load of snow right now instead of dirt." He hands me a pair of leather work gloves. "Pull the weeds. Loosen the soil twelve inches down. I'm going to get your brother ready for school."

Dad heads back into the house. I jab at the hard ground with the shovel and manage to loosen a few dirt clods. I pick up one that's the size of a baseball with clumps of dried grass sticking out of one side, like hair. A lump on it could almost pass for a nose. I hold it up, closing one eye. It looks an awful lot like Norton. I chuck it against the side of the house where it explodes like a grenade.

PENNY

EIGHT

IF IT WEREN'T FOR Jake Dillinger, today would have been the perfect day. It's beach weather (despite being the middle of December), I got an 'A' on my history essay, and for once, my lab partner in Biology actually completed her half of the assignment. At lunch, I bolt from the lab and head for the cafeteria to cram for the Spanish midterm with Tali. I'm practically at a run when I turn a corner and career into Kennedy's unofficial Brat Pack—Jake and his basketball minions.

"Well, if it isn't Penny Tate," Jake says, combing his fingers through his cropped red hair. "Coming to the big game tomorrow night?"

Jake is starting point guard on the boys' varsity team. He and Brett have been friends since the second grade, though now that Brett and Jake's sister, Celine, have split, I suspect things are going to be different.

I try to push past him, but Jake is a good six inches taller and forty pounds heavier than me. Getting past him is like trying to sail around an iceberg in a dinghy. Before I can protest, he scoops his arm around my neck, gripping me in the crook of his elbow. Then he gives my head a good, hard knuckle-rub.

"Make a wish, Acosta!" he shouts at one of the other boys.

"Let me go, Jake!" I beat on his thigh with my fist, but he just laughs.

"Oh, c'mon! It's for good luck!"

Eddie Acosta laughs. "You're an idiot, Dillinger."

This beyond childish ritual started two summers ago when Brett and Jake were at our house watching a baseball game on TV. The score was tied at four runs at the bottom of the ninth against Pittsburg with the Dodgers up to bat. I was sitting on the floor in front of Brett with one hand buried in a bowl of popcorn. Just before the pitcher let the ball fly, I felt four bony stubs pressing circles into my skull.

"Come on!" Jake said.

"Knock it off," I said, brushing his hand away.

"You're good luck, Penny. You know—find a penny, pick it up, and all that day you'll have good luck."

Sounded stupid to me, but then *crack*! As the bat smashed the ball over the wall at center field, Brett and Jake screeched with victory. And the knuckle-rub thing stuck.

I had hoped that since Brett and Celine had broken up that Jake would leave me alone, but now he's an even bigger jerk than usual.

I manage to wriggle free from his elbow and shove him away. "Brett told you not to do that anymore."

He raises his hands, fake innocent-like. "I was just playin', and besides," he adds with sudden venom, "I don't listen to that crazy brother of yours anymore."

He takes a swipe at my head, then wanders off with his friends, all howling like a gaggle of demented geese. I start again for the cafeteria, but I don't get far before I spot Brett sitting by himself in the quad. A few weeks ago, he would have been with Jake. But today he's alone, hunched over a red spiral notebook.

I text Tali to let her know I'll be a few minutes late and then head for the quad, which is really nothing more than a square slab of cement near the library. But it's shady, the perfect spot on a day like today, at least it would be if lowerclassmen were allowed to enjoy it. I'm in enemy territory just being here.

As I near Brett, I see that he's scribbling furiously in the notebook, his forehead creased in deep thought.

"Since when do you do homework during lunch?" I say when I reach him.

He shuts the notebook and slips it into his backpack before extracting a bag of Fritos instead. "Actually, I'm eating. Mom sent a tuna sandwich and a box of apple juice."

"Me too," I tell him. "She thinks we're still in first grade."

He laughs a normal, comfortable laugh, so I relax a little, but what was he so focused on writing before?

I sit beside him on the concrete bench plastered with petrified gum wads from generations of students long past. Brett opens his Fritos and pours half the contents into his mouth.

"I was wondering if you could do me a favor," I ask, scanning the area for prowling seniors who might come to defend their terrain. "I'm having trouble with this essay I'm writing for Mr. Winters' class. It's due after vacation, and—let's face it—I suck at grammar."

Brett squints, an amused smirk on his face. "*You*—suck at grammar? Penny, you talk like Shakespeare in drag. What do you need my help for?"

"You passed sophomore English, that's what, and you've had Winters before. You know what he expects. Could you just read it over? Tell me if I'm on target or not?"

The truth is, I really don't need his help. I've got the highest scores in just about every class, including English. It's just that Brett's been so down lately. He used to be really social, had lots of friends, and was so fun to be around. All that changed after Dad left. At least he had Celine, but now I guess that's over too. No wonder he's been so hard on himself. Maybe if I show him how much he's needed, he might snap out of it.

Brett finishes off his Fritos. "Yeah, sure I'll read it."

I unzip my backpack and slide out the paper. He takes it from me, giving it a once-over. "I'll look at it after school."

"Thanks. But remember it's just the rough draft."

Brett folds the paper into quarters and slips it into his back pocket just as Lea Pachero and her groupies materialize beside us. Lea tosses her head to the side, tails of dark curls bouncing against her shoulder.

"Hello, Brett," she says with a voice so fake I could scratch it off with the edge of a dime. "How's it going?"

Brett looks up at her, and in that sliver of a moment, his eyes grow cold and distant, like he's just erected an invisible barrier around himself.

"Fine, Lea," he says. "I'm just fine."

"You sure? You look to me like you could use some company."

His eyes flicker from her to the girls behind her, all of whom stare at him with varying levels of playful pouting—except one. Celine Dillinger, Jake's sister, hangs back from the others. She's strawberry blonde, blue-eyed, pretty, and a lot nicer than most of Lea's friends.

Brett's eyes find her, lingering a few moments before he blinks and looks away. "I got plenty of company," he says.

Lea's gaze shifts to me. "What are you doing here? The quad is restricted. Juniors and seniors only."

"I'm eating lunch with my brother." I try to sound braver than I really am. I wait for Brett to say something in my defense, but he doesn't. Instead, he stands and walks away, leaving me to face the pack of female hyenas alone.

Lea watches Brett meander across the lawn for a moment and then fixes her glare on me. "Let me give you some advice," she says. "Your brother may be a senior, but he's an outcast. You'd be better off here without him."

"You didn't seem to think he was an outcast when you flirted with him all last year."

The hyenas give a collective gasp, and fury burns behind Lea's eyes.

"Listen, you bald-headed freak. You and your creep of a brother had better stay out of the quad and away from us. Now, get-the-hell-out." Her words are so sharp, I think if I don't leave this second, she'll hit me, or more hyena-like, bite me. Either way, I know she's serious. So, I grab my backpack and leave.

I don't get far before someone grabs me by the arm. Thinking Lea has followed me wanting to stir up trouble, I spin around, ready to lash out. But it isn't Lea. It's Celine. Her eyes dart back to the quad, like she's scared she might be seen with me. But Lea and her hyenas are clustered together, squawking over who knows what.

"Is he—" She glances across the lawn to where Brett now sits under a tree, his head down on his knees. "Is he okay?"

She sounds sincerely concerned, and in truth, I am too.

"Why don't you ask him yourself?" I suggest.

She lowers her eyes. "Jake'd flip if he saw me talking to him."

Behind her, I notice Lea looking in our direction. Celine tenses, like she can feel the other girls watching her.

"That's all right," she says. "I'd better go."

She turns to leave, but I have to ask. "Celine, what happened between the two of you?"

She glances at me, her eyes moist, but she says nothing and hurries back to Lea's gang.

As I start toward the cafeteria, I look at Brett. Though I'm kind of ticked that he didn't stick up for me with Lea, I'm still worried. I can't help but think about Celine's question: *Is he okay?* But I know he's not.

I consider trying to talk to him about it, but a text from Tali reminds me that I have other obligations to keep. So, I leave my brother to himself for now—but for the rest of the day, I can't shake the feeling that something bad is lurking just around the corner.

RYAN

nine

AT 3:45 PM, I CLOSE my laptop and head out the front
door for the community center. It's busier than it was
yesterday, with kids playing ping-pong and watching TV.
No one is at the desk, so I hang out in the lobby for a few
minutes waiting for Penny to show up. To pass the time, I
look over the fliers pinned to the board. There's a photo of
a German shepherd with the caption "Have You Seen
Me?", along with several ads for piano lessons, private
tutors, and even a dog walking service. In the middle of
them all is a full-color poster with an image of a drum set
on a lighted stage. Above the stage are bold letters in
shimmery gold:

BANDMASTERZ – WINTER SESSION

I scan to the bottom of the flier where the details are
printed in smaller text, but before I can read it, the door to
the center snaps open, and Penny walks in.

"Hello, Ryan," she says in what I can tell is a forced
acknowledgment of my presence. She opens a cabinet and

grabs a net bag filled with half a dozen basketballs. Then she leans over the desk, taking a clipboard with a ballpoint pen tied to it with string.

"Fred, I've got it!" she hollers.

Fred's voice echoes out of the back office. "Yeah, all right!"

Then Penny heads out the door. I follow her to the basketball court where I met her yesterday. A group of kids has gathered under one of the baskets. There are ten of them, boys and girls, ranging in age from around eight to maybe twelve or thirteen. One is in a wheelchair, his arms bent at odd angles. The others are also disabled, including two with Down Syndrome.

Penny marches right up to the kids and tosses a basketball to one of the boys. He catches it awkwardly and hugs it to his chest.

"Good catch, Robert," says Penny. "You guys ready to play?"

The kids all giggle.

"Okay," continues Penny, "but first we have some introductions to make." She glances at her clipboard. "We've got two new teammates today."

The boy in the wheelchair raises one of his stiff hands in the air. It looks like the move takes a tremendous amount of effort. Garbled words come out of his mouth, what sounds something like "I'm Danny", and a string of saliva drips from his lips.

Penny smiles warmly at him. "Welcome, Danny. And Alice?"

A black girl at the end of the line nervously waves her hand. Penny beams at her. She makes several check marks on the roster clipped to the board, then hands it to me.

"We have one more newcomer," she continues. "This is Ryan. He's going to be helping me out for a few weeks."

"Hi, Ryan." The kids wave enthusiastically.

Despite the fact that Penny doesn't seem to want me here, she doesn't show it in front of the kids.

"So, let's get started," she says.

For the next hour, I watch as Penny coaches this ragtag team of disabled kids, teaching them how to hold the ball, helping them line up shots, showing them how to dribble. It is, in reality, a disaster. Balls bouncing off the rim, though most of the kids can't even shoot that high. Balls rolling away off the court. I spend most of the time retrieving them and throwing them back into play. But the kids have a blast. They laugh the whole time. They cheer for each other and applaud every effort.

When parents begin arriving to pick up their kids, each team member hugs Penny goodbye. She returns their embraces and calls them by name.

"Your aim is really improving, David."

"You almost made that last basket, Sarah. Next time for sure."

I hang back, collecting the stray balls and scooping them into the bag. When the kids have gone, Penny and I head back into the center. She hands the clipboard to Fred, who's leafing through some papers at the desk.

"Did you give my message to Brett?" he asks Penny.

She opens the cabinet and stuffs the ball bag inside. "Sorry, but he said no. Busy year for him."

"Well," says Fred with a disappointed sigh, "we're still a player short. Got a few weeks to change his mind."

"I'll try."

Fred turns to me, holding out his hand. At first, I'm not sure what he wants, but then I remember the form. I pull it out of my pocket and hand it to him. He unfolds it and writes today's date on the first blank line. Then he signs his name and hands it back to me.

"You play?" he asks.

His question takes me by surprise. "Oh, well, I *was* on a team once in fifth grade—"

"I meant music." Fred points at the BandMasterz poster on the board. "I'm looking for a bass guitarist."

"Actually, I used to play a little," I tell him, though I'm hesitant to admit it. "Bass, I mean. Piano too."

"Well, we got six bands registered. Plenty of guitarists, but only five bassists. How 'bout I sign you up?"

Two years ago, I might have jumped at the chance, but not anymore. "Sorry, can't," I tell him. "It's been a long time, and I'm kinda busy."

Fred straightens the edge of his papers against the desk and then shoves them into a manila envelope. "Too bad. I guess we'll have to cut one of the bands. Kids'll be disappointed."

"You've still got a few weeks before it starts," offers Penny. "Somebody will step up."

"Yeah," says Fred, but he doesn't sound too hopeful.

Penny and I head outside again. The afternoon has cooled, and so has Penny's attitude. She starts toward her house without so much as a second glance at me. I'm kinda surprised since she was nice to me in front of the kids.

I decide to play it light. "Aren't you going to kiss me goodbye?"

Penny cuts me a sharp look. Oops. I guess she's not in a joking mood. I try to laugh it off. "I mean, c'mon. Don't I at least deserve a thank you?"

"Thank you," she says curtly, and continues on her way.

I watch her for a few seconds, but now I'm offended. Where does she get off treating me like that?

"What's your problem?" I call after her. "You clearly don't like me."

Penny stops and looks back. "Maybe I don't."

"But you hardly know me."

"I know enough." She closes the space between us. "That form in your pocket? I don't need someone like you hanging around here, not with my kids."

"Someone *like me*? What? You think I'm some sort of delinquent?"

"You got expelled from school."

"Not quite."

"Not quite? So, you just decided to volunteer because it's the noble thing to do—and complete a MANDATORY COMMUNITY SERVICE HOURS form for the hell of it."

"You don't know what you're talking about."

"Then why did you get in trouble?" she asks me point-blank. "Cheating? Vandalism?"

"No! Nothing like that. I wouldn't do that."

"Drugs?"

The same heat I felt yesterday in Norton's office instantly scorches me from the inside out. I feel my face turn red. Penny smirks at me, which just makes it worse.

"It's not what you think," I tell her.

"No?" she says smugly.

"No. I mean, I'm actually a good guy."

Why am I letting this bald girl get under my skin? To hell with her stupid basketball class. But like it or not, I need those volunteer hours, which means I need her to trust me.

Penny moves closer and tips her head to the side, studying me through narrowed eyes. "You're a *good* guy?"

"Well, yeah. Sure."

"Then prove it," she says, crossing her arms.

Prove it?

I glance across the street at my house. The minivan isn't there, which means Dad left to take Justin to scouts and won't be back for a while.

"Okay," though I haven't a clue what to do next. She wants me to prove I'm a decent person. How do I do that?

"How about you come over to my place?"

Penny backs up a few steps, huffing. "I don't think so." She starts walking off again.

"Not like that," I sputter. "I meant, like for a glass of lemonade or something. My mom makes it from scratch, fresh lemons from our tree. It's really good."

Penny pauses and gives me a wary look, but I hope I'm breaking through her shell.

"You—want to try some?" I gesture toward my house, feeling more awkward than ever. This girl hates me, and here I am luring her into my house like some lunatic stalker. I try to give off "safe" vibes, if that's even possible, sure that any second Penny is going to turn and run away in horror.

I pull a double pointer, like the Scarecrow in *The Wizard of Oz*. To my surprise, Penny laughs. She's got a nice laugh, light and bubbly—like Coke fizz.

Across the street, the house with the red door opens. Some guy steps out onto the porch and lights a cigarette. He's wearing a black T-shirt and jeans, dark hair hanging loosely around his face. He blinks up at the sky, then scans the park. When he spots Penny and me, his expression hardens, and he crushes his cigarette against the side of the house.

Something about Penny changes, like yesterday when she missed that basket. She starts tugging at the hem of her shirt and gnawing on her bottom lip. The guy fixes a searing gaze on me, like he could kill me.

"I gotta go," says Penny abruptly.

"Sure. Okay." What else can I say? "See you next Tuesday?"

But she's not hearing me anymore. She jogs across the park to the guy on her front porch. He juts his cigarette butt in my direction, and they exchange sharp words. Then they both vanish inside the house.

I don't know how long I stand there, watching that red door. Maybe I'm waiting for Penny to come outside again, to tell me she'll have that lemonade after all. Not that it really matters, I guess. Like I said, I need those volunteer hours, but there's nothing that says I have to get along with this girl. If helping her doesn't work out, I'll just go somewhere else. No big deal.

I head back to my house. Norton called earlier to tell me the school board approved my joining the independent study program. After I worked in Mom's garden this morning, I spent a few hours messing with the website, trying to figure everything out.

I open my front door, pausing to look across the park at Penny's red door again. Thinking about her is starting to irritate me. What right does she have to judge me? I don't have to prove anything to her. What I do and what I've done is none of her business.

I step inside and slam the front door behind me.

Screw the lemonade.

PENNY

TEN

I DON'T OFTEN GO to the boys' basketball games, but Tali's got her eye on Connor Smith, the starting center. Accompanying her to ogle him from the sidelines doesn't sound too unpleasant, so after some intense pleading from Tali, I finally agree to go to Friday's game.

When we arrive at the school, Tali parks her Dad's borrowed Mustang in the most remote corner of the parking lot. Then we trudge toward the gym where shouting and band music spills from the open doors. By the time we find seats near the top of the bleachers, it's already ten minutes into the game. I spot Connor on the court, taking a pass from Jake. He shoots and sinks it. The audience roars. The score is already five to four with our team in the lead.

Tali leaps to her feet, cupping her hands around her mouth. "Connor! You're a God!"

He actually kind of looks like one, with his wavy golden hair and near-perfect physique.

Connor glances in our direction and gives a quick wave. Tali sinks onto the bench beside me and sighs. "I swear that boy is Apollo himself when he's on the court."

"When are you two actually going to make it official?" I ask.

"We will, eventually. I told him we'd meet him at Vinny's Pizza."

"We?" Vinny's is where the Kennedy Cougars gather to celebrate, or mourn, after a game. But since I haven't been too successful at "making friends" with my teammates, I haven't bothered going.

"Yes 'we'," says Tali, bumping me with her shoulder. "You didn't think I'd let you slink away from another victory party, did you? It's time you joined in the fun, Penny. Get out of that shell of yours."

I consider telling her that I got out of my shell in seventh grade. Still, gorging myself on ice-cold Coke and pizza does sound kind of fun. And besides, if I don't go with Tali, I'll just end up at home watching TV with Brett.

As expected, we destroy the opposing team. Afterward, half the school invades the pizza parlor, the team whooping and giving each other congratulatory slaps on the back. Tali and I order a medium combo and a pitcher of Coke, then take our number to the table nearest the team. Connor, his hair still wet from his after-game shower, joins us, straddling a chair.

"Hi, Tali," he says through a mischievous smile, revealing a set of perfect teeth. I wonder how long it's been since he's worn braces. "How'd you like the game?"

"You were spectacular." She runs a finger through the hair over his ear.

"Yeah?" he says.

"Yeah."

The complexity of their conversation is enough to make me gag. I reach for a cup and fill it with Coke.

"You know my friend, Penny." Tali points a thumb at me. Connor nods, a strand of wet hair flopping across his forehead.

"You're on the girls' team, right? I've seen you play. You're good."

I grip the plastic cup. "Uh, thanks."

Connor nods again, or I should say he's still nodding. His head has this perpetual gentle bounce to it, like he's bobbing up and down with an ocean current.

A server delivers our pizza. The scent of sausage and green peppers wafts off it. But before I can take a piece, a hand reaches over me and snags a slice. I whip around to see Jake shoving MY pizza into his big mouth.

"I paid for that," I tell him.

"Thanks!" He takes another bite then shouts to the room. "You guys! I told you it would work!"

Most of the eyes in the room focus on me. I shoot Tali a questioning look, but she just shrugs.

Jake keeps talking. "I propose we elect Penny Tate here as Kennedy's new mascot! What'dya say?"

The room explodes with cheers and laughter, but Jake's up to something.

Connor, who's also helped himself to my and Tali's pizza, pumps his fist in the air. "Penny! Penny! Penny!" he shouts, and a chorus of voices join him, chanting my name.

Jake leans in close. "I told you, Penny. You're my good luck charm. Thanks to you, we won the game." Am I the only one cluing into his sarcasm?

He moves too fast for me to react, sliding his arm around my neck in a chokehold. He pulls me up out of my chair and knuckle rubs my head.

"Stop it, Jake!" I try to wriggle out of his grip, but I can't. He's got me so tight, I'm gasping for air. All around me, I hear laughter. And then I feel more hard swipes at my scalp. Wet hands, sweaty and sticky with Coke and pizza sauce, knuckles, palms, fingertips. What? The whole team's doing it now?

"Knock it off, Jake!" I hear Tali shout. "Connor, do something!"

"C'mon, man," says Connor. "This isn't cool. Let her go."

Jake releases me. The moment he does, I pull in a deep, desperate breath—and then I run for the door.

The laughter follows me outside but starts to fade the farther from the restaurant I get. I'm running—in which direction, I have no idea. I just want to get away from here. My eyes sting with tears, but I don't bother wiping them away.

I'm about a block down when Tali's car pulls up beside me.

"Get in," she says through the window. I pull open the door and drop into the seat. Tali glances at me, but I don't dare look back.

"You shouldn't let Jake get to you. The guys were just fooling around," she says. "Okay. Fine, they're a bunch of dickheads. Well, Connor isn't a dickhead."

I know she means well, but I'm not really in the mood for talking.

"I'm sorry, Penny," Tali continues. "If I'd known this would happen…" She doesn't finish. When she lays a hand on my shoulder, I can't help it. I curl into her and burst into sobs.

"It's all right," says Tali. "You go on and cry as much as you want." She takes a package of tissues from her glove compartment and hands it to me. "Jake is such an idiot."

I dab my cheeks and blow my nose as discreetly as possible. "Thanks for coming for me."

"No problem. When you ran out, Connor called Jake a jerk, but Jake just brushed him off."

I take another tissue and hand back the package. The car idles at the corner, a block from Vinny's. Behind us we can see the kids from Kennedy through the restaurant window.

"Celine and Brett broke up," I say.

Tali gasps. "They did what? Are you serious?"

"I think Jake's taking it out on me."

"What a prick."

We sit quietly for a few moments. I'm not sure what I should do now. Get out of the car and walk home? I can't go back into the restaurant. But maybe Tali wants to.

"Tali, maybe I should—"

"Hold on," says Tali, her face lighting up. "I have an idea."

She taps three numbers into her cell phone.

"Who are you calling?"

Tali shushes me. "Hello? 9-1-1? I'm calling from Vinny's Pizza at—" She glances back at the oversized address printed on the restaurant's front door. "—2110

Burbank Drive…Yes, that's right. I'm reporting a public disturbance."

"Tali? What are you—"

"A bunch of local hoodlums are tearing the place apart. One kid in particular, I think I heard someone call him Jake? He seems to be the instigator. You better send the authorities right away before they hurt someone!"

Then Tali slaps the phone against the window a few times for effect before ending the call.

Tali turns her eyes, wide and panicked, on me. Then we both burst into hysterical laughter. The shriek of a distant siren cuts it short. Tali releases the emergency brake and hits the gas, burning rubber as she speeds away.

"What was that?" I say, laughing again. "I can't believe you! What balls!"

"*Balls?* I'm offended!" shouts Tali. She rolls down her car window and hollers at the top of her lungs, "I am woman! Hear me roar!" Then she shoves her hand out the window, shooting the bird at the diminishing image of Vinny's. "Take that, Jake Dillinger, and shove it up your—"

"Wait! Wait!" I giggle. "What if he gets arrested?"

"He won't," says Tali, rolling her window back up. "They'll figure out it's a prank."

"But he'll know it was us."

"So what if he does? What's he going to do about it? Winter break starts in a few days. After that, you won't see Jake for three whole weeks. By then, he'll have forgotten all about it."

I don't know what Jake will do or if he'll forget about it, but I can't worry about that now. I have to admit it feels good to have gotten some revenge, however slight.

"Where do you want to go?" asks Tali.

"I don't know. Home, I guess."

"Are you kidding?" Tali slaps the steering wheel with both palms. "It's too damn early to go home! I don't know about you, but I'm hungry. I had high hopes for that pizza we abandoned back at Vinny's, you know. You up for a burger?"

"Yes," I tell her. "Yes, I believe I am up for a burger."

"Great," says Tali, cranking up the volume on the radio. "But you're buying!"

Tommy's makes the best chili burgers, hands down. I don't exactly know what about the gloppy, greasy mess is so appealing. It just is.

I scoop a stray blob of chili off the wrapper with my finger and slide it into my mouth, then pop in a yellow pepper. I chase it all down with a slug of ice-cold root beer.

"I could eat a gallon of chili cheese fries," says Tali, spearing a wad of grease-soaked fries with a plastic fork.

"An all-time favorite." I help myself to one of her fries, and she takes one of my peppers. "I'm curious," I tell her, "what's really going on between you and Connor? It's pretty obvious you two are crazy about each other."

Tali twirls her fork in the cheese. "Kinda weird, isn't it? Actually, we've talked about going out a couple of times, but his parents are sort of—"

"Sort of what?"

She lets out an exasperated huff. "Let's just say they have their hearts set on having blonde, blue-eyed grandbabies someday, and I don't fit the bill." She gestures to her face and her dark, Tongan features.

"And Connor's all right with that?"

"No, he is not all right with that." She stabs her fries, releasing her vengeance on them. "But we're taking it slow. He'll tell them about me when it's the right time."

I finish my burger and crumple the cheese-smeared wrapper into a tight ball. Then I chuck it at the trash can.

"Two points!" I shout. Tali high-fives me, then tries the same maneuver with her wrapper—and misses. We clean up our table and head back out to the car.

"It's your turn," says Tali, starting the engine and shifting it into gear.

"My turn for what?"

"To reveal your innermost secrets."

"I don't want to talk about me."

"You *never* want to talk about you."

She's right. But after what she did for me tonight, I guess I can spare some transparency.

"Fine. What do you want to know?"

"Nothing important. Just boyfriends and stuff."

"What? You haven't noticed the harem of men following me around?"

"I'm serious."

"Just stuff," I tell her. "No boyfriends."

"Really? I find that hard to believe."

We pull onto the main road, heading in the direction of my house. I'm actually starting to feel wiped out and am looking forward to a long, undisturbed night of sleep.

"Well, believe it," I say, running a palm over my scalp. "I don't know too many boys who prefer bald to blonde."

"Oh, c'mon, Penny. You don't give yourself enough credit."

"But it's true."

"Fine. Then which guys do you find attractive? Got anyone on your radar lately?"

"No," I tell her. "No one."

"No one?" Tali casts me a seriously doubtful glance. "You mean to tell me there isn't a single solitary member of the opposite sex in your life?"

We pass by the street with Vinny's, but the restaurant is closed now, its windows dark. Whatever trouble Tali's call might have caused is over now. I'm almost sorry to have missed the show.

"There's my brother, Brett."

"He doesn't count! Try again."

"Well, there is this one guy at the community center."

"All right," says Tali eagerly. "Now we're talking. What's his name?"

"His name's Ryan, but he's a loser. Got himself kicked out of school."

"Oooh! A rebel. Is he cute?"

I hadn't really considered whether Ryan was cute before, but I suppose he sort of is. "He's got nice eyes, but he's really not my type."

She *tsks* at me. "Maybe you should give him a chance. Bad boys aren't always what they seem."

I think about how I treated Ryan yesterday. I wasn't very nice to him. True, he all but admitted he got busted because of drugs, but other than that, what did I really know about him? He was actually pretty good with the kids, and his invitation to hang out seemed sincere enough. Still, it'd be best to keep my distance.

"It just wouldn't work," I tell Tali, laughing at the idea of me and Ryan, or me and *anybody*.

"Why not?"

"We're just different, that's all."

Tali pulls the car into my driveway. I look across the park at Ryan's house, at least I think it's his house. It was the one he was pointing to when he asked me over for lemonade. All the windows are dark except for one on the second floor. I wonder if that's his room.

What am I thinking? I shake it off. Nuts to all that.

I open the car door and step out. "Thanks for the ride home."

Tali leans across the seat to look up at me. "Thanks for the chili fries. And, Penny," she says with a wink, "don't dismiss that guy so easily. Sometimes different isn't so bad."

RYAN

ELEVEN

SATURDAY, MY PARENTS give me the day off schoolwork and chores, but Mom insists I accompany Dad to physical therapy because the library is across the street and I need to pick out a book for English. I think she just doesn't want me hanging around the house alone for the two hours she and Justin are gone grocery shopping. Like, what am I going to do? Scurry off to the local strip club, or shoot up and get high or something? Town is eight miles from our house, and I have no wheels, no money, no nothing. I'd probably just climb into bed and take a very long nap.

Dad and I stop at the post office and then head downtown. We park outside the clinic, and Dad juts a thumb at the library.

"You can hang out there for a while," he says. "Find that book you need. Then how about I take you to lunch?"

"Sure." I try not to sound too bored.

I climb out of the car and zip my hoodie. The car beeps when Dad hits the auto lock on his key chain. Then he heads into the clinic.

I stand on the sidewalk staring at the library, a two-story building with wide, smoky windows and doors that look like a castle archway. Mom used to bring me here when I was a kid, before Dad's injury. She still brings Justin once in a while on her days off. He's always got a stack of cellophane-covered books in his room.

I head inside and start browsing a display of hardcovers. My course requires I read one text of my own choosing, but it has to be a "classic." I scan some of the titles, like *Catcher in the Rye* by J. D. Salinger. Read that in 9th grade. Next.

Night by Elie Wiesel. Good book, but I think I read that in 4th grade.

I move to the next display and pick up two John Steinbeck books, weighing them in my palms. *The Grapes of Wrath* and *Of Mice and Men*. Decisions, decisions. At 465 pages, the first book is a brick. Pass. The other's got just over a hundred pages. No contest.

I carry *Of Mice and Men* to the checkout counter. The librarian, a large man with a bad comb-over, informs me that I need a library card. I had one once, but who knows where that ended up. He looks me up in the system and issues me a new card, warning that the next replacement will cost me a dollar.

I thank him, tuck the book into my hoodie pocket, and head out the door. I'm not in the mood to just sit here and read. I prefer to do that at home in my room, where there are no distractions.

The street is lined with lots of shops, a café, and a grocery store. The community theater is down a few blocks. When I was younger, Mom took me to shows there—until I got too old and lost interest in people bursting into song at the drop of a hat. Now, like the library, she takes Justin. Last month, she took him to see *Hairspray*, one of her favorites. When they came home that night, both were belting out "I Can Hear the Bells" at the tops of their lungs. I called Justin a sissy, which sent him into a sullen slump and Mom into a fuming finger-wagging lecture about name-calling. But the truth was—and I'd never admit this to anyone—seeing all the fun they'd had together—the kind of fun Mom and I used to have—I was kind of jealous.

Curious what's playing at the theater now, I start off down the street. Along the way, I pass the Army surplus, Easy Pickins Pawn Shop, and a bunch of boutique stores displaying everything from collectible coins to cookbooks in their windows.

Before I know it, I reach the theater. There's an acrylic display out front with playbills and posters. I pick up a brochure from the lobby, then head back the way I came. The hour is almost up, so I'd better get back. Halfway to the library, I pause in front of Easy Pickins and look in the window.

The shop isn't very big, just a hole in the wall really, a narrow room lined with shelves. There's a massive grandfather clock near the door and two glass display cases stretching from one wall to the other. There's some pretty cool stuff in there. I glance back toward the clinic. No sign of Dad yet, so I slip inside the store.

The smell of *old* permeates the air. I browse a shelf where dozens of antique cameras are arranged, some probably at least a hundred years old. The display cases, on the other hand, are filled not only with all kinds of jewelry and watches, but also iPods, cell phones, video cameras, gaming devices, and more.

But what really catches my attention are the guitars. One whole wall is covered with them—acoustics, classicals, and electrics in every style and color. A virtual rainbow of sleek, shiny instruments.

I think about what Fred asked me the other day at the community center. Did I play bass guitar? The truth is, I wasn't half bad when I did. I dreamed of playing in a professional band someday. But that was a long time ago, a silly wish. I've got more important things to worry about now, like school.

Still…

I step up to the counter where a man with wrinkles as deep as the Grand Canyon asks if he can help me.

"Are any of those bass guitars?" I ask.

"Yup," he says. He reeks of tobacco. "Just got two. Don't get too many in here. Wanna see 'em?"

"Sure," I say.

He lifts two black guitars from their brackets on the wall. He hands me one of them over the counter. It's got a thin scratch down one side and the paint's dull from years of wear, but it feels heavy and solid in my hands. I pull my thumb across the four thick, metal strings which emit a deep, serious hum. I flip over the price tag tied around the neck: $79. A new bass guitar, on the low end, costs at least $250.

"What about the other one?" I ask.

We trade instruments. This one looks a lot like the other, but it's obviously much newer—shiny and not a nick on it. The price of the Fender is twice as much as the first, and no wonder. I pluck at the strings, imagining Les Claypool of Primus tearing out a killer riff.

When Dad got hurt, I just couldn't play anymore. So I sold my bass to a friend for twenty bucks. After Dad recovered from his accident enough to come home, he asked me what happened to it. I told him it broke. Neither of us ever brought it up again.

I guess time gets away from me, because when I finally stop playing, I look up to find my dad watching me through the store window. I hadn't even noticed him walk up. For a second, a jolt of shame shoots through me. I'm supposed to be at the library. He must have gone there looking for me, then headed down the street to find me goofing off.

I hand the bass back to the sales clerk and thank him. Then I head for the door, expecting Dad to lecture me. But instead, he asks if I found what I was looking for. I show him the library book, and we go to lunch.

PENNY

TWELVE

IT'S BEEN DAYS SINCE the post-game fiasco with Jake Dillinger, but I can't stop thinking about it. I spend Monday and Tuesday evading him in every way possible. I begin to feel like a ghost, an invisible being haunting the halls. Even Tali notices. A few times during practice, she asks if I'm okay. I lie and tell her I'm fine, but the truth is I'm scared. Jake's got to know Tali and I called the cops. He's bound to find some way to get even.

So, I'm glad when Tuesday's final bell rings. After school, I head over to the center, grab my clipboard and ball bag, and meet the kids on the court. I'm actually looking forward to seeing Ryan again, talking to someone who doesn't know me well and who doesn't have any pre-conceived notions about me. But Ryan is nowhere to be found. Typical. I guess I had him pegged right after all: just a run-of-the-mill loafer. Who needs him anyway?

I hand out the balls to the kids and begin coaching them on dribbling. We've gone over this several times this month, but it isn't easy for them. Most have trouble with hand/eye coordination, and about half can't even catch the ball due to physical disabilities, like Danny, who has cerebral palsy. But that's okay. The kids try their best and laugh easily at themselves when the ball goes flying into the bushes or gets tangled in their feet. For the few kids who have dribbling down, I move them to one end of the court to practice shooting baskets. It's a rare occasion when someone makes one, and when they do, everyone cheers. It's honestly impossible not to have fun doing this.

About five minutes into practice, I notice the door to Ryan's house open. Ryan bursts out of it and sprints across the park like he's got wild animals at his heels. He comes to a halt on the court, doubles over with his hands on his knees, and wheezes for breath.

"Sorry," he gasps. "Sorry I'm late."

I pull a ball from the bag and pass it to him, harder than I probably should. He catches it with a grunt.

"Go help the kids under the basket," I tell him. Then I turn my back to him and focus on the dribbling.

During practice, I avoid making eye contact with Ryan or even speak to him, except for occasionally assigning him a new task. I don't know if I'm angrier that he was late or that he showed up at all. I silently chide myself for thinking, even for a second, that he might be an okay guy.

But when I glance at him from time to time to make sure he's doing what he's been told, he is. And while last time he held back a bit, just running rebound mostly, today he's actually interacting with the kids. He's making an effort to learn their names, and he compliments them on their effort. The kids seem to like him, which, for some reason, makes me even madder.

After the kids have gone home, Ryan corrals the balls into their bag. No words pass between us as we enter the community center.

While Fred signs Ryan's form, he asks me about Brett. "Any chance that brother of yours'll change his mind about BandMasterz?"

I feel bad for Fred. He was counting on Brett to play again this year. I hate having to give excuses for him, but Brett said no, and that was final.

Dejected, Fred hands back the form, and then Ryan starts for the ball cabinet.

"Not today," I tell him. "I'm taking the balls home for disinfecting. Some of the kids have weak immune systems, so I try to keep them clean."

I reach for the ball bag, anxious to get home, but Ryan slings it over his shoulder like Santa carrying a big sack of toys. "I'll carry them."

"I can manage."

"Really. It's no problem."

"Have it your way."

We leave the center and start across the park, heading toward my house. After a few minutes, Ryan starts talking.

"Can I ask you a question? What's BandMasterz?"

I'm not really in the mood for conversation, but whatever. "It's for teen musicians," I tell him. "The center organizes them into bands. They practice for a few weeks and then put on a concert."

"How much does it cost?"

"Nothing. It's a service provided by the community, although people who attend the concert are encouraged to make a donation, which funds programs like the one I teach."

Ryan shifts the heavy bag to his other shoulder. I remember he told Fred he played the piano, so I say, "They have enough keyboard players, by the way."

"But they need a bass player, right?"

That's right. He had mentioned bass, too. For a split moment, I think maybe this guy might have something to offer after all.

"You want to join up? They could use some help."

"I don't know," he says. "It's been a long time."

"So, you *don't* play."

Ryan rubs a hesitant thumb over his lips. "I don't even have a bass anymore."

Seriously?

"Sorry to burst your bubble," I tell him, "but these bands need *real* musicians."

"Yeah," he says. "You're right. Forget I asked. It was a dumb idea anyway."

I stop walking and spin back to face Ryan. I've had enough of this guy for today. "Hand over the bag. Volunteer hours are over, Ryan. Go home."

He pauses as if waiting for me to say something else, like maybe I'm joking. I'm not.

"Sorry," he says finally. "I didn't think you'd mind my walking you home. I thought maybe we could hang out?"

His comment takes me off guard. It's not every day guys want to spend time with me. But I don't know anything about him except that he's a screw-up needing to make peace with his school.

But he's a nice screw-up, I guess.

What have I got to lose? Brett's probably still in one of his moods. His car is gone, so who knows where he's run off to. Mom won't be home for hours. Nothing for me to do except homework and Netflix. But then again, what if Ryan gets the wrong idea?

I picture my own image: smooth head, alien face. Wrong idea? I don't think so.

"Fine," I say finally with a resigned breath. "Just—fine."

We take our time walking across the street. Neither of us talks much until Ryan says something about how one of the kids, Julie, seems to love playing basketball. Then he asks me how I began working with them, and that gets me started. I can't help myself—I tell him how a year ago I was feeling kind of depressed, and my mom told me I should stop thinking so much about myself and "give back to the world." I started volunteering at the center months before we moved into this neighborhood, and it's made a big difference for me.

Ryan listens, and then before I know it, we're at my front door.

"That was fast," Ryan says, smiling. It's a nice smile. And suddenly I remember everything I told Tali about him. I can't believe I said he has nice eyes!

Even though he does.

He stands there, leaning against the door jamb, one hand shoved deep into his pants pockets the other gripping the ball bag. He's wearing Levi's, a ratty pair of Converse, and a snug T-shirt. I hadn't noticed before, but he's ripped. I force my eyes from his biceps back to his face. He smiles at me, looking way too cute for a guy like him. But he was pretty great with the kids today, and he's lugged that cluster of basketballs all the way from the community center.

I unlock the door and push it open, thinking about what Brett would say if he found some strange boy in our house. But it's not like I get a lot of visitors. And it's just for a few minutes. No harm in that.

"You want some cookies?" I ask.

"Sure," he says. "How can I say no to cookies?"

Ryan sets the balls down in the entry and then follows me into the kitchen. I retrieve my stash of Thin Mints from the cabinet along with a gallon of milk and two mugs. He takes half a dozen from the box and pops one into his mouth.

"I didn't think it was Girl Scout cookie season yet."

I take a cookie, snap it in two, and slide one half into my mouth. "Believe it or not, these are from last year. My mom stocks up," I say once I've swallowed. "She buys, like, a thousand boxes, hides them away and brings out one box at a time."

"So, she's like a cookie squirrel."

"A what?"

"You know, squirrels hoard nuts for the winter."

"Oh, right. I get it." I offer him another cookie.

"You got any Samoas?" asks Ryan. "They're my favorite."

The irritation I felt during the basketball class has melted. "Mine too," I say, laughing. "And Mom's. She hides those so well, I've never been able to find them."

"You've tried?"

"Of course, I've tried. But not even Nancy Drew could find those suckers. This year, Mom only gave my brother and me one box to share, and when those were gone, they were gone. The rest are hers. Hands off or else."

"Don't get between a mom and her Samoas."

"Right."

We finish off the box of Thin Mints without saying much else. When we're done, Ryan takes both our mugs and rinses them in the sink. Then he turns to face me, drying his hands on a dish towel.

"So," he says, "you wanna shoot some hoops?"

I can tell by the grin on his face that he's joking. "How about a video game instead?" I offer.

Ryan considers this for a few seconds. "I've got a better idea," he says. "When does your mom get home?"

"She's a nurse at the hospital. Tonight she's got the late shift. Why?"

"Good. Then we've got all the time in the world. How about we hunt for those Samoas?"

I'm tempted to explain that I've already scoured every inch of the house a dozen times over. But why should I tell him?

"Sure," I reply, repressing a grin. "Sure. Why not?"

Ryan rubs his hands together and starts systematically opening the kitchen cabinets. I lean back against the counter to observe his search. I'll let him explore for a while before I suggest he give up. In the meantime, I'm having fun. More fun, I have to admit, than I've had in a long time.

RYAN

THIRTEEN

HOMESCHOOL SUCKS. After almost two weeks of it, my brain has decomposed into something like the peach Jell-O salad we ate at dinner last night. It isn't the studying so much as the studying *alone*. No one to talk to except Justin, when he's home. No one to team up or hang out with. The word boring is a serious understatement. I want my friends back, my phone back. I want to play *Fortnite* on my freakin' PS4!

Mom's chores are another thing. So far, I've spent a total of nine mornings in that stupid garden of hers, pulling weeds, digging up rocks, building one of those white picket fence borders. I dread to see what else she has in store for me.

The truth is, I can't focus. Not today, the two-year anniversary of Dad's accident. No one in the family talks about it, pretending it's just like any other day. But it invades my every thought. And to make things worse, I can't stop thinking about that bass guitar I saw at the pawn shop over the weekend, because two years ago today was also the last time I played. My mind drifts to what it felt like to hold an instrument again, the weight of it in my arms, the slick finish against my skin. But then reality hits me, everything I have to do to prepare for that meeting with the school board. I can't waste time dreaming about music. I gotta get back into Middleton.

I work on the computer for another half hour before saving my progress and logging off the school site. Dad's gone to pick up Justin from school, so he's not here to peer over my shoulder or offer for the umpteenth time to help me with math, which is a joke because he was never any good at it, even in college.

I stare at my dull, gray ghost of a reflection in the dead computer screen. That stupid guitar keeps picking at my brain. Finally, I can't fight it anymore. I turn the computer back on and go to YouTube, something I haven't dared to try yet due to my parents' constant hovering. Maybe the Web Watcher thing will block it, but no. I'm in luck. Mom probably has it set to block out only the really nasty stuff. But she and Dad will be able to see the history. They'll know what sites I've been to. But there are links to various websites in my online lessons. I could claim I was doing research for school. Just to be on the safe side, I type 'American Revolution' into the YouTube search engine and scan through a bunch of docu-snoozes. I find one that's two minutes long and watch it with half-hearted interest. Now if Mom confronts me, I can show her this.

When it's over, I type in the name of my favorite band. The music explodes from the computer speakers. Oops. If Dad walks in and hears this, I'm screwed.

I run upstairs to my room and grab a pair of earbuds. I leave one bud dangling, so I can hear when he comes home. Then I lean back in my chair to watch Vampire Weekend's Chris Baio slamming out "Campus's" sweet bass line.

I love the bass guitar. There's something about the thrum of those deep, low notes that literally makes your bones vibrate. I know the lead guitar always gets the glory, but it's the bass line that gives every song its soul.

It wasn't that I lost interest in piano or guitar. Music was everything. But after Dad's accident, things changed. My priorities changed. I had to let something go.

I listen to a few more songs, and then I hear a car door slam outside. I close YouTube and return to the school site just as Dad and Justin come in.

"We're home, Ryan. Did you get your assignments done?" asks Dad.

"I think so," I reply, casually shutting down the computer. Watching Dad limp into the kitchen, a grocery bag in each arm, immediately sends a wave of guilt through me. What was I thinking? I don't have time to mess around with music anymore. Dad deserves better from me.

While Dad starts putting stuff away, Justin wanders over with a Twinkie in each hand. "Want one?" he asks.

He and I have this thing about Twinkies. A few years back, when Hostess stopped making them, we set up this wish jar in his room. Every day we'd drop a penny in and make a wish that Twinkies would come back. It was more of a joke than anything else, something silly to keep us occupied. But after a few months, we started taking it seriously, collecting loose change wherever we could find it, not just pennies, but quarters, dimes, nickels. Justin even wrote a letter to Hostess explaining all the reasons why America needed Twinkies. I guess it worked because they eventually did come back. I'm sure it had nothing to do with the letter. The whole thing was just some major marketing ploy to boost sales. But Justin and I were happy to have our little golden buddy back. It was the one thing we had in common, and the one thing I could count on to keep Justin as my ally. The money jar still sits on his windowsill, nearly full to the top with all that change.

After removing the plastic sleeve, I bite off one end of my Twinkie and suck out the cream filling. "So, you wanna help me in the garden this afternoon?" I ask with intentional indifference. I don't want to appear too desperate, or Justin might catch on to the fact that I hate working out there alone.

"Why?" Justin asks.

"I wanna finish what I started this morning before Mom gets home. Just thought maybe you'd like to join me."

He finishes his Twinkie before answering. "I dunno. Maybe. What are you doing?"

"Just digging out a few more rocks and mixing in some fertilizer."

Justin squishes up his face. "Yuck."

That's what I thought too.

"It isn't so bad," I tell him. "C'mon. With two of us working, it'll take half as long."

"But doesn't Mom want *you* to do it? You know, to teach you a lesson or something?"

"I guess, but what am I going to learn by playing in the dirt? What she really wants is a garden, right? Somewhere to grow zucchini and carrots and stuff."

"Yeah?"

"You know she gets off on being self-reliant and all that. So, what'dya say, Justin? You with me on this?"

He hesitates, but I can tell he's liking the idea of getting involved in something other than homework and practicing piano. I'm sure he's about to say yes when he gets this doubtful look on his face.

"What about Dad?" he asks.

"He won't care. In fact, he might appreciate us working together to get the job done faster."

Justin considers this for a second. "But I get to wear Dad's work gloves."

"Whatever you say, bro."

Justin's been digging in the dirt for half an hour, completely intent on building a pile of stones in the corner of the yard and oblivious to the fact that I'm just sitting here watching him. There's only one pair of gloves, so we agreed to take turns with the hoe. I worked first to appear fair, but after about ten minutes, Justin was getting bored, so I graciously let him take over. And boy, can that kid dig. The way he hammers the blade into the ground, you'd swear he has a vendetta against it. He grunts with every downward swing, the hoe hacking away at dirt clods and clinking against rocks, which Justin plucks up and studies like an archeologist. Then he sets each one on his stone heap, which is looking more like an Egyptian pyramid with each passing minute.

I figure I'd better do some of the work myself before he starts to get wise about my little scheme.

"Okay, bro, why don't you let me take over for a while? You're all hot and sweaty."

Justin hands me the hoe and the gloves and then takes a seat on the front steps. I slide on the gloves and start whacking away at the now mostly cleared soil. Justin did a pretty thorough job. Mom should be pleased when she gets home tonight. Setting the hoe aside, I head for the 25-pound bags of fertilizer piled up against the side of the house. I heft the first onto my shoulder and just reach the middle of the garden when I get an uneasy, creeping feeling up the back of my neck—the kind you get when you know someone's watching you.

Thinking maybe Mom's home early from work, I drop the bag and turn to face her, but it isn't Mom.

"Hey, Andrew," I say.

"Hey," he says back.

Andrew is a friend from Middleton. Back in the day, we were in the same band. Now we just light up together sometimes.

Justin stares at him suspiciously.

"Justin, why don't you head inside and get some of Mom's lemonade," I tell him. "You've been working hard."

"I don't wanna go inside," he whines.

"Just do it. Okay?"

He gets up from the step and drags his feet all the way into the house. Soon enough, I'm alone with Andrew.

He's taller than me, just shy of six feet, but thin as a broomstick. His brown hair is cropped military style, like all the boys at Middleton. He's only a year older than me, but he looks twenty. He's got his longboard under one arm.

"Wanna ride?" he asks.

I haven't heard from this guy in almost two weeks. Now all of a sudden, he's on my doorstep, acting as if I didn't fall off the face of the planet. I know why he's really here, and it isn't because he wants to skateboard.

"Man, I can't," I tell him. "If you hadn't noticed, I got kicked out of school. My parents are watching my every move."

He eyes me sympathetically. His pupils are blown. He's already high, just doesn't want to enjoy it alone.

"Yeah. All right," he says. "Listen, Ry. The guys and I are gonna meet at the park tonight around eleven with some other kids from school. I'll save a spot for you. K?"

A shot of adrenaline pulses through me. Hanging out with my friends would be the perfect cure for my boredom—and the memories this day has dumped on me. I'm about to say yeah, I'll be there, but then I think of the school board and Mom's rules, including no hanging out with friends. And I remember what got me into this mess in the first place.

I really want to go, but I've got too much at stake.

"Thanks for the invite," I say to Andrew, "but I've got tons of homework. Maybe next time."

Andrew tips his head back and sucks air through his teeth like he's just received bad news. "It's just that, well, I promised the guys you'd come. They miss you, man."

"Yeah, but my parents—"

"Who says they have to know? Wouldn't be the first time you snuck out. C'mon," he adds, poking my shoulder with his forefinger, "you deserve a night out."

He's got a point. Maybe I could go, for a little while, spend an hour with some actual human beings and revive my sanity. What could that hurt?

Andrew raises a fist. I bump it with my own. "Can't promise anything," I tell him, "but I'll try to make it."

Andrew leaves, and I watch him skateboard down our street. I want more than anything to be out there with him. On my board. Cruising the neighborhood with my phone plugged into my ears rocking to the Chili Peppers.

I'm still gazing after Andrew when Dad appears at the door.

"Who was that?" he asks.

Without a pause, I tell him, "Nobody. Just someone asking for directions."

Dad hardly hears me. He's busy extracting mail from the mailbox. "That's nice," he says. When he heads back inside, his prosthetic catches on the threshold. He stumbles forward, off balance. I move to help him, but before I get there, he's caught hold of the door and stopped his fall. Still, I hate seeing this once strong, independent soldier struggling to take a simple step.

"Damn leg," he mutters before going inside and shutting the door.

That's when I make my decision. I'm going to the park. No matter what.

Mom comes home from work looking miserable. Her shoulders are slumped, and her head droops. She shuffles into the house and drops her keys on the entry table.

"Hi, Honey," says Dad, kissing her.

Mom rubs her left shoulder. "I pulled a muscle. I swear those Amazon boxes get heavier every day."

Dad disappears into the kitchen and returns with a cup of water and two orange pills in his palm. "Here," he says, holding them out to Mom. "Take these, then upstairs to bed. I'll get the heating pad and the muscle cream."

Mom groans. "I promised we'd decorate the Christmas tree tonight."

Decorating the tree is one of Dad's favorite activities—second only to doing up the front yard for Halloween. He has a massive collection of holiday stuff, which he stores in rubber bins in the attic. Everything is labeled and color-coded. Dad takes his holidays very seriously.

"The boys can decorate the tree," Dad says. "You go rest."

Justin and I trade worried glances. Us? Decorate the tree? Without Mom around to dictate where every single ornament is supposed to go?

Mom groans again, and then Frankenstein-monsters it up the stairs. I normally hate it when she isn't feeling well, but maybe this time it will work to my advantage.

Dad sends me up to the attic for the bin of ornaments, which I drag through the house and park beside our fake tree.

"You know how it goes," he says, popping off the lid and leaning it behind the piano. "Make sure they are spaced evenly apart, and don't let the tinsel cover up the special ones. And put the lights on first."

"We've got it, Dad." I pull out the first ornament, a ceramic rocking horse with Justin's birth date painted on its rump. Dad spies it and gets a nostalgic look in his eye. That's all I need, to have him getting sentimental when there's work to be done. I've got to distract him. "Dad, the heating pad?"

Dad snaps back to attention, and a moment later, he's headed upstairs with his cache of medical aids for Mom's shoulder.

Justin and I have the tree trimmed and lighted in forty minutes flat. We stand back to admire our accomplishment. I start to think maybe Justin and I are a good team. Garden. Christmas tree. But then Justin turns on the gaming console and dives into Mario Kart. I would give just about anything to play a video game right now, but I know not to bother asking for permission. At least I can sit and watch him play.

After a while, Dad comes downstairs, a concerned look on his face.

"How's Mom?" I ask.

He blinks and sighs. "Sleeping finally. She really did a number on herself. She might have to take a few days off work."

He tells Justin to turn off the game and go to bed.

"I'm going to study," I tell him. I grab a textbook from the dining table and hold it up as evidence. "Got a quiz coming up."

"Don't stay up late," he says, then follows Justin upstairs.

I wait out the next two hours with the patience of God before quietly heading upstairs to check on everyone. Justin's lying in bed wearing ear buds, probably listening to a book on his iPod. Dad's binge-watching *CSI* on Netflix next to Mom, who is so deep asleep she looks dead. If I slip away for a bit, no one will miss me. If they do, I'll just tell them I was out in the garden doing some late-night weeding or something.

Weed. That reminds me.

I step into my bedroom, quietly closing the door. Then I go to my dresser. I know it's sort of cliché to stash secrets in the sock drawer, but I've got mine taped to the underside. Impossible to spot unless you take it out and flip it upside down.

Mom has searched my room a couple times since I got suspended from Middleton. I know because I've found certain things slightly off kilter from where I'd left them before. But so far, she's come up empty-handed.

I start for the baggie with the pair of joints, lighter, and pills—today of all days I could use them—but then I think better of it. Since I've been home, Mom's tested me three times, all negative, of course. The guys tonight are sure to be smoking. I wonder if second-hand pot will result in a positive reading. Just to be on the safe side, I'd better steer clear of the weed and just enjoy the social stuff. I'll stop by long enough to say my hellos, let everyone know I'm not dead, and then come home.

Things are well underway by the time I arrive at the park at a quarter past eleven. Andrew sits on one of the picnic tables, strumming a steel-string guitar. He's singing a very off-key rendition of "Little Drummer Boy" with some other kid failing miserably at a David Bowie impression. About a dozen other kids are here too, some sitting, some standing. I recognize most of them from school and around the neighborhood. A few I've never seen before.

I mosey up to Andrew, and we do our customary fist bump. "Ry, you made it," he says in a relaxed voice. He reeks of pot. He grabs the shoulder of the boy nearest him, a guy built like a truck. "This is my cousin, Benji. He's visiting from Nebraska. Where the hell is Nebraska anyway?" Even though the kid's big, he's at least a year or two younger than me.

"Yeah," Andrew says to his cousin, "this here is Ry. He and I and some of these other guys used to play in a band together. We rocked, man."

At the mention of the band, Pete and Darren come over to say hi. To my surprise, Chris Segarra is here too, our old drummer who sold me and Jenn the pills at school. With his clean-cut polo shirt style, it's no wonder he got away with dealing for so long. After turning him in, I didn't think I'd ever have to face him again.

The air is colder than I anticipated. I zip my hoodie and stick my hands in my pockets.

"Good to see you, man," says Chris.

"You too," I reply, trying not to show how anxious I feel.

Pete tips back a beer, taking a long swallow. "How's it goin', Ryan?" he asks, wiping his mouth on his sleeve. "So, where've you been? I haven't seen you in, like, forever."

"You know what happened," says Chris. "Same that happened to me. He got kicked out." He laughs like it was all a big joke.

Pete lands a soft punch on my arm. "Way to go," he says. "Wish I'd had the guts to stand up to Norton like that. Tell him what I think of his dumb school."

I try to laugh.

"I thought the two of you'd be arrested for sure," says Pete.

"Nah, man," says Chris. "I didn't have any hard stuff on my person, if you know what I mean. I would've been fine if someone hadn't squealed on me."

Pete shakes his head. "I'll bet Jenn spilled everything."

Chris reaches behind him and pulls a beer out of a cardboard case, pops it open, takes a swallow. He looks at me over the rim, and for a second, I wonder if he knows about what I told Norton.

"My parents wouldn't believe any of it," Chris says. "Instead, they accused Norton of running a second-rate school. So, my mom pulled me out and transferred me to Mission, that brainiac school downtown. Now I'm surrounded by dickheads all the time."

"Should feel right at home then, right Chris?" Darren busts up at his own joke. Chris just shakes his head.

"What about you?" Pete points his can toward me. "You at a new school too?"

"No," I tell them. "I'm, uh, being homeschooled."

There's a pause as everyone stares at me and gawks.

"That sucks," says Chris finally.

"Yeah." I pick at a loose thread inside my hoodie pocket. Wanting to shift the attention off me, I change the subject. "So, what about Jenn? Anybody seen her?"

Everyone goes quiet as Pete slides a hand across his bristly red hair. "I've seen her. Came back to school after a few days in the hospital to empty her locker. Got a concussion is all. I heard she transferred."

I'm relieved that Jenn is all right, though it's too bad she couldn't stay at Middleton. Like me, she had a good shot at getting into a top school. I wonder what she'll do now.

Chris reaches into his jacket and pulls out a Ziploc baggie. He leans close to me. "Here," he whispers, sliding it into my hand. "This is for you. In honor of the good old days."

I look at the baggie. Inside are half a dozen pills, but it's so dark now I can't even tell what color they are.

"Thanks, but I'm not partaking tonight, if you know what I mean." I try to hand them back, but Chris won't take them.

"They're harmless," he says, jabbing a thumb towards Andrew, who's now crooning "White Christmas" like a sick puppy baying at the moon. "Andy there took one and is feeling just fine."

"I can't, man. My mom's been drug testing me."

"How often?"

"She tested me this morning, so it'll probably be a few days before the next one."

Chris takes another gulp of his beer. "*No problemo*. By then, any trace of this will be long gone from your system."

I open the baggie and take out one of the pills, cradling it in my palm. I see Jenn lying on the floor—and the blood—it all comes back to me.

"C'mon, Rojas," Chris coaxes. "You used to be adventurous. Live a little, why don'tcha?"

I blink away the image of Jenn. Then I stuff the bag back into Chris's pocket. "No thanks, man."

Andrew, Darren, and the others all stand around drunk or high. I look at my watch. I haven't been here more than a few minutes, and I'm already done.

"I'm going home," I tell the guys.

"So soon?" asks Chris. "You just got here. I was hoping maybe we could coax you to play a few songs with us for old time's sake. Andrew, hand over that guitar!"

Chris knows I play bass, not guitar. He's just egging me on, I see that now.

I try to laugh it off. "I don't want to risk getting caught on my first night out, you know?" But the truth is, I just don't want to be here anymore.

Chris snorts, like he can't believe what he's hearing. He holds out a beer. "Have a drink with us first," he says. His eyes lock on mine, like a challenge. "What's one beer gonna do?"

I look at the can, Chris's fingers spread open around it. I think of the disappointment in my dad's eyes that day in Norton's office, and how he almost fell today.

Today.

Two years ago today, I was with these same guys: Andrew, Darren, Pete, and Chris. This isn't a coincidence, I realize. It's a set-up.

"How's your dad these days?" Chris asks like he's reading my mind.

A hot brick forms in my gut. I'm starting to want that beer. A few sips won't do any harm. Just drink something, let them think I'm still part of the gang, and then I'll head home.

So, I take the can, which has already been opened, and swirl it around a bit. "It's half empty," I say.

Chris laughs. "Yeah, well, I guess I spilled some." Then he holds out the baggie with the pills, dangles it in front of my face.

The guys are all looking at me now. Even Andrew is smirking.

"Just one," says Chris. "Then you can slink off to your little homeschooling party."

He says this with thick sarcasm that twists inside me. I shouldn't have told them about being homeschooled. I'll never live it down.

"What is it?" I ask.

Chris shrugs. "Does it matter?"

Darren cackles with laughter. "See, I told you," he says, spittle flying from his mouth. "He's a pussy!"

Chris sways the baggie back and forth in front of me. When he starts to pull it back, I reach out and grab it. I pull open the bag, pluck out a pill, and pop it into my mouth. I take a swig of the beer. Then I take another. It's cold and smooth going down. I finish it off, crush the can between my palms, and toss it back to Chris. He's grinning like the Joker.

We stand around for a few more minutes. Andrew is singing again, but the words are so messed up, I have no idea what song it is. Some of the other guys join in, a mangled chorus of God knows what. Pathetic.

After a while, I turn back to Chris. "Thanks," I tell him. "And when he's sober, let Andrew know I appreciate his inviting me tonight."

I start walking toward my house, but it seems farther than usual, like the grass has stretched way out in front of me. I squeeze my eyes shut and open them again, but it doesn't help. What was in that baggie? I look down. The grass swirls around my feet and sways up and down in waves.

I realize that someone is walking beside me. It's Chris, and he isn't smiling anymore. I think maybe he's going to help me. I feel odd, like the world is melting away, but I keep walking, trying to get home. Halfway across the park, Chris steps in front of me, blocking my path. He leans in close and whispers in my ear.

"You pretend to be all high and mighty, some devout school boy trying to make his crippled dad proud. But you haven't changed one bit, Ryan. You're still just like the rest of us."

Then he shoves my chest—hard—and I stumble back. The ground feels like Jell-O under my feet. I go down. And then Chris kicks me in the ribs. A sharp pain stabs into me.

He bends over me, breathing hard. "It wasn't enough that you broke up the band. You had to try to take me down too."

Chris kicks me again, but I can't fight back. I can't move.

"Nighty, night, snitch." He wriggles his fingers in my face, then everything goes dark.

PENNY

FOURTEEN

"WHATCHA WATCHING?" Brett drops down on the couch beside me and pops open a Coke. He slurps loudly, doing his best to annoy me.

"C'mon, Brett. Really?"

He leans in close enough to lick my ear if he wanted and guzzles from the can. I guess this is better than him fuming and ignoring me like he has the past couple weeks.

I jab him in the ribs with my elbow.

"Ow!"

"Go watch something in Mom's room," I tell him. "I'm trying to have some quiet time."

"I thought you were going out with Tali tonight. Weren't you supposed to go shopping or something?"

"She cancelled. Her boyfriend's parents are out of town, so they made last minute plans, which don't include me."

Brett finishes off his drink and crushes the can. I've never understood what it is about boys and erroneous displays of masculinity. What does squashing a hollow object made of the lightest metal on earth prove anyway?

He tosses the Coke can behind him and misses the garbage by at least a yard. It clatters against the tile floor, and I imagine the drops of Coke leaving behind a sticky residue that I'll end up having to clean in the morning.

"You're going to pick that up, right?"

He groans, but to his credit, he does get up to rescue the stray can, dropping it into the trash. I hear the fridge open, and Brett pops open another can. Next, I hear the sound of paper shuffling on the kitchen counter.

"What are you doing?" I call out. "You'd better not be messing with my homework."

He's not above doodling on my History assignments.

"Mail," he says. "Nothing for me as usual. But hey…"

He returns to the living room with an oversized marketing postcard in his hand. "Did you see this, Pen? It's another invitation to that basketball camp you've been raving about all year."

"Yeah, I saw it."

He hands it to me. I meant to throw it out earlier, like everything IMG sends me, but I forgot. I wad the stiff paper into a ball and chuck it into the trash. My aim is better than Brett's.

"I told you before," I say. "Not happening."

Brett frowns. "You should apply. You're really good, good enough for a scholarship."

If only he knew the truth about IMG already offering me one, but he can't know. Not ever.

"Or you could ask Dad to pay for it. He did offer once. Remember?"

"I wouldn't ask Dad for a dime!"

I don't mean to shout. Brett clams up quick. He knows how I feel about the man who calls himself our father. We both feel the same way. But my decision is not about Dad or the money. It's about Brett, but I could never tell him that.

We sit quietly on the couch for a few more minutes, Brett drinking his Coke, me trying to think about anything else, when Brett asks, "Why don't *I* take you shopping?"

Did I just hear an invitation coming from my brother's mouth? My brother, who has his own car, a thousand dollars in his savings account, and a credit card?

"It's too late," I tell him. "It's after eleven."

"Walmart's open 'til midnight."

I'm off the couch in a nanosecond. "You sure?" I'm already halfway down the hall to my room. "I mean, really. Only if it isn't any trouble."

"It's no trouble," says Brett. "I gotta shop, too. I need a present for Mom. What do you think she'd want for Christmas?"

A son in a good mood, but I don't say that. "I dunno. A new umbrella? Maybe California will actually get some rain this winter."

My room is in the front of the house with a sweeping view of the entire park. Mostly, I keep my blinds closed because who wants a bunch of weirdos looking into my room all the time? I grab my wallet and a sweater when I hear a commotion outside. Music, if you can call it that, a guitar maybe. And something like singing. What's going on out there?

I step to the window and pull back the curtain. Sure enough, there's a bunch of idiots at the picnic tables. One of them, clearly drunk, is serenading some other equally out-of-it boys. I can't tell if they're high or motion sick.

Brett hollers at me from the other room. "I just texted Mom to let her know we're going out. Okay? Penny?"

The light at the park isn't that great. There are a couple of old streetlamps along the sidewalk that cast a faded yellow glow. The groupies sit under one of them. There are maybe a dozen kids in all.

Brett appears in my bedroom doorway. "Something wrong?"

"No. Just a bunch of screw ups getting drunk out there. That's all."

I'm about to let the curtain fall back into place when I notice two of the guys break away from the group, heading toward the far side of the park. Normally, I wouldn't care what these idiots are doing, but something about one of the guys seems familiar, so I keep watching. When they pause under a street lamp, I realize that one of them is Ryan.

To think I let that guy work with my kids. And I let him in my house! I am definitely going to complain to Fred after Christmas.

Ryan seems off balance. *Serves him right.* But then the guy he's with shoves him, and Ryan falls. The guy kicks him a few times in the gut. What the hell?

Brett appears at my elbow and glances over my shoulder through the window. "What's going on?"

Something is very wrong, though my brain screams at me that it shouldn't matter. I shouldn't give a damn. But my conscience gets the better of me.

I drop the curtain back into place and tell Brett, "I'm going out there."

RYAN

FIFTEEN

"GET UP! GET THE HELL UP!"

Something sharp digs into my ribcage, followed by a ferocious push that sends ripples of pain through my back and chest. I swat at whatever's attacking me, but my arms feel heavy, and lifting them feels like I'm lifting a pair of wet mattresses.

"Gowray." My words come out garbled. So, I try again. "Leavemarone."

"I can't understand a word you're saying, you realize that?"

I know that voice, though it sounds sort of distant, like it's coming at me through a long tube. The sharp pain hits me again.

"Owww," I say, though it kinda sticks in my throat.

Then I feel something slide beneath both my arms, pulling at me. That's when I realize I'm lying face down on the ground. I groan as the mysterious—whatever—gets me into a sort of slumped-over sitting position. Something digs in my pocket like a chipmunk. I slap at it.

"Would you stop that?" the voice barks.

I hear the sound of plastic crinkling. I crack open my eyes and see a hand shaking a plastic baggie in front of my face. There are some little pills inside.

"What did you take?" asks the voice, which now sounds way too close.

"Stop shouting," I say, wiping dribble off my chin with my sleeve.

"I'm not shouting, you imbecile. What did you take?"

"Who cares?"

The voice huffs. "Because if you're gonna O.D. on me, I'll have to call 9-1-1. That's why."

"I dunno. I dunno." Hearing 9-1-1 scares me. What happened? I remember feeling really woozy, still do. Chris...saying something...

With my eyes open, I take a second to identify the source of the voice. Big blue eyes. Bald head. Penny.

"Did you take these?" She shakes the baggie in front of my face again.

It looks familiar, so I nod, at least I think I do. With the swirling ache in my brain, it's hard to tell.

"How many?"

"One," I manage to mumble. "Or maybe two?"

I want to close my eyes. I feel dizzy and out of it. Then I start to panic. How long have I been laying here?

I groan. "I gotta go home."

I try to get my feet under me, but the world has tipped to one side, and I can't keep my balance. I'm about to crash back to the ground when something grabs me hard around the waist.

"I got him," says a new, deep voice.

"Thanks, Brett," says Penny.

The voice called Brett slings my arm around his shoulder and pulls me upright. We start walking, though my feet refuse to do what they're supposed to. And I still feel off-kilter and sleepy. So very sleepy.

I want to ask Penny where we're going. Are they taking me home? Mom will be pissed when she realizes I snuck out. Dad'll be disappointed. I wasn't going to take anything. I swear. Just hang out a while.

I wasn't going to. . .

When I wake up, my eyelids feel like lead. I struggle to open them and keep them open. My eyesight is blurred, and the inside of my mouth is dry. I blink hard several times to clear my head. To my surprise, I'm on the couch. *My* couch. The overstuffed brown leather sofa in my very own living room. And there's my Christmas tree in the corner. The decorations Justin and I slapped on it blink at me in the sunlight, which pours in through the front window.

How the hell did I get here? I try to remember if I walked home from the park last night, if I somehow miraculously dragged myself up the steps, across my yard, and into the house. I don't think so. But I do have a half-formed image of someone standing over me, saying something I can't quite remember.

When I sit up, pain shoots through my body. My left side hurts like someone took a sledgehammer to it. I lift my shirt and find an ugly black bruise across my ribs. What the hell?

I start to get up from the couch, and that's when I see her. Penny. Lying sound asleep in my dad's recliner. She's curled up under an afghan, snug and snoring softly, like a girl would snore, I guess.

Penny.

Penny's asleep in my living room.

A bolt of anxiety zips through me. I look at my watch. Nearly seven in the morning. Crap! Mom and Dad are going to wake up any minute, if they haven't already. How will I explain…?

"Penny," I whisper harshly. "Penny, get up. You've got to go home. Penny."

She murmurs something incomprehensible and pulls the afghan tighter around her.

It all comes back to me. Sneaking out. Andrew playing that stupid guitar. Chris. The beer. I am in deep, deep…

"Ryan, you're up." Dad's voice severs my thoughts like a blade. I can actually feel the sweat forming on my skin. "I'm craving pancakes this morning. How does that sound?"

He comes downstairs wearing the reindeer PJs Mom bought him for Christmas last year. He normally only wears them on Sundays, so the fact that he's got them on today must mean Mom stayed home from work.

I cast a nervous glance at Penny's sleeping form.

"Sure. Pancakes would be, uh, great."

Dad passes by the living room and into the kitchen. Not a glance, not a gasp. Did he really *not* notice the bald girl lying in the chair?

Penny stirs, rubs her eyes.

"Penny," I whisper as quietly as I can. "Penny, shhh."

She yawns. "Shhh? Why shhh?"

Under the circumstances, her voice might as well have been a jet engine. I'm frantically trying to think of a solution when Dad's head pops into view, peering around the corner.

"Penny, do you prefer syrup or whipped cream on your pancakes?"

"Whipped cream sounds perfect," says Penny, stretching her arms and yawning again. "Do you have any bananas?"

"I sure do," says Dad, swirling a plastic spatula around like it's a magic wand or something. "I'll slice some right up."

When Dad's head disappears, I look at Penny with what I'm sure is an expression of utter shock. She mouths, *Just follow my lead.*

Dad comes in and hands both me and Penny a glass of orange juice. I take a sip. It's freshly squeezed. When is the last time my dad actually squeezed juice for me?

"Did you sleep all right, Penny?" he says, sitting on the arm of the couch. "Sorry about not having a guest room, but I swear that recliner is way more comfortable than any bed."

"Oh, it is," says Penny. She downs half her juice and continues talking. "Thank you so much for letting me crash here last night. I can't believe I locked myself out of the house."

"We've all done it," says Dad. "My wife locked herself out of the house once when Ryan was a toddler. Did she ever tell you about that, Ryan?"

I shake my head, too in shock to speak.

"Ryan wasn't even a year, not walking yet. I was on tour in the Middle East. Marissa took the trash out to the can, and the door closed behind her. Ryan was still inside. She could see him through the front window, crawling around searching for her." Dad laughs. "She completely panicked. Called the police from our neighbor's house. They brought a locksmith and let her in. From what she told me later, the whole thing was over in ten minutes, but it was the longest ten minutes of her life." Dad grins like a kid with a secret. "Don't tell Mom I told you about that, all right?"

Penny finishes her juice and hands the cup back to my dad. "Thanks again. That was really delicious. But my mom should be home from work by now. I'd better be getting back."

Penny gets up and folds the afghan, which my dad takes from her and lays across the back of the couch. "I'm just glad Ryan heard you knocking last night and let you in. And Ryan," Dad adds, "that was nice of you to stay down here with her instead of letting her sleep in a strange house alone. I have to admit, I was surprised to find her here this morning, but Penny explained that you two work together at the center and how you helped her last night."

Dad beams at me proudly, like I've just won the science fair or something. He turns back to Penny.

"Why don't you have a plate of pancakes, and then I'll have Ryan walk you home."

The fragrant smell of Dad's cooking permeates the air. My stomach rumbles. So does Penny's. Our eyes lock, and as if rehearsed, we both reply together, "Okay."

PENNY

SIXTEEN

"WHAT HAPPENED IN THERE?" Ryan asks outside on his porch.

I feel like I'm the one who should be asking that question. Frankly, the whole morning has been seriously awkward. It was clear from the way Ryan's father peppered me with questions and kept giving Ryan sidelong glances that he assumed, or at least hoped, that there was something going on between us. Of course, nothing could be farther from possible. Neither of us could get out of there fast enough.

Ryan struggles to keep a straight face.

"Why are you laughing?" I ask.

"Nothing," he replies, rubbing his ribs. He's probably still sore from where that jackass kicked him. "It's just the way my dad went so nuts over you, is all. You'd think General Patton was sitting at the table."

"Who?"

"Patton. American General from World War II? He's my dad's favorite."

"You're comparing me to a war general?"

Ryan's face turns pink. "I meant a celebrity or something."

It *was* pretty funny. Ryan's dad even wore an apron while he cooked us pancakes. He was actually really nice, not what I expected from a former Marine, which was how he introduced himself to me. "I'm Ryan's dad—Marine. Well, former Marine," he'd said with an apologetic glance at his leg.

"What *did* happen?" Ryan asks again. "I don't remember much, except I snuck out to see my friends, and the next thing I know I'm on my couch."

"You were completely out of it when we found you," I tell him. "I spotted you with that group of boys. *All* idiots, in my opinion." I glare at him, hoping he'll catch my meaning. "When I saw that jerk lay into you, though, I had to do something."

Ryan smirks at me. "You were watching me?"

Now it's my turn to blush. "I happened to see you through my window. I was getting ready to go shopping."

"At eleven o'clock?"

"In any case," I continue, "Brett and I ran out there shouting that we were calling the cops, and everyone took off. Brett thinks the pills in the baggie are of the date rape variety."

Ryan slides his hands into his hoodie pocket and leans against the porch column. "I didn't know. A friend—well, ex-friend—gave them to me." He pauses, the space between his eyebrows crinkling. "Who's Brett? Your boyfriend?"

His question catches me off guard—not that he thinks Brett's my boyfriend, but that he even thinks I *have* a boyfriend.

"He's my brother," I reply, "and the one who got you home. Luckily, you'd left your front door unlocked. He carried you in and put you on the couch."

"But *you* stayed with me. Why?"

"Brett told me I should," I answer, unwilling to admit how worried I was. "He wanted to make sure you were okay. You said you only took one, but we weren't sure. If anything went wrong, someone needed to be here to explain what happened to your parents. But you're fine now. You just needed to sleep it off."

I start down the front steps, and Ryan begins to follow. But I turn to him, setting my palm against his chest to stop him.

"Can't I walk you home?" he asks.

"Not this time."

"You mean not after last night."

In truth, part of me wants to smack him and tell him not to bother coming back to the community center. He's got issues, and my kids don't need guys like him around, but that's not what comes out of my mouth.

"What you did was stupid," I tell him, "and dangerous."

"It wasn't my fault."

"It *was* your fault. You said you snuck out. And *you* took the drugs."

"I know. But I honestly didn't plan for any of that to happen."

Not far from us, a group of kids climb into the park swings. The chains start creaking as they move back and forth.

"But it did happen," I say. "And apparently, it's not the first time."

"I'm sorry. Really." Ryan scratches at his ear and breathes out heavily. "You forgive me, right?"

I say nothing.

"I mean, we're still friends, aren't we?"

For some reason, this whole thing just pisses me off. I stomp down the steps and get a few yards before I turn back. "Just so there's no misunderstanding between us," I tell Ryan, "you and me? We're not friends. In my book, you're just another bonehead trying to avoid the consequences of his stupidity and who doesn't give a crap about anyone but himself."

"Wait a sec. You don't know me—" he starts to say, but I cut him off.

"I don't have to know you. I know your kind."

"And what kind is that?"

Now, he's asking for it. Since the moment I met him, I knew I shouldn't trust him, but I got sucked in. The truth is, I'd started to actually like him. I should have known better.

"Answer me this, Ryan. Why did you talk to me that first day on the basketball court?"

"I told you. I wanted to volunteer."

"I mean after that. Why did you go into the bushes after my basketball?"

"Your basket—?"

"Or walk me home the other day and help me hunt for Samoas?"

"I was trying to be pol—"

"You felt sorry for me, just like everyone does. Well, I don't need your pity. So, I'm bald. Big deal. For your information, I have Alopecia Universalis, which means my body thinks hair is some kind of alien invader. I'm over it. And I don't need jerks like you pretending to be nice to me to make me feel good about myself. And I really don't need to be bailing you out of your own problems."

Ryan raises his hands defensively. "Whoa! Hang on a minute. Enough with the holier-than-thou judgments. Like I said, I was just being nice. At least let me thank you for helping me last night."

"I wasn't trying to help *you!*"

Ryan lets out an aggravated breath. "Then why did you go through all that trouble of getting me home?"

"Because no parent should have to find their kid dead at the park!"

There's an uncomfortable pause as Ryan takes this in. He tries to laugh it off, but I can hear the unease in his voice. "I wasn't going to die—"

"You don't know that," I snap. "You have no idea what might have happened if Brett and I hadn't come to your rescue. That guy could have really hurt you, or worse, you might have O.D.'d or something!"

I squeeze my eyes shut, then take a slow, deep breath. Is this guy really so thick? When I found him lying there at the park, it was like a bullet punched right through me because for a split second, it was like I was seeing Brett on the ground.

Yeah, I helped him out—but for his family's sake, not his.

I open my eyes and peer sternly into Ryan's. "Swear to me you won't do that again—ever." Unwanted tears burn at the backs of my eyes.

"Yeah. Sure, I promise," he says, but I can tell he doesn't grasp the seriousness of what I'm asking. I don't even know why I'm asking it—of *him*—a guy I shouldn't care less about. But for some reason, I feel driven to extract an oath from him.

I march back up the steps until we're standing face to face. "I didn't ask you to promise." I stab my finger into his chest. "*Swear!*"

"Ow! All right! I swear!"

"And if you ever break that vow, Ryan Rojas, I will never forgive you."

He rubs the spot on his chest where I poked him. "Can I still volunteer with you?"

Instead of answering, I growl in frustration. Then I turn and run across the park.

When I get to my house, I hurry inside and slam the door behind me. Brett's in the living room watching TV. He looks up at me, but I'm not in the mood to explain. I need to cool off first. So, I make a beeline for my room. I'm not in there ten seconds before there's a knock on the door.

"Decent?" Brett asks, poking his face into my room.

"Why do you bother asking when you can see for yourself that I am?" I reply, irritated. "What would you do if you opened that door and found me stark naked?"

Brett comes in and flops backward onto my bed, arms outstretched. "My eyeballs would shrivel up like prunes, and my brain would explode out of every orifice."

I pick up a bath towel from my floor and chuck it at him. It lands on his face, but he makes no move to take it off.

"What do you want, Brett?" I ask, not-so-eager to get on with my morning. Being as it's Saturday, Mom's sure to have a list of chores waiting for me. For both of us. After that, I want to head to the mall to go Christmas shopping, since we didn't get a chance last night.

Brett lifts the towel by its corner and drops it over the side of my bed. "I want to talk to you about that guy."

"You mean Ryan." I start steaming again just saying his name. "What about him?"

"You know what about him." Brett rolls to his side, his head propped on his hand, and glares at me. "Didn't you say he got kicked out of school? He's got problems, Pen. The park thing proves it."

Brett's right, but for some reason, I start to feel guilty. Was I too hard on Ryan? Was I unfair to judge him so harshly? I really didn't give him much chance to explain.

"I know what happened last night looks bad," I start to say. "Okay, it *was* bad. He was an idiot, *is* an idiot, but maybe he's not as *troubled* as I thought."

"What, you're defending him now?"

"No! Of course not, it's just—" It's just *what?* "He's great with the kids in my class, and he's been nice to me."

"So that's it," says Brett, getting up on his elbows. "Some druggie douche bag with pretty eyes shows you a little kindness, and you get all flirty with him."

That hurts, and I cut Brett a sharp look to let him know it.

Brett takes a quick breath. "Sorry, Pen. That's not what I meant." He sits, pushing his fists into my mattress. "I worry about you, that's all. I don't want you to get hurt."

"There's nothing between me and Ryan." Brett raises his eyebrows doubtfully, so I add, "And there never will be."

Saying those words makes me sad because I know from experience how true they're bound to be.

Satisfied, Brett gets up, wraps his burly arm around my neck, and gives my head a quick rub. Then he kisses me, right on my crown.

"I love you, you know that?" he says. Then, before I can reply, he turns and strides out of my room.

Brett can be pretty cool—sometimes. Other times, he's like a grenade with the pin pulled. It's just a matter of time before he'll blow. I know this sounds weird, but when he's really nice—like right now—when things seem exceptionally good, and I start to think, "Yes! Progress!"— that's when I start to feel sick inside, when my guts twist, and my mind churns with anxiety. When Brett smiles more than usual, jokes more than usual—it's the calm before the storm.

RYAN

SEVENTEEN

UNBELIEVABLE.

Will Mom ever let up with the chores? It's not enough that I've installed new sprinklers, built a fence, and dug up half the front yard for her dream garden, now she wants me to *plant* the garden for her, too.

She's mail-ordered dozens of packages of bulbs: daffodils, tulips, crocuses, and hyacinths. She wants them in rows along the perimeter of the garden so that when they bloom in the spring, it'll add color to the yard.

I get to work digging the holes and dropping in the bulbs, which have to be planted with the pointy end up at just the right depth. It's not the easiest thing to do with bruised ribs.

Once the bulbs are in, I add some plant food and cover them up with soil. I spend two hours on the job, and the whole time I'm thinking about Penny. She didn't have to help me out last night. Who am I to her? She could have—maybe should have—left me there to deal with the consequences of my own stupidity. But instead, she not only got me home, she covered for me so my parents wouldn't find out. I would call that a friend, but apparently, I'm not good enough for that title.

When I'm finished with the bulbs, I actually feel kind of proud of what I've done. I have to admit the house and yard are looking pretty impressive. But what happened with Penny overshadows it.

I start putting away the tools and empty bulb packages when the front door opens, and Dad sticks his head out. "Ryan, don't you know what time it is?"

I shake my head. I didn't bother looking at the clock when I came outside.

"It's almost nine. Did you forget about your Skype interview with Commander Norton today?"

Crap! How could I forget? Norton set up this appointment to check up on me.

"C'mon," says Dad. "Clean yourself up and let's move."

I drop my shovel and the packaging and hurry inside. No time for a shower, I wash my hands at the kitchen sink and head to the dining table to turn on the computer. Two minutes later, I get a notification that a call is coming in. I answer, and Norton's face pops up on my screen.

"Good morning, Cadet Rojas," he says. I can see the back wall of his office behind him. "I'm glad you could meet with me this morning."

I can't really explain it, but the way Norton talks to me, the way he looks at me makes me feel like a loser.

"Hello, Commander Norton."

"So, let's get right to it, shall we? Tell me how things are going."

I take a few minutes to talk about English, Math, and my other classes. I try to sound enthusiastic, though I really don't feel it. He fires question after question, wanting details about specific assignments and tests. How do I think I did on this? How do I feel about that? During the whole conversation, Norton looks annoyed and bored, like talking to me is the last thing in the world he wants to do right now.

Finally, he asks about my volunteer hours.

"I'm helping out with disabled kids," I tell him. "We teach them how to play basketball."

"We?"

I explain how Penny is the coach, and I'm her assistant, how we work together to help the kids develop coordination and skills. Though I've only done it a few times, I'm actually excited to share this information with Norton. I like working with the kids, and I guess it must show in my voice and my face because Norton looks more interested, too.

When I'm done talking, he writes some stuff on a notepad. Then he starts tapping his pencil against the desk. "Well, it seems you're on the right track," he says finally. "Your assignment scores are excellent so far. Just keep up the good work. And you'll need to circle the third Saturday in February on your calendar."

"Why?"

"Because that's the date you'll be meeting with the school board."

Norton thanks me for my time and ends the call. I lean back in my chair, relieved the interview's over.

Dad comes into the dining room and takes a seat across from me at the table. "How'd it go?"

I'm not sure what to say. Norton clearly doesn't like me, but when I talked about the kids at the community center, he seemed sincerely interested. So, maybe he'll change his opinion of me over time—if I keep my act straight. I'm determined to do that, not just for him, but for Penny too. I swore to her I would.

Dad asks again, "What did Norton say? Tell me what happened."

I lean back into my chair. Part of me feels irritated that I ever got myself into this mess, but another part wants to shout out the good news.

"The meeting with the school board," I tell Dad with a laugh, "is on!"

PENNY

EIGHTEEN

IT'S HARD TO BELIEVE there are just four days until Christmas, and we still haven't gotten our decorations out of the storage closet. After a lot of coaxing from Mom, Dad promised to fly in on Christmas Eve. Even though it's Mom's year, she knows how much it means to Brett for all of us to be together. I honestly couldn't care less.

Mom managed to get off work early this afternoon, so we could at least get our tree. Maybe with some luck, we'll actually be ready by the time Dad arrives.

Brett grabs some rope from the garage, and we head for the tree farm near the highway. At the first intersection, we stop at a red light. A small crowd of people wait at the bus stop. Brett rolls down his car window and bellows, "Happy Kwanza! Merry Boxing Day!"

The bus stop people gaze at my brother, dumbstruck. Some laugh. Others look away, like they're embarrassed. Brett waves at a little boy, but when the boy waves back, his mother pushes his arm down.

Mom playfully smacks Brett's shoulder. "Brett!" She laughs but rolls down her window too. At the next stop, she calls out to an old man on the corner, "Merry Christmas!"

"Merry Christmas!" the man calls back.

Mom gives Brett a smug look to which Brett responds by leaning over her and shouting through the window, "Happy National Date Nut Bread Day!"

The man's expression morphs into bewilderment. The light turns green, and Mom hits the gas.

"Date Nut Bread Day?" I ask.

"Yeah," says Brett. "I looked it up on Google. Every day in December is National something or other day. Today is National Date Nut Bread Day."

"What in the world is Date Nut Bread?" asks Mom, sending Brett and me into hysterics.

The tree farm is packed with people, all scouring the diminutive evergreen forest for the perfect tree, even though hundreds have been there before us. Only stumps remain of what were likely the fullest and most ideal conifers.

Bundled in matching green and red striped scarves and beanies (gifts we got from Grandma three years ago), Brett and I tromp through the trees shouting, "Here's one!" and "This one looks good!" We've had a drier winter than usual, and the air is still a balmy seventy-five degrees when the sun begins its descent. But Brett and I won't let a little warm weather thwart our holiday spirit. We examine at least a dozen trees before settling on a seven-footer.

Brett crawls beneath the lower branches and hacks away at the trunk with a hand saw provided by the farm.

"Timber!" I shout when it starts to tilt to one side.

"Grab it!" says Brett. But instead, Mom manages to shift the massive wagon, also farm-owned, beneath the flailing tree just in time.

Brett gets up and proudly inspects the raw, sap-oozing wound. Then, shoving his fists into the air, he screams, "I'm the king of the world!" and darts off through the trees, leaping and whooping like a wild gibbon. The other tree patrons respond to his antics with varying degrees of amusement and irritation.

I bend over to grasp the wagon handle when I notice Mom. She's watching Brett with a grim expression.

"Did he take his pills today?" she asks.

I try to remember if I saw him take them. "Doesn't look like it," I answer, kicking myself for not checking earlier.

I haul the wagon to the register, where Mom pays with a credit card. One of the employees shakes the dead needles out with this giant vibrator and wraps the tree in netting before hefting it onto the top of our car and tying it down with the rope we brought.

There's no sign of Brett.

"Should I go find him?" I ask.

Mom shakes her head, but I go after him anyway.

Making my way through the maze of trees, I start calling his name. "Brett? Brett!" But he doesn't answer.

I finally find him in a field beyond the forest, a vast wasteland of tree stumps from Christmases past. He's just standing in the middle of it all, the hack saw hanging limply from one hand, his phone in the other. The sun has almost completely disappeared by this point, and all the colors of the world have faded to a muddled gray.

"Brett?" I approach cautiously, stepping in front of him. He stares off at nothing. "Mom's waiting in the car. Are you all right?"

At first, he doesn't seem to hear me, but then he hands me his cell phone.

"Dad's not coming."

I read the text still highlighted on the screen, an apology from Dad and a one-line explanation about an unexpected business trip.

Bastard.

"I'm sorry, Brett," I say, slipping the phone into my own pocket. I'll have to show Mom later.

Brett grips the hack saw tighter in his fist and shifts his weight from one foot to the other.

"Do you ever wonder what comes after this?" he asks.

"After what?"

"This!" He swings the saw in a circle in front of him, indicating the hundreds of stumps dotting the ground. I have to take a step back to avoid getting severed in two. "How long do you think that tree we cut down has been alive? Five years? Six? Ten?"

"I don't know." I glance back toward the parking lot, wondering how long Mom will wait before she comes looking for us.

Brett holds up his free hand and presses the tips of his fingers and thumb together. I can hear the sticky sound of sap as he pulls them apart. "Tree blood," he says.

I slide my hand through his elbow and turn him toward the forest. We stroll along the path, passing families eagerly chopping down their trees of choice. One man glares at Brett, and I wonder what my brother did to make him angry.

Brett doesn't say anything on the way home. When we get there, he heads to his room and locks the door behind him. After I tell Mom about Dad's change of plans, I go to my room too, where I lie in bed and stare into the darkness for most of the night.

Brett doesn't emerge from his room the whole next day. Mom left a box of tree ornaments in the living room. Must have dug them out of the closet last night after I went to bed.

I spend most of the day watching Christmas specials on TV and decorating the tree. I actually consider going over to Ryan's house just to have someone to talk to, but what would I say? "So, Ryan, I know I treated you like dirt the other day, but you wanna hang out?" Every outcome I think of is absurd, so I ditch the idea.

At noon, I knock on Brett's door. "I made you a sandwich."

Nothing.

"It's turkey and tomato, your favorite," I say.

"Go away!" The door muffles Brett's voice, but his tone comes through crystal clear.

"Are you okay? I can bring you whatever you want. Cookies?" *Your medication.*

There's a sudden loud *thump* on the other side of the door as if something's been thrown at it.

"I'll take that as a no."

I go back to the living room and turn on another movie while I devour Brett's sandwich. After that, I work on finishing our tree—alone.

At about five o'clock, I hear the front door open and the jangle of Mom's keys being dropped onto the counter. I turn off the TV and find her sitting at the kitchen table, her head in her hands.

"Hard day?" I ask.

She peers up at me. "I had the patient from hell today. Criticized everything I did, but I managed to get through it without throwing a bedpan at her. I'm really glad to be home."

I fill a glass for her with ice and water from the sink, where the dirty dishes from yesterday are starting to smell.

"Where's Brett?" she asks, sliding a finger down the condensation on her glass. "It's his day to clean the kitchen, isn't it?"

The lines on her face are taut. She's had a bad day, but it's about to get worse.

"Mom—"

She gets up and stomps down the hall, rapping on Brett's bedroom door. "Brett, could you come out and do the dishes? I need to get dinner started."

I hear his voice from inside the room. "I'm busy."

Mom sighs. "Well, whatever you're doing, I'm sure you can spare a few minutes to come do what you should have done this morning."

I should warn her, tell her he's been in there all day. But I just can't get the words out.

A few seconds pass before Brett's door opens, slamming against the wall. The sound startles Mom. Brett pushes past her and marches, soldier stiff, to the kitchen and starts attacking a frying pan with a scouring sponge.

Mom and I stare at him. We know this scene all too well. We're powerless to stop it, but Mom tries anyway.

"Brett," she says in an insanely calm voice. "Honey, you don't need to do that right now. I don't mind."

"No!" he shouts. "It's my chore. I'll do it!"

He shoves the clean pan into the dish rack on the counter and reaches for a plate. That's when I see the red droplet hit the floor. Mom sees it too, and we share desperate glances.

Several more drops of blood burst against the tile, like tiny red stars.

Mom takes a cautious step toward him. "Brett, what did you do?"

Brett rinses the plate and tries to add it to the rack, but it slips from his hands and shatters on the floor.

"Damn it!" Brett shouts. "F—"

Brett turns to face us, but he doesn't see us. He's so deep in his own pain he can't see anything else. He slides to the floor, his back pressed against the cabinet, and squeezes his eyes shut. I can't tell if he's going to scream or cry.

When he raises his hands to his face, that's when I see the crisscross of crimson slices on the inside of his left arm.

Mom's eyes widen, but she says nothing. Keeping her focus on Brett, she moves cautiously toward him like she's approaching a wild animal.

I can hardly breathe. I don't dare move for fear of startling him, of setting him off again. Scenes like this have played out a dozen times before, but there's never been so much blood. My eyes burn. I blink hard and bite my bottom lip to keep from crying.

"It's all right," Mom coos gently. Her expression is surprisingly pleasant, a mask of utter self-control. Her voice is gentle and low.

"I broke the plate!" Brett shouts.

"Don't worry about it," Mom says. "It's no big deal."

"It's ruined!"

"We've got plenty more."

I can't help it. A muffled cry bursts out of me. Mom cuts a serious look in my direction. *Hold it together, Penny. Hold it together.*

"Leave me alone!" Brett screams. "Just leave me alone!"

Mom freezes mid-step, her palms out in the universal sign of *don't do anything we'll all regret.*

"Brett, you're bleeding, Honey. I just want to stop the bleeding. If you don't let me help you, I'll have no choice but to call 9-1-1. The sheriff will come again. He'll handcuff you. You don't want that, do you?"

Brett shakes his head. "No." He starts to weep. His chest heaves as he gasps through tears. "I'm sorry, Mom—" he says, "I'm so sorry—"

Mom takes another two steps and kneels beside Brett. "Penny, get a towel."

I hand her one, and she wraps it around Brett's arm. He sobs like a scared little boy. Mom strokes his hair with one hand and applies pressure to the towel with the other. The tone of her voice is as calm and low as it was before, but the look in her eyes is urgent.

"Penny," she says, "get my keys. Start the car."

Tears burn behind my eyes. "Okay, but—"

"You'll have to sit with him in the back seat," Mom adds. "Keep pressure on this. Can you do that?"

A dark red circle seeps through the towel on Brett's arm. I rush down the hall to the front door, snatching Mom's keys off the table on my way. I also grab a stack of clean dish towels from the counter.

In the car, I grip the steering wheel as the engine comes to life. *Please God...Please God...Please God...* I try not to cry, but it does no good. I force myself to take slow, deep breaths to calm myself, to get my tears under control. I can't let Brett see me like this. It would just make things worse.

The front door to the house opens, and Mom comes out cradling Brett's head against her shoulder. His arm, wrapped in that bloody towel, is pressed against his chest. They walk together, Mom guiding him down the steps and across the driveway. I get out of the driver's seat and open the back door. Mom helps him in, her hands covered in blood, and I climb in behind him. I wrap a clean towel around the one he's got, pressing my palm against it. As Mom climbs into the driver's seat and backs the car out of the driveway, Brett turns his face to the window, staring out as if nothing's there.

RYAN

NINETEEN

I HAVEN'T SEEN PENNY for a few days. The community center is closed for Christmas break, so no chance of finding her there, and her house is dark. No car in the driveway. But it's Christmas Eve. She and her family probably just went out of town or something, which is too bad because I've been hoping to talk to her and apologize again for the park thing.

Dad pulls out his DVD of *The Nightmare Before Christmas*, his all-time favorite, and brings home a bag full of junk food from the market: microwave popcorn, Red Vines, Oreos, and a seven-layer dip with a giant bag of corn chips.

"You're going to make yourselves sick," says Mom with an eye roll.

"That's the whole point," says Dad, popping open the chips with a dramatic flair.

When Justin comes in and sees the stash, he freaks out. "All right!" he shouts and does his wacky dance of joy in the middle of the living room. I fold my arms and shake my head, embarrassed for the little guy. He has no shame.

"What?" asks Dad. "You don't remember doing the dance of joy when you were younger?"

"Me? I never acted like that."

Dad snorts. "Where do you think Justin learned it? We used to have this music video, some animation thing that would set you twirling like a top and jiving all over the place."

"I never jived, Dad."

"Oh, yes you did. I have a video of you somewhere. I'll have to dig it out and show it to you."

"Please, don't."

I have this horrible vision of Dad playing old videos of me as a kid, and me being forever humiliated. It's time to escape before that nightmare comes true, so I head for the stairs.

"Where are you going?" asks Justin.

"I'm not allowed to watch TV, bro," I tell him. "Mom's orders."

Dad slides the DVD into the player. Justin turns to him, a frantic plea in his voice. "Daaaaad, Ryan has to watch with us. Pleeeze?"

I can hardly believe what I'm seeing. My little brother pestering Dad—on my behalf.

"Ryan's grounded," Dad says.

"But it's Christmas." Justin's voice rises to an obnoxious pitch. "We always watch movies together for Christmas! Mom?"

Through the doorway to the kitchen, I watch Mom take down two bowls from the cupboard. She intentionally ignores Justin.

"Mom, can Ryan watch the movie?" Justin asks again.

The muscles in Mom's jaw tense. She closes the cupboard and carries the bowls into the living room. I can actually feel my palms grow sweaty as I await her verdict. All eyes are on her: mine, Justin's, even Dad's. After what seems an eternity, she shrugs resignedly.

"Fine," is all she says, but it's enough.

I leap over the stair rail and plop down on the sofa next to Justin. I ruffle his hair and whisper, "Thanks, bro."

Mom opens a bag of Doritos and pours it into one of the bowls. She fills the other with cheddar popcorn. It's been weeks since I've been allowed to watch TV or do anything other than chores and homework, so I expect Mom to lecture me about how generous she is for allowing me the privilege of viewing a movie with the family. But all she says is, "Screw my diet. Pass the Oreos, Ryan, and get the milk."

After I fill four mugs, I carry three of them to the living room. I pass them around and go back for mine. I hear the opening music to the movie, and Dad applauding, and Justin munching loudly on popcorn, and Mom shushing them both. And I feel something I haven't felt in a while. Happy.

I pick up my mug and head back to the TV, passing the Christmas tree and living room window on the way. I take a look through the window at our neighborhood, all lit up with green and red and white lights. Like a winter wonderland. Except for Penny's house. They never got their lights up. Maybe they won't be home for Christmas. Maybe they're visiting relatives or something. Or maybe they will be home, but they've just been too busy. Their dark house seems out of place among the giant Santas, and snowmen, and nativities on everyone else's lawns.

The movie has started. On the TV screen, the wolfman guy pulls a cart with a scarecrow on it. The music builds. This is my favorite part, not because of the movie, but because of my dad. Dad, who two years ago was fighting for his life in a hospital bed, struggling to recover from his injuries. Remembering that time shoots spasms of nausea through me. But I shake it off. I hate thinking about it. Can't think about it. Anyway, it's good to see Dad enjoying something again.

Dad leans forward with the anticipation of a kid, and when the scarecrow catches fire and Jack the Pumpkin King emerges from the well, his face lights up, he slaps his real knee and laughs with an "I-just-knew-it-was-Jack!" heartiness.

I wait until Dad settles down again. Then I ask, "Hey, Dad? You know those extra lights we put away?"

"Yeah?" he answers, his eyes glued to the screen.

"Can I have them?"

"I guess. Sure. They're in that red plastic tub in the garage. There's some other stuff in there, too, if you want it. But what for?"

I look out the window again across the street at Penny's house. "I have an idea."

Christmas morning dawns bright and sunny, just the way it does every Christmas in Southern California. Mom says that in all the years she's lived here, she can't remember a single gloomy Christmas. Same goes for New Year's Day. The really cold weather won't hit until late January. Though she and Dad moved around a lot because of the military, she grew up here, which is why they chose to come back during Dad's last deployment.

Justin and I are already checking out our presents under the tree when Mom wanders downstairs in her bathrobe and slippers.

"Boys, you know the rules. Breakfast first, presents after."

Mom has this stupid tradition that carries back to when she was a kid—eating breakfast as a family BEFORE opening gifts. It's torture. By the time we're barely clearing our dishes to the sink, all the other neighborhood kids are outside playing with their new toys. She does let us open our stockings at least, which we've already done. Justin and I got mostly the same stuff: a giant candy cane, iTunes gift cards, yo-yos, new video games, and socks. Why she always gives us socks, I'll never know.

Mom takes her sweet time making cinnamon rolls, bacon, and fruit salad. Dad comes downstairs to give her a hand. We eat. We clear the table. Mom insists on rinsing the dishes and loading the dishwasher. By now, Justin and I are going crazy. I could swear she drags out this whole breakfast thing just to see us suffer.

Finally, around nine o'clock, we make our way into the living room and gather around the tree. Justin begs to be

Santa this year, which is fine by me. I'd rather open presents than hand them out to everyone else. Justin passes around the gifts, and we all start tearing into them, which drives my mother crazy. She has this other tradition—that we should all take turns opening one gift at a time, "So we can appreciate what everyone's gotten," she says. To hell with that! Luckily, Dad (being a guy) agrees with me and Justin. The fun of Christmas is ripping open our gifts as fast as possible, then spending the rest of the day appreciating them all at once.

While Mom tries futilely to keep all the wrappings and trash contained, the rest of us are *oohing* and *aahing* over our presents. Dad gets the typical stuff from Mom: cologne, a tie, a sweater, stuff like that. Mom also bought him a digital watch (from me and Justin), which he thinks is pretty cool. For Mom, we picked out some perfume and jewelry, which Dad paid for, along with a KitchenAid mixer, which I think Dad really wants more than Mom. But she gives him an enthusiastic hug and kiss for it just the same.

Justin is overjoyed with his new longboard and the latest *Diary of a Wimpy Kid* book. I also get a long board with a new helmet (which I'll never wear), a Rosetta Stone German computer program (yippee), a microscope, and several other homeschool-type things. I mean, am I really supposed to shout for joy over *curriculum*? I do my best to sound enthusiastic when I thank my parents for the gifts. At least I've got the long board, though how much good will it do me when I'm not allowed to ride it anywhere?

Mom finishes stuffing all the bows and torn-up packaging into the trash while Dad munches on a can of mixed salted nuts he got in his stocking, and Justin assembles his Lego Millennium Falcon.

"Want me to install that for you?" asks Mom, pointing to my yellow Rosetta Stone box. "It's all three levels. The equivalent of three years of German. Of course, you're only required to have two years for high school."

"Sure," I say. "Thanks."

Feeling bummed, I gather up my new homeschool stuff and carry it to the dining table.

"Ryan?" Dad calls from the living room. "Can you give me a hand here? This is kind of heavy."

I turn back and see Dad reaching behind the Christmas tree. "I think we missed one."

He pulls out something about three feet long made of black nylon mesh with a zipper along its side. A giant red bow has been stuck onto the front of it with an equally giant cardboard gift tag that reads: TO RYAN.

Dad sets the end of it on the floor. "I think this is yours," he says. As Mom slips the Rosetta Stone disc into my computer, she casts Dad a puzzled look. Apparently, this is something he didn't clear with her first.

I pinch the zipper between my fingers and pull it down. The fabric falls away, revealing a black bass guitar. It's not new (Dad couldn't afford a new one). It's the used one I played in the pawn shop a few weeks back.

"What do you think?" Dad asks eagerly.

I hesitate. Two years ago, I got rid of my old bass for a reason, but Dad doesn't know that reason. Never needs to know.

"It's awesome," I tell him, forcing a smile. "Thanks so much."

It's not that I don't like the gift. I've been dreaming about it ever since I first saw it. But it reminds me how I let my parents down—how I let *him* down. I can't ever let that happen again.

PENNY

TWENTY

AFTER THREE DAYS in the psych unit, Brett is ready to come home. Since the hospital where he was admitted is nearly two hours from our house, Mom and I stayed at a hotel, so we could see him every day. When we check him out, Brett's arm is still bandaged, and his mood is subdued. The drive home is a quiet one, just holiday music on the radio. I'm pretty sure we're all thinking the same thing: what a way to spend Christmas Day.

We stop for dinner at McDonald's, literally the only place open tonight, and eat in the car. Mom tries to cheer us up by ordering two kids' meals and giving us the little plastic toys inside.

"Merry Christmas," she jokes, and we finish our fries.

By the time we pull into our street, I'm ready to just go to bed. But we all see it at the same time. Mom slows the car to a crawl as we approach our driveway. The house — *our* house — is ablaze with blinking colored lights.

"What the hell?" says Brett, his first words of the day.

Mom parks, and we all climb out of the car and gape at the spectacle. Strings of lights adorn the edge of the roof and the outline of our door and front windows. And there's a huge plastic star hanging on the garage that fades from one color to the next.

"Who did this?" asks Mom. Her voice breaks, and I see that her eyes are tearing up.

But neither Brett nor I answers. We just gaze at the lights, saying nothing. After a few minutes, I feel Brett's arm, the one not bandaged, slide across my shoulders. He gives me a gentle squeeze and then heads into the house. Mom kisses my cheek and follows him. I decide to stay outside a little longer. Maybe I'm just not ready to face what's waiting for me inside—a half-decorated tree, unwrapped gifts, dirty dishes from three days ago. Brett's blood is probably still on the floor, waiting for me or Mom to wipe it up.

I'm still standing there, uncertain about what to do next, when I sense someone approaching. I turn to see Ryan Rojas, his hands buried in his pockets as usual.

"Kinda pretty, don't you think?" he asks, bumping me with his shoulder. "I was outside and saw you drive up. Thought I'd say hi."

I bump him back. I should have guessed he was the one behind the lights. "I wonder who did this?" I tell him with as much drama as I can muster. "I mean, what a cruel joke to play on a family of Buddhists."

The blood drains from Ryan's face. "Buddhists? Are you serious?"

I'm trying really hard to look mad, but I'm sure the quiver in my chin gives me away. "Nah," I say. "We're Jehovah's Witnesses."

"Oh," says Ryan.

"I'm kidding!" I grab Ryan's arm, laughing. "Really. It's beautiful. Thank you for doing this. My mom was so shocked when we pulled into the driveway tonight, you literally made her cry."

"I did? I mean, she cried? Why?"

I wonder how much I should tell him, about the ten hours we spent in the ER with Brett strapped to a gurney, the hopeless look on his face in the psyche ward, the dirty motel room. It's really none of Ryan's business, but what he's done is beyond the normal level of nice.

"It's been a long week, that's all," I tell him. I just don't want to talk about it. Not with Ryan, anyway. Maybe not with anyone. "What did you get for Christmas?" I ask, changing the subject.

Ryan's expression falters, and I catch a glimpse of self-doubt before it's replaced with a smile. "I'll show you," he says, "but it's on my porch."

"What is it? A potted cactus?"

"Just come and see."

I follow him across the park to his yard. We climb the steps to his porch, where he proudly motions toward something leaning against the house.

"Ta da," he says half-heartedly.

I decide to mess with him. "Nice," I tell him, "but aren't guitars supposed to have six strings?"

"It's not a guitar."

"Could have fooled me. Sure looks like one."

"It's a bass guitar."

"Right. That's what I said. A guitar."

"*Bass* guitar. The anchor of any rock band. Flea, Les Claypool, Nick O'Malley."

"Nick O'Malley. Arctic Monkeys."

"You've heard of them?"

"They're my favorite band."

Ryan picks up the instrument. "My dad gave this to me. I know it's used, but it was nice of him just the same." He strums his thumb across the strings.

"I think it's broken, Ryan."

"It's not broken."

"It's not making any sound."

"Yes, it is." He strums it again.

I lean in close, so my ear is inches from the strings. "Barely," I say. I'm trying hard not to bust up laughing. He's taking this so seriously!

"It's not plugged in," Ryan explains. "The amp is inside. When I plug it in, it actually sounds awesome."

I give him a skeptical glare. "I'll believe it when I hear it." That's when I break. I just can't keep the façade any longer, and I start to laugh. Ryan looks bewildered by my reaction.

"You're teasing me," he says, still uncertain. "Right?"

"Of course, I am. You really think I don't know what a bass guitar is? My brother Brett's been playing most of his life."

"I'll have you know," Ryan says, "I wasn't half bad myself before I quit."

"Why *did* you quit?"

My question takes him by surprise. He lowers his eyes and hugs his instrument close. "I got busy," he says, though that doesn't feel like the whole truth.

Now it's his turn to change the subject. "I haven't seen you for a few days. Were you out of town or something?"

"Or something," I reply, glancing across the park. From here, my house looks like all the other houses: happy and full of holiday spirit. "What you did—the lights—that was nice."

Ryan shrugs. "I've been trying to think of a way to thank you for helping me that night."

"You don't need to thank me."

"Then consider it my Christmas present to you."

A Christmas present? If Ryan really knew what the past few days have been like, if he understood what every day is like in our family, then he'd know that these lights mean so much more than that. Now, when I look at Ryan, it's like I'm seeing him for the first time. Not the moron dropout I saw before, but someone with a heart. Someone who actually gives a damn.

How can *I* thank *him*?

I reach into my shirt collar and slide out the necklace I've been wearing for years. I pull it over my head and hold it out to Ryan.

"What is this?" he asks, taking it from me.

The metal chain is the kind you'd wear with dog tags, only instead of dog tags, there's a pendant—half a pendant, really. A jagged half circle with the word FRIENDS engraved on it.

"A girl I knew had the other half, the part that says 'Best,' but she moved away a few years ago and I haven't talked to her since. Consider it *my* Christmas present to *you*."

I don't tell him that the girl didn't actually move away. We just aren't friends anymore. Haven't been for a long time.

I remember when I told Ryan we weren't technically friends. I'm hoping he'll get the message that I've changed my mind.

"Thanks," he tells me, and then slips the chain into his pocket.

"Listen, Ryan," I say, "we just got home, and I'm pretty beat. If you don't mind."

"Sure. I'll walk you back."

"No," I tell him, but then I add, "thanks, but I can find my way. I'll just . . . follow the star." I point at the lighted star on my garage.

I walk down the steps and start across the park, in no hurry to get home. When I reach my house, I glance back and see Ryan sitting on his porch, strumming his bass. As if he senses me watching him, he lifts his eyes to meet mine. Then he smiles, or at least I imagine he's smiling. It's too far and too dark to tell for sure, but somehow, I know he is.

I turn back to the house, pausing to touch a corner of the star before letting myself inside.

RYAN

TWENTY-ONE

AFTER CHRISTMAS, the week goes by way too fast. Justin is home for winter break, and Mom's taken the week off work, which means two early morning drug tests and extra chores. Luckily, the tests Dad bought don't include Rohypnol, so despite my taking Chris's pills a couple weeks back, they both turn up negative. The upside to all this is that Mom decided it would be best to move the computer from the dining table to my room—to minimize distractions. With the increased privacy and the fact that my parents have started to slack off somewhat on the Web Watcher thing, I've started spending time online with Penny.

After what happened at the park, I haven't bothered contacting any of my old friends, if I can call them that, which I guess I can't. So, Penny has become my fallback, now that she actually is a friend. With Mom home all day on vacation, I avoid going to Penny's place. No sense making Mom suspicious, and I don't want to have to explain myself. But Penny has come here a few times. Dad likes her, which means Mom tolerates the visits. In fact, when Penny's here, my parents treat her like the daughter they never had and seem convinced something is going on between us. Dad gives me a thumbs up every time Penny isn't looking. Mom is polite but indifferent, which is to be expected, I guess. But most days, Penny has basketball practice, and when she's not at practice, I'm doing schoolwork or chores.

After Christmas, I hung Penny's 'Friend' pendant on a thumb tack over my desk. She says she doesn't expect me to wear it since guys don't wear stuff like that. But I look at it a lot. Why did she give it to me instead of somebody else?

I never got her a present. I said the Christmas lights were my present, but still, I feel like she deserves something more. But what would I get for a girl like her?

New Year's Day starts off boring. Dad and Justin get up early to watch the Rose Parade on TV, but there's no way I'm getting out of bed that early to do anything. By the time I do wake up, they're watching the replay.

Mom's left a plate of apple crepes on my desk, which are now cold, and the whipped cream she sprayed on top has morphed into a puddle of goo. I take a bite anyway, and they don't taste too bad.

Over the past few days, I've debated what to do about the bass Dad gave me. I want to play it. No denying that, but whenever I pick it up, the memories of the day Dad got hurt rush back to me. But if I don't play, he'll know something's up, and I don't want to explain. So, I start working on some songs I've always wanted to learn. I'm a bit rusty, and I hate to admit it, but it's great feeling the strings under my fingers again.

After I finish off Mom's crepes, I decide to watch music videos to pick up some new bass moves, so I shift the mouse, and the computer screen comes on. I'm in the middle of a clip of Muse in concert when a window pops open with a message from Penny.

Penny: Busy?

Me: Just watching YouTube.

Penny: Can I come over?

Me: Sure.

Penny: Great. I'll be there in 5.

Five minutes? My messy room materializes before my eyes. Boxers and dirty socks and T-shirts lay inches deep on my floor. After chucking them into my closet and smoothing out the covers on my bed, I head for the living room to wait for Penny. She knocks on the front door a few minutes later.

"Hi," she says, stepping into the entry. Dad, still watching the parade, waves as she comes in. Justin doesn't even look up, he's so engrossed in it.

"Sorry, I forgot to mention the living room is sort of occupied," I tell Penny. "Wanna go upstairs?"

Penny follows me up to my room. We pass Mom on the way, carrying a basket of dirty laundry. "Happy New Year, Mrs. Rojas," says Penny.

"Same to you, Penny." Mom continues on her way downstairs but adds, "Leave the door open, Ryan."

So, I do because that's the rule in my house. The doors stay open when friends are over, especially if that friend happens to be a girl. Even though she's been over before, it's her first time upstairs.

Penny roams around my room, casually inspecting the new territory. She reads the little plaques on my trophies, studies the pictures on my walls, runs a finger across the spines of the books on my shelves. I'm glad I took a minute to pick up before she came, or she might have sorted through my dirty clothes.

"You ever been?" she asks. "To the parade, I mean."

"No. Dad says it's too cold, and we have a much better view of the floats from home anyway. You?"

"Almost every year. You should go sometime."

She spies the 'Friends' pendant hanging above my desk, then glances questioningly at me.

"I keep it there, so I can always see it," I tell her.

She moves on to my bass guitar, running a finger down its fretboard. "How's the music coming along?"

"I'm working on two songs, 'Can't Stop' by the Peppers and 'Reptilia' by the Strokes." I pick up the bass and play a few measures for her. "At least I've got the basics down."

"Not bad," she says. "Actually, it sounds really good." She lowers herself into my desk chair and digs the toes of her shoes into my carpet, pushing the chair from side to side.

"I watch a lot of videos of bass players," I explain. "How their fingers move across the strings. It's like their instruments are an extension of their bodies. And they all move the same way, not how a guitarist moves. Bass players have this subtle head nodding thing they do, like they really feel the music. Those low notes just flow out of them as naturally as their own heartbeats. Here, listen to this."

I turn up the volume on my speaker, though not loud enough to be heard downstairs. I've been working hard at trying to match Flea's riff note by note. It hasn't been easy, but I've got most of it down. I make a few mistakes playing it for Penny, but overall, it's not too bad. When I'm done, I look at her, waiting for her response.

She leans her head back against my chair, her eyes closed. Has she fallen asleep? Am I that bad? The next few moments pass in awkward silence. I wonder if I should say her name to get her attention, but then she opens those blue eyes of hers and studies me. I squirm uncomfortably, like when I'm sitting in a cotton robe in a doctor's office. Finally, she speaks.

"Why bass guitar?" she asks. "I mean, why did you pick *this* instrument over something else, like a regular guitar or drums or the clarinet?"

Her question surprises me, but I know the answer because it's something I've thought a lot about, especially since I gave it up.

"It's the bass line that really makes a song," I tell her. "Some people don't bother paying attention, but when it comes right down to it, those low notes that vibrate in your gut, quiet and woven into the background of the music, are what make a song truly memorable." Then I add, "I guess I wanted to be memorable."

"Wanted?" she asks.

I set my bass back in its stand. "It was a silly dream. I've got more important things to do now."

Penny rotates the chair toward my desk, traces some of the keys on my computer with her fingertips.

"Like school?" she says.

I don't know if the sarcasm is real or if I'm just reading more into those two words than Penny intended. Either way, I suddenly feel annoyed. So I screwed up before. I've done nothing but homework and chores for three weeks solid. I'm working my butt off to get back into Middleton. What's it going to hurt if I play a little music once in a while? It's not something I feel like discussing with Penny anyway, so I change the subject.

"Why didn't you go to the parade this year? You said you go almost every year, why not today?"

Penny turns the chair back to face me. She crosses her knees and lays her hands over the tops of them, squeezing her fingers together. "Things didn't work out for us to go this year. But we're going later," she says, brightening. "To see the floats, I mean. After the parade, they display them in Red Grove Park. People come from everywhere to look at them up close. Did you know that every single square inch of a float has to be covered in flowers or leaves? I worked on a float a few years ago with Brett. There were these beautiful orchids, white with just a blush of pink, and their stems were in these plastic vials of water to keep them alive. The float had thousands of holes, and we had to carefully insert every single vial into a hole. Took hours. But the finished effect was breathtaking. Funny thing was, we were too tired after to stay and watch the parade. We drove home that morning and slept through the whole thing."

Penny looks up at me, smiling. She has a really nice smile, slightly off-kilter like she's amused about something known only to her. "Anyway," she continues, "we're driving down after lunch to see the floats. Why don't you come with us?"

"I'd really like to, but. . ."

"But what?"

My shoulders sag. "You know I've sort of been under house arrest. It's one thing walking thirty yards to the community center, but I'm not allowed to go anywhere else, let alone all the way to Pasadena."

Penny starts moving the chair back and forth again. She leans back, narrowing her eyes, and responds with a thoughtful "hmmm." A moment later, she stiffens like a mannequin in her chair, a fiendishly happy look on her face. Then she bolts out of my room.

"Penny?" I call after her. "Where are you going?"

I hear her loudly whisper from the hall, "I'm going to ask your Dad if you can go!"

"What? No!" I go after her, but she's already reached the bottom of the stairs. I stop halfway down. Dad is still watching the parade. I can't see him. He can't see me, but I can hear their voices.

Penny: How's the parade, Mr. Rojas?

Dad: Pretty great this year. James Franco is Grand Marshall.

Penny: I can't wait to see it up close.

Beat.

Dad: You're going?

Penny: Yeah. My mom takes us every year. If we don't make it to the parade, then we at least go see the floats on display. You ever been?

Dad: I went to the parade a couple of times when I was young. Marissa and I have never taken the kids. (*His voice lowers.*) She hates being tired and cold.

Mom (from the kitchen): Don't listen to him, Penny. He's the wimpy one.

Penny: My family's going right after lunch. We'll just be there for a few hours and come right home. *Beat.* Could Ryan come with us?

She says it all so casually, like it's no big deal. But there's no way my parents will bend on this. No way in hell.

Dad (loudly): Marissa?

Beat. Another beat.

Mom: I don't know.

At first, Dad doesn't say anything. He just waits, like he knows it's just a matter of time. But after a few minutes, he tries again.

Dad: Marissa?

Mom: What?

Dad: The floats? Ryan?

An excruciatingly long silence passes while some marching band belts out the theme of *Indiana Jones* from the TV.

Mom: He's got homework. And I need the driveway hosed off.

Dad: It's New Year's Day.

I can hear it in his voice, that gentle way he has with her. Then I hear Mom sigh.

Mom: Fine. He can go. But—*she adds, calling up the stairs to me as though she knows I'm listening*—he'll have to get right back to work tomorrow. No slacking off.

If she says anything else, I don't hear it. My heart thumps so hard, all I can hear is my own blood rushing through my ears. I hurry back to my room and lean against the wall like I've been there all along. A minute later, Penny comes in all casual like.

"So?" I ask, trying not to look overly excited.

"Don't pretend you weren't listening," she says. "You're going. No big deal. Really, Ryan, you talk about your parents like they're ogres. They're actually really cool."

And that is that.

Penny stays for a plate of Mom's crepes. Then, a while later, we get ready to leave. On my way out the door, Dad calls me over to the couch. *Oh no. Here it comes,* I think. *They've changed their minds.*

Dad locks me in his sights. "I'm putting my trust in you," he says quietly so Penny—and Mom—don't overhear. "Don't blow it." Then he steps over to the bookcase and retrieves something from the top shelf—my cell phone! So, that's where he's been hiding it.

He places it carefully in my hands like it's the Holy Grail or something and says, "You will return this to me when you get home. You are to use it only for emergencies. I *will* check your call history. Got it?"

"Got it," I reply, hardly believing my good fortune.

"All right then. Have fun." Then Dad turns his focus back to the TV.

I'm so stunned, I just stand there frozen. I want to say thank you, tell him what an amazing Dad he is, but I can't seem to form the words. And if I wait too much longer to follow Penny, Mom might change her mind. So, I run for the door before she has the chance.

TWENTY-TWO

THE FIRST FEW MINUTES with Ryan in our car feel kind of awkward. Other than a quick hello between all of us, we don't have much to say to each other. Brett, who's driving, doesn't have anything to say at all. Finally, Mom breaks the painful silence.

"So, Ryan, are you having a nice Christmas break?" she asks, turning slightly toward him from the front seat.

"Break?" says Ryan. "What break?"

I jab an elbow into his ribs.

"I mean, yeah. I guess so. I'm being homeschooled right now, so I don't really get an official vacation. But I did have a nice Christmas. Thanks for asking, Mrs. Tate."

Ryan looks at me, raising his eyebrows in a silent *Was that good enough?* It is. And I let him know by smiling.

"Please call me Joelle," says Mom. She must like him right off, because she never tells my friends to call her by her first name. I hope she isn't reading more into this than there is.

"Okay," says Ryan, though I can tell by the way he says it, he feels weird about it.

"Ryan got a bass guitar," I tell Mom, hoping to kickstart some kind of conversation.

"Really? Brett used to play bass, didn't you, Brett?"

Brett keeps his eyes on the road. We turn onto the freeway, and my body presses against the back of the seat as the car accelerates to move into traffic. Brett didn't want to come today, but Mom talked him into it. Then, when he saw Ryan getting into the car, he gave me a scathing glare, but to his credit, he kept quiet.

Mom, oblivious to Brett's discomfort, continues. "Brett took lessons for years. He's very good. You still have it, don't you, Honey?" she asks, placing a hand on Brett's shoulder. He tenses. Mom notices and pulls back. "I think I saw it in his closet the last time I cleaned up in there, which was a while ago."

"Bass guitar, huh?" says Ryan. "Did you ever play in a band?"

Brett glances at me in the rearview, a warning not to go there, but Mom plows on, excited now. "Did he ever! They were called The Muckrakers, and they performed at Vinny's Pizza Parlor on Friday nights. Remember, Brett? How all your friends from school would come just to hear you guys play? They were great."

"What kind of music did you play?" Ryan asks.

I start to giggle. I can't help it. Talking about Brett's one stint in a *real* band always strikes me as funny. I take my pack of gum from my jeans pocket and slide a stick into my mouth, but it doesn't help. And Mom's giggling too.

"Zydeco," I finally say, and then I burst out laughing. Even Brett, who has so far been as solemn as a cement wall, cracks a smile. I can see it in the mirror, along with an eye roll.

"Zydeco?" asks Ryan. "You mean that weird, zippy, Louisiana Bayou music?"

"They were good," says Mom defensively. "Really, really good."

"Yes, they were," I agree.

"But why Zydeco?" Ryan says. "I mean, that seems an odd choice for a California-based band."

"The lead singer was from New Orleans," I reply, offering some gum to Ryan. "And they needed a bass guitarist, so Brett took the gig. He was just a freshman then, but The Muckrakers were all the rage for a while."

Brett shakes his head as if to say he thinks his little sister is crazy. But the mood in the car has lightened, so for that, breaking Brett's silence is worth it.

"Cool," says Ryan, and he seems sincerely impressed.

"He didn't just play Zydeco," says Mom. "He played lots of things, didn't you, Brett? What was that one song you used to play over and over again? You know. By that group Inky-something?"

"Incubus." It's the first word Brett has said since we got in the car.

"That's right," says Mom, and then as if on cue, she and I break into song, just like in the movies:

I'm on the road of least resistance
I'd rather give up than give into this
So promise me only one thing, would you?

And to my surprise, Brett joins in:

Just don't ever make me promises.

No promises, no promises.

The three of us dissolve into laughter, like we possess some sort of magic that only we share. For that moment, it's like old times again, before Dad left. Before the fear really set in.

Then Ryan asks, "Why'd you stop playing?"

Our laughter dies away, and a strange hush falls over the car. I can't meet Brett's eyes again, so I focus out the window where barren hillsides glide by.

"My dad took off," says Brett, his first words of the day. The silence continues for a few minutes longer, and the same tension we felt when the trip first began is back.

"I hope they still sell kettle corn at the park," says Mom, clapping her hands together and rubbing them briskly. "Ryan, do you like kettle corn?"

"Yeah," Ryan replies. "Sure, I do."

But he sounds uncertain. So, I'm pretty sure he's never had kettle corn in his life.

RYAN

TWENTY-THREE

IN PASADENA, PENNY'S family and I spend a couple hours roaming a field crammed with massive parade floats, each one bigger and more colorful than the next, with larger-than-life trees and animals and faces all decorated with a gazillion tiny blossoms. And there are people everywhere. More people than I've ever seen in one place, except for maybe Disneyland, all gazing at the floats with awestruck expressions.

After we've seen most of the floats and the sun has gotten too warm for comfort, Mrs. Tate offers to buy us all lunch. Brett and I settle at a picnic table while Penny and her mom stand in line at the nearest food vendor. They return a few minutes later carrying four cartons of what look like brown, gloppy lumps. Mrs. Tate passes them around.

"Hope you like chili dogs!" she sings, jabbing a white plastic fork into each one.

Before I can reply, Penny shouts, "Mom, there's the kettle corn!" as she points across the park to a line of people snaking through the crowd. Her mom perks up, just like a prairie dog, peering over everyone's heads.

"Really? Where?"

"There! Come on, Mom. We've got to get some to take home."

Mrs. Tate turns to me. "Will you two be all right for a minute?"

Penny grabs her mom by the hand, and the two of them blend into the sea of bodies.

Across the table, Brett takes a massive bite of chili dog. Bits of onion and sauce plop onto the napkin below. He chews, lost in his own world.

"You like chili dogs?" I ask, poking at mine with the flimsy fork. The truth is, I've never had a chili dog before. Not too fond of beans, actually, or unidentifiable fragments of meat guts died pink and formed into something that resembles a penis. I saw this episode of *How It's Made* a few years ago that demonstrated the process. Let's just say it was not very appetizing. I haven't eaten a hot dog since.

Brett says nothing but takes another bite of his lunch. I'm thinking about Penny's mom and how excited she was to buy food for me. When she asked me if I was hungry, I could have said no. And when she put this thing down in front of me, I could have said something like, "I'm so sorry, but I'm allergic to beans" or "Did I ever mention I'm a vegetarian?" both of which are lies, but instead I said nothing, which automatically obligates me to eat it.

I stab the fork into the mess of chili, fishing around for something solid. Then I twist it, breaking off a segment of meat and bun, and lift it halfway to my mouth.

"You don't have to eat it, you know." I look up to find Brett staring at me, an amused smirk on his face, but his eyes say—*Go ahead. I dare you.*

So, I do. I open my mouth wide and shove the dripping, greasy glop of over-processed pig guts inside. Brett's eyes remain fixed on my face. What is he doing? Waiting to see if I'll spit it out? Is my hatred of hot dogs that obvious?

When I swallow the whole mass down, Brett raises his eyebrows in approval. Then he does something that takes me totally by surprise. He reaches for my plate and pulls it across the table in front of him. Then he removes a ten-dollar bill from his wallet.

"I estimate you've got about eight minutes before my mom and Penny come back," he says, holding the money out to me. "The line at Zorba's is the shortest. They've got a mean chicken gyro."

What's he up to? But with only eight minutes to spare, I really don't have time to question his motives. I take the money and get up from the table.

"Thanks," I say and jog off to the Greek place. And he's right. The gyro is delicious, even if I just scarfed it down in two minutes flat. When I get back, my plate—my *empty* plate—is back across the table. Penny and her mom are munching on popcorn.

"You find the bathrooms?" Penny asks.

"Huh?"

"Maybe you can point the way for me."

Brett must have covered for me, telling them I'd gone to the restroom. I try to recall if I'd spotted one earlier.

"Yeah, but they're just porta-potties. Not very clean. You'd be better off waiting," I say as casually as I can.

"We do need to be heading back," says Mrs. Tate. "I promised to get you home at a decent hour."

On the way home, we listen to music on the radio. Turns out Brett and I like a lot of the same music. Once we've reached Penny's house, we all get out of the car. Mrs. Tate gives me a hug goodbye. Brett fist bumps me.

"See you around," he says.

Penny walks with me across the park to my house.

"I had a great time," I tell her. "Thanks for inviting me."

"No problem," she says. "It was fun."

"Your family's nice."

As we pass one of the pine trees, Penny reaches up, plucks off a needle, and holds it between her teeth like a toothpick. "Brett seems to like you."

"He does?"

"Yeah."

"How can you tell?"

She takes the pine needle out of her mouth and twists it into a tiny pretzel. "I just can."

We walk a little farther, but our steps are slow, like neither of us wants to actually get anywhere.

"So...the holidays are officially over," says Penny. "What's next for you?"

I notice the park grass has become brown in spots, normal for this time of year. "Well, helping you out with the kids, for one thing, and more schoolwork."

"How long will you have to be homeschooled?"

I slide my hands into my pants pockets. "Dunno. I'm supposed to meet with my school board in February, beg them to take me back."

"You don't sound too enthusiastic about it."

Is that how I sounded? I look up at Penny. Now she's got the pine needle pinched between her upper lip and nose, like a green, pointy mustache. She crosses her eyes at me. I laugh.

"Of course I want to go back," I tell her. "Why wouldn't I?"

Penny tosses the pine needle away. We've reached the end of my driveway. "Well, at least you like school," she says.

"You don't?"

"Not always." She looks away, her eyes drifting back across the park toward her house.

"I don't always like school either," I tell her, afraid of losing her attention. For some reason, I want her to look at me again. When she does, the sunlight hits her eyes just right, so that the blue in them sparkles.

"*You* don't like school?" she asks, like she doesn't believe me. "But you're always going on about how you gave up music so you'd have more time to study. I'll bet you've got your whole future mapped out—scholarships, Ivy League university—"

"Kings Point, actually."

Penny makes an exaggerated face, like some goofy royal snob.

"I'm not a total geek, you know," I tell her. But now she just looks skeptical. "I'm not! If everything was about school, would I be stuck at home right now?"

"What I think is that you tried too hard, and the pressure got to you."

Her accuracy stuns me. How is she so good at reading me like that?

She goes on. "You know, Ryan, there's more to life than homework and studying for exams."

"Okay," I say, knowing I'm setting myself up. "Like what?"

"Music, for one thing. From the few times I've heard you play, I'd say you're pretty good, better than you give yourself credit for."

"I shouldn't be wasting my time on it."

"Wasting your time? Or your parents' time? Don't forget it was your dad who bought you that bass for Christmas."

My dad. If only he knew the real reason I quit playing, he would have left that thing hanging on the store wall.

"You're an enigma, Ryan," says Penny. "A paradox."

I realize that Penny's studying me again, her blue eyes trying to penetrate some invisible outer shell. For a second, I'm tempted to let her in.

"Why?" I ask instead.

"Because I don't think you really know who you are. A rebel who pops pills behind his parents' back, or a geek who inhales academics like it's just another drug."

"I told you, I'm not a geek," I say, laughing.

"I'm not convinced."

"What do I have to do to prove it to you?"

Penny considers my challenge. "What's your *least* favorite school subject? Or do you even have one?"

"Math."

"That's a given. No one likes math."

"English, then."

She seems surprised. "Really? Why?"

"All those novels. I'd rather spend my time doing anything else besides read."

"I'm offended," Penny says, sticking her nose in the air.

"I take it you *like* to read?"

She lowers her nose, peers at me with her laser eyes. "Maybe you're just not comprehending what you're reading. Name a book you've read, one you really didn't like at all."

"I just finished *Of Mice and Men*."

She gasps. "I love that book!"

"It's depressing. Why would anyone intentionally subject themselves to that?"

Penny gets this determined look in her eyes. And she does this thing with her hands, waving them around for emphasis. "It is tragic," she says, "and beautiful."

"Beautiful how? George kills Lennie. He didn't have to do that."

Her voice gets higher, more insistent. "If he hadn't, the townspeople would have done something worse to Lennie."

"Worse than dying?"

"Maybe. I don't know."

My question seems to frustrate her, and she turns away again. But now I'm curious. "I think George should have tried talking to them, you know? He could have explained to them what happened, that Lennie didn't mean to hurt the girl. It was an accident. They might have understood."

Penny continues to look at her house, its red door practically screaming at us. At first, she doesn't say anything, but then she turns her gaze back to me. She's calm again.

"George did what he did because he knew they *wouldn't* understand. People like that don't get people like Lennie. All they see is what they want to see, and in the end, someone always gets hurt."

I'm not sure how to respond, but she doesn't seem to want me to. After a moment, her expression softens.

"I'll see you later," she says. "Thanks for coming with us. Today was a good day."

Then she turns and jogs across the park.

I watch her go, feeling more confused than ever. I obviously said something that upset her, but what? I dunno. Maybe she has a thing for Steinbeck. I feel bad that the day ends this way. Maybe I can make it up to her somehow.

I come into the house and find Dad sprawled on the sofa, an empty Coke can clutched in his hand. And he's snoring—loudly.

"Where's Mom?" I ask Justin, who's busy piecing together a jigsaw puzzle at the dining table.

"She's upstairs taking a nap," he says. "Did you see the parade?"

"No, just the floats. But they were pretty cool."

"I wish I could see the floats." Justin connects two long trains of puzzle pieces with a corner piece, then sifts through a pile of them with his index finger.

"Maybe next year you and I can go," I tell him.

"Sure," he says. "Cool."

I head for the kitchen and pop open the fridge. The gyro I ate earlier was good, but I could use a snack right about now. I grab a Coke and a cheese stick.

"Listen," I say, turning back to Justin. "You know that old jar of change? You've still got it in your room, right?"

"Yeah?" he asks warily.

"How much do you think is in there?"

"I dunno. Why?"

"Penny gave me a present at Christmas, but I still haven't gotten her anything."

Justin scoops the puzzle pieces into the empty box, then fits on the lid. "So, go get her something."

"That's just it. I don't have any money. If you haven't noticed, Mom's been heaping on the chores but hasn't paid me a cent. I'm flat broke."

"That's not my problem." Justin gets up from the table. He opens the game cupboard below the china cabinet and slides the box inside.

I'm getting irritated now. Those pennies have been collecting dust for years. At best, maybe there's ten or fifteen dollars, enough to get Penny a gift card or something. After what she did to get me out of the house today, I owe it to her.

"C'mon, Justin," I say in my nice-big-brother voice. "It's not a big deal. Most of those pennies are mine anyway."

Justin's eyes dart up, shooting invisible daggers into mine. "Those are *our* pennies, Ryan. We collected them together. They're our wishes."

"Justin, we were wishing for Twinkies!"

He pushes past me, stomping up the stairs. "You can't have them!" he shouts, then slams his bedroom door shut.

From my parents' room, Mom calls out, "What's going on down there?"

"Everything's fine, Mom," I tell her.

Except Justin's acting like a total dick, that's all.

PENNY

TWENTY-FOUR

AFTER OUR VISIT to the New Year's parade grounds, the rest of the week feels almost surreal, the way it does when the holidays are behind you, and you have to face real life without the lights and Christmas music. It's kind of anti-climactic. We spend months anticipating it, and then it's all over in a day.

On Friday, Mom asks me and Brett to take down the lights from the front of the house, the ones Ryan put up in our absence. In truth, we haven't had Christmas lights since Dad left two years ago, and we hadn't intended to put any up this year either. But after spending three nights in a sketchy motel room to be close to Brett while he was in the hospital, coming home to those lights was spectacular. I think seeing them changed us all for the better. For the first time in a long time, Christmas felt at least a little like Christmas.

So now, taking them down and putting them in a box feels sort of sad. I almost want to keep them, but I've been assigned the task of returning them to Ryan's family.

Brett unhooks the last string of lights and snakes it down to me while I wind the cord around my bent elbow.

"Need help?" He flaps a hand at the cardboard box at my feet, the one filled with the rest of the lights and decorations.

"It's not heavy," I say. "I'll just run it over, and then I'm helping Mom with dinner."

"What are we having?"

"I think she said something about split pea soup."

Brett makes a face. He hates soup.

"I'm kidding! We're having chicken and rice."

His face changes to a "so-so" expression as he makes his way down the ladder. "Do me a favor," he says. "Give this to Ryan, will you?"

He pulls a piece of paper from his back pocket. It's not folded in half or quarters like normal people would do. No, it's folded into some badly executed origami star. My hands are full with the box, so Brett wedges it between two of my fingers.

"What is it?"

"Fred left it for me. He keeps pestering me about doing the band thing."

"Sorry. I've told him no every time he's asked."

"It's okay. But I thought your friend might be interested, though."

The box of lights is heavier than I expected, so I say a quick goodbye to Brett and head over to Ryan's house. Balancing the box on my knee, I ring the doorbell. Ryan's dad answers.

"Hi. Um, we wanted to thank you for the lights," I tell him.

Mr. Rojas studies me for a second. Then he shouts over his shoulder. "Ryan! It's for you!" His voice is so deep and strong, it startles me. But when he turns back to me, I notice a sparkle in his eye. "Keep the lights," he tells me. "You can use them again next year."

Then he limps out of the living room.

A moment later, Ryan comes to the door red-faced and breathless. "Penny. I didn't expect you."

"Hi. Are you all right?"

"I've been out back digging holes for new fence posts. I'd just gone upstairs for a shower when Dad called me back down. Just need to catch my breath." He pauses, then gives me a funny look. "Are *you* all right?"

"Other than the fact that this box is starting to feel like a flat of bricks, I'm fine."

"Oh geez, let me get that." He takes the box from me and sets it on the porch. My arms ache with relief.

"You carried that here on your own? I could have come over for it. But did I just hear my dad tell you to keep it?"

"Yes," I say. "That was really nice of him."

"He's just happy to have more space in the attic for the new fake tree he bought on clearance. I'll carry the box back home for you, if you like."

"Sure, thanks."

There's this awkward pause where neither of us says anything. I'm wondering if Ryan plans to take the box now, or if he wants me to stay and visit. He starts to pick up the box, but then I hold out Brett's funky folded paper.

"My brother sent this for you."

Ryan takes the paper and unfolds it, smoothing it out on his thigh. "It's a BandMasterz flier. This says practices start next week." He glances at me with hopeful uncertainty. "You think they still need bass players?"

"I'm sure of it, or else Fred wouldn't have asked Brett—again."

"Your brother doesn't like the program?"

"He did them for years, but not since our dad—you know. So, you gonna sign up?"

For a second, Ryan's face lights up, but then all of a sudden, the enthusiasm drains from his face. "I can't," he says.

"Why not?"

"It's been two years since I've played. Even then, I wasn't all that great."

"Fred might be desperate enough to take you anyway."

I playfully bump against Ryan with my shoulder. He's reading the flier again.

"I'm supposed to be getting ready to meet with Middleton's school board. Between homework and volunteering, I wouldn't have time to practice." He hands me back the flier. "Even if I could, my parents would never go for it."

I'm not sure if he means what he says, or if he's using his mom and dad as an excuse.

"Are you sure? I mean, seems like when you want to do something, you do it."

"I don't want to do it."

I don't believe him. I sense there's something else going on he doesn't want to tell me. But it's none of my business.

"Bummer." I take the flier from his hand. "Fred'll be disappointed."

Ryan picks up the box, grunting from the effort. "This *is* heavy." He laughs a little. "Tell Brett thanks for thinking of me, but I'll leave the performing to the real musicians."

Ryan follows me back across the park and deposits the box on my porch. I'll ask Brett to find a spot in the garage for it later. I expect Ryan to say goodbye, but he lingers. And oddly, I linger too.

"You want to come in?" I ask.

Ryan shakes his head. "Mom was cool about me going with you to see the floats on New Year's, but I'd better not push my luck, if you know what I mean. But she goes back to work on Monday. Maybe we could hang out then."

The disappointment I feel surprises me. "That's my first day back at school, and I have a game that night. You want to come? To the game, I mean. Six o'clock at the school auditorium. And it's free."

"Wish I could, but the *being grounded* thing. I'm lucky my leash stretches this far. But I know you'll kick butt."

I laugh. "I always do."

Ryan turns away, but before he leaves, I stuff the BandMasterz flier back into his hand.

"Penny, I can't—"

"I know," I tell him. "Just take it anyway. For Brett."

He stares at it a moment, then folds it and slides it into his pocket.

We say goodbye, and I step inside the house and close the door, but not all the way. Peering through the narrow opening, I watch Ryan kick a stray rock across my driveway. The realization that I actually like him fills my stomach with light, little bubbles. For a second, I feel happy, giddy even.

I shut the door, but as I turn for the living room, I catch a glimpse of my reflection in the entryway mirror—the alien blue eyes, the sunburned scalp. Sometimes I still forget I don't have hair.

I turn from the mirror, the bubbles inside me bursting all at once.

RYAN

TWENTY-FIVE

MONDAY NIGHT. Worst night of any week. Worst because the weekend's over. And worst because even though I've survived the weekend being over, the rest of the week is just beginning. That makes Monday nights my least favorite because I can't relax, not like on Friday nights, when (before I was grounded) I could watch TV or play video games or hang out with my friends with no guilt. Monday night means a week's worth of assignments and chores still ahead of me.

Justin's sitting in the living room binge-watching *SpongeBob* on Amazon. I'm sitting at the dining table working on the second draft of my Steinbeck essay. After my chat with Penny over New Year's, I decided to take it from a different angle than I did before. I've been tweaking my outline all day, and now I'm ready for the rewrite.

"You're still at it?" asks Dad, reaching for his coat draped in its usual spot over the back of a dining chair. "Your dinner's getting cold."

Mom made meatloaf, but I didn't want to break my concentration, so she stuck it in the microwave for me.

"Soon," I say, briefly glancing up from the computer screen. "Going somewhere?"

Dad slips on his jacket. "I'm taking your mother out to dinner."

Mom comes in dressed to kill. She's wearing one of her nicer outfits, with a pearl necklace and lipstick. "I'm taking *you* out for dinner," she says. Then she adds, "We're celebrating."

"Oh?"

Mom's beaming. "Remember last month I applied for a window? Well, I got it. As of next week, no more 'rain and snow' routes and reams of useless junk mail to deliver. I'll be working indoors."

"That's awesome, Mom. Congratulations."

"And that's not all," Mom continues, cutting a sneaky glance at Dad. "Wanna tell him?"

"It's nothing," says Dad, but the proud look on his face tells me it's anything but nothing. "I'm going to start assisting at the gym, that's all. Helping other wounded vets get in shape. It's just a few hours a week, and I'm not getting paid or anything—at least, not yet."

Dad, who never was one to draw attention to himself, immediately turns his focus to Mom. "Are you ready to go?"

"Just a minute," she says, then turns a skeptical eye on me. "We're going to Spaldings for dinner and then a movie. Will you watch Justin?"

Justin is almost eleven and quite capable of watching himself, but I agree anyway. "Sure. Have a good time."

They say goodbye to their other son, but he doesn't even notice when they've left, he's such a TV zombie. He'd probably stay up all night watching that crap if I let him. But this is my chance to make good with Mom. I'll let him watch for another hour, then insist he go to bed and read. That's what she always tells him to do.

I turn back to the computer, but now my focus is shot. Damn. Leaning back in my chair, I glare at the ceiling as if the ideas that escaped me might be floating around up there. No such luck. So instead, I get up and head to the kitchen, punch two minutes into the microwave and turn it on. The numbers count down, and when they hit zero, the microwave beeps. I pop it open, retrieve my plate, and shove the door closed again. That's when I notice them—the numbers on the clock. Of course, they've shifted from cook time to real time. 5:43 pm. What time did Penny say her game was tonight? I'm pretty sure she said it was six.

Opening the drawer under the microwave, I grab a fork and prod the pile of mashed potatoes. I could go to the game. The school's a bit of a walk, but I could take my new long board, be there in ten minutes tops. Watch the game. Ten back. I'd be gone an hour and a half at most and be back in time to put Justin to bed.

Wait. Stop it, I tell myself, twirling a nugget of meat through some gravy. Last time I snuck out, I nearly got myself into a heap of trouble.

But I'm not sneaking out. Not really. And I'll be right back.

But still…

I stick my plate back in the microwave, then I head to the bookshelf in the living room and fetch my phone from the top shelf, where Dad stashed it after New Year's. I speed dial Dad's number. Since this whole thing is about Penny, I figure I at least have a shot at him giving me permission. But instead of hearing Dad's voice on the other end of the line, it goes right to voicemail. He's probably still driving to the restaurant, and the ringer's most likely off or else Mom would have answered for him. I consider calling Mom's cell instead, but two things stop me: first, the phone's down to just 1%, which means Dad never bothered recharging my phone, and it's about to die; and second, the time. It's almost six. If I don't leave now, I might as well not bother.

So, I put the phone back on the shelf and grab my longboard out of the hall closet.

"I'm going out for a while, bro," I tell Justin, whose eyes are still glued to the TV. "I won't be long. You don't mind, do you?"

"Where are you going?"

"Just out. I promise I'll be back soon. Sure you're okay?"

Justin glances in my direction just long enough to shrug, then returns to the screen.

"All right," I tell him, "you know what to do if there's an earthquake or a fire?"

I laugh at myself because I'm starting to sound like Mom. Justin doesn't respond. So, I take one last look at him as if doing so magically guarantees that I'll find him in this exact same spot when I return. Then I open the door and step outside.

TWENTY-SIX

"HAVE YOU KISSED HIM YET?"

Tali snaps her rat-tailed T-shirt at me, stinging my forearm.

"Ow!" I rub the spot and throw a playful punch in her direction, which she dodges easily. "It's not like that. Ryan's just a friend—sort of."

"How can someone be a friend, *sort of*?"

"I mean, we get along and have a few things in common."

"Like what?"

I pull off my T-shirt, tossing it into my locker, and tug on my white and blue jersey while Tali's question bounces around in my brain.

"We both like Girl Scout cookies," I finally answer, pulling on my sneakers. "Samoas."

Tali rolls her eyes. "Big freakin' deal. Half the country likes those best. The other half, including moi, prefer the subtle snap and coolness of the Thin Mint."

"We like those too."

"I'm sorry, Penny, but you have to come up with something better than refreshments."

It's been three days since I saw Ryan. School's back in session. Vacation's over. Though Ryan and I did chat online over the weekend, I can't get his face out of my brain. But I won't admit that to Tali, or to anyone.

Coach comes in, the game ball tucked in the crook of her elbow. "Okay, ladies. Game's about to start. Let's warm up."

Tali and I jog onto the court with the rest of the team. The bleachers are already half full of parents, friends, and teachers, all here to root for the home team. When we make our appearance, they hoot and stamp their feet. The sound reverberates through the gymnasium, sending spears of adrenaline through me. I glance up and see Connor waving at Tali. Mom and Brett are in their usual spots near the top. Brett gets to his feet and cups his hands around his mouth.

"Go Penny!" Only it comes out more like a war cry than a shout of confidence. But it makes me feel good just the same.

Lea Pachero smirks at me before passing me the ball. Even though things between us get heated during practices, games are another matter entirely. On the court, we share a common enemy. No time for petty rivalry here.

I manage to shoot a few before the ref's whistle blows, announcing the start of the game. Half our team takes their seats on the sidelines. The rest of us take our places on the court. Lea faces off against Bakersfield's center, ferocity and focus in her eyes. The buzzer sounds. The ref tosses the ball, and both girls leap, slapping at it. Lea, a few inches taller than the other girl, takes the ball and hurtles down the court toward the basket. The ball slamming against the floor is one of the best sounds in the world, that and the sound that comes next. *Whoosh!* Lea sinks the ball with almost no resistance at all.

But we can't rest on the laurels of an early lead.

Tali throws the ball in to Natalie, but she's soon hemmed in by red and gold jerseys. The high-pitched squeaks of ten pairs of sneakers against the polished court can't drown out the shouts from the crowd.

"Come on, Natalie!"

"Pass it! Pass it!"

Nat's face glistens with sweat. She looks for a break and finds it between numbers 24 and 17. She passes the ball to me right between them. The taller one, 24, tries to snatch it as it rockets by, but misses. A second later, the ball arrives confidently between my palms.

I love the feel of a basketball, the thousands of tiny rubber bumps gripping my skin, allowing me to hold it in ways no other ball can. I love the way it comes back to me when I shove it down against the court. A basketball is like a pet dog, loyal and obedient.

I'm focused now, my eyes lining up the basket before I even reach the key. I dodge right then left, just like a football player on the field, edging my way closer to the basket. But what the opposing team doesn't know yet is that I don't need to get that close.

I wait for just the right moment and then fake a shot. Number 9 falls for it, leaps up to block. On her way down, I take aim and shoot.

The ball sails in a perfect arc between my fingertips and the basket. It doesn't even touch the rim going in. *Swoosh!*

4 – Nothing. A good start to the game.

The ref whistles.

Bakersfield calls a time-out, and Coach signals us in.

That's when I hear someone screaming my name like a banshee from the back row. I look up, expecting to see Brett, wondering if he's having one of his episodes again. I do see Brett, and he's grinning like the Cheshire Cat and pointing with both hands at the boy sitting to his left, who's stomping and hollering louder than anyone. He pumps the air with his fist and gives a few more whoops.

I can't believe it.

It's Ryan.

Coach calls my name.

"Oh, uh, sorry," I say, getting back into the game. I glance over at Tali, and she's got the biggest smirk on her face ever.

The final buzzer sounds, and the dejected Bakersfield team lines up to shake our hands. Everyone else swarms the court, congratulating us on our win. Connor leaps over three bleachers and scoops Tali into his arms, screaming, "You won! You won!"

Tali made the final shot of the game, so she's the one swallowed into the mass of crazed basketball fans. I'd be a part of that too, but instead, I pry myself away from the crowd and make my way to the sidelines where Ryan's waiting.

"Hi," I say, giving my head and face a quick swipe with a towel first. "I can't believe you made it."

"I wanted to see you in action," Ryan replies. "Are you surprised to see me?"

"Are you kidding? I was so shocked to see you in the stands, I nearly forgot about the game. I can't believe your parents let you come."

Ryan's eyes dart to the side, and he fidgets with his hoodie zipper.

From the center of the court, Tali shouts, "Penny, get over here!"

"I guess you better join in the victory," says Ryan. "Are you going to Vinny's? That's where you guys usually celebrate, isn't it?"

In truth, Vinny's is the last place I want to go, not after what happened with Jake last time. "Or maybe," I reply, "we could go out for ice cream instead."

What? Did I really just ask Ryan out? I feel my face flush with heat. "I mean—what I meant to say was—" I try to back pedal, but Ryan's grinning at me.

Before he can respond, Brett comes up behind me. He slips his arms around my waist and lifts me off the ground with an animal-like growl. "Congrats, Pen," he says, kissing the back of my neck. "You were awesome out there."

Mom gives me a squeeze. "So proud of you, Honey." She turns to Ryan. "I hope you had fun."

"Thanks for letting me sit with you guys," he says.

"Anytime," Mom replies. "Well, I've got to get to work. I hate night shift, but I take whatever overtime I can get these days. Bed pans won't empty themselves, you know."

"All right, Mom." I laugh, giving her another hug.

"I've gotta go too," says Ryan, glancing at his watch.

I look back toward Tali, still the center of attention. Lea, Jake, and Celine are all there. Brett and Celine's eyes connect for just a moment before Jake notices and pulls Celine away into the crowd.

"You know, I'm not really in the mood for pizza," I say.

"You—not in the mood for pizza?" Brett drags his attention back to me, pretending to knock an invisible something out of his ear. "Did I really just hear you say that?"

I slug his arm. "Ow!" he says. Then he turns to Ryan. "Sounds like Penny here doesn't want to mingle with the victors tonight. Let's say we go back to our place and watch a video. Wanna come?"

The gym door opens, and the crowd starts to leave. "Wish I could," says Ryan, "but I'd better get going."

"Too bad," says Brett. "Since Penny doesn't want pizza tonight, I'm ordering Chinese." Brett pulls out his phone and starts dialing, stepping outside to handle the call.

Ryan looks at his watch—again. He seems jumpy.

"You okay?" I ask him. "You keep looking at your watch."

"I'm fine," he says. "Mind if I catch a ride back with you guys, though? I have my longboard, but it'd be faster to drive."

"Sure." We start for the gym door, through which I hear Brett placing our order. "Moo Shu Pork! Not *fork*. P-o-r-k."

"I think this is going to take a minute. Can you hang on a second?" I ask Ryan. "I'm just going to let Tali know what's up."

I weave my way through the thinning crowd to Tali, who's tangled with Connor, their lips smashed together in a kiss.

"Uh, Tali?"

Tali peels herself off Connor to look at me. "Yeah?"

"Brett and I are gonna pass on Vinny's tonight. That all right with you?"

Her eyes dart from me to Ryan. "Is *that* all right with me? If you're choosing that guy over some insanely crazy victory party, then—hell, yeah, it's all right with me!"

Tali kisses Connor again, and they gaze at each other as if they're the only people in the whole world. I'm all but forgotten. I can't help feeling envious.

I'm about to go back to Ryan when someone's hand drops onto my shoulder. I turn and find myself face-to-face with Jake Dillinger.

"It was you, wasn't it?"

I look around for Celine and the others, but they've gone already.

"Was what?" I ask, though I know exactly what he's talking about.

"The cops—Vinny's. I know you called them that night."

"I didn't do any such thing." Tali and I share a brief conspiratorial glance.

"We were just fooling around," he continues, his voice low and harsh. "You couldn't take a joke, could you?"

"Are you all right, Penny?" Ryan comes up behind me.

"She's fine," Jake snaps. "This is between us."

From the corner of my eye, I see that Brett's stepped back into the gym and is watching us. He stays near the door, but his knuckles are practically white, he's clutching his phone so tightly.

Jake sees him too. "Hey, moron," he sneers, "we were just talking about you. Me and the guys? We all voted you Most Likely School Shooter."

He laughs, but Brett says nothing.

"Oh, and Penny," adds Jake, "your ball needs a polish," and swipes a rough hand over my skull.

I'm used to Jake's ribbing, but apparently this is too much for Ryan. "I don't know who the hell you think you are," he says, stepping close to Jake, "but you're going to apologize for that."

Jake sizes up Ryan, amused. Then he closes the gap between them, so they're almost nose to nose. "I don't think so."

"Ryan, it's not a big deal," I start to say, but what comes next happens before I can finish my sentence. Jake gets up in Ryan's face, and Ryan pushes him back. Not hard, just enough to make some space, but that's all the excuse Jake needs. His knuckles strike Ryan's left eye, snapping his head back. Ryan grunts from the force of it but then turns a hard, vengeful glare on him. Thankfully, Connor has reappeared and steps in between them.

"Jake! That's enough! Leave them alone."

"He hit me first!" says Jake. "You saw it!"

"He hardly touched you, man." Connor's trying to calm him down. "C'mon. We've got a party to catch."

I grab Ryan's arm, pulling him away. "Let's get out of here."

Jake flips his middle finger at Ryan. "Yeah," Jake spits, "he's not worth it. None of you are worth it." He says this last bit while staring daggers across the gym at Brett. Then he stomps through the locker room doors. Tali takes Connor's hand and follows Jake. She turns back to me and mouths *sorry* before leaving the gym.

I turn to Ryan. "What were you thinking?" I say, running a delicate touch over his eye, which has already begun to swell.

He flinches.

"Sorry. But that was beyond dumb, shoving Jake Dillinger like that."

"He deserved it."

"I don't care, Ryan. He's a jerk—and a lot bigger than you. You're lucky Connor called him off."

We head across the gym toward Brett, who whistles when he sees Ryan's face. "That's one helluva mark," says Brett, but I'm miffed. Jake is *his* ex-best friend. He should have been the one to deal with him, not Ryan.

"Hope you're hungry," Brett adds.

"That's an understatement," I say, deciding to keep my mood to myself. "When Brett orders Chinese, it's enough to feed the entire neighborhood and half of China."

Ryan doesn't even seem to hear the joke, let alone respond to it, not that it was all that funny anyway, but it's not like him to ignore my pitiful attempts at humor. He glances at his watch again.

"I need to get home," he says.

"It's not even seven-thirty," I tell him. "What's the matter? You've been ogling your watch like it's a naked woman. Maybe it *is* a naked woman!"

I reach for his wrist, laughing. But he pulls away.

"I'm sorry, Penny. But I really have to go."

Ryan heads for the door at practically a run. Then it hits me, and I'm too stunned to even say it, but I have to.

"You snuck out, didn't you?"

Ryan stops. He doesn't answer me, which is as good as a confession.

"Again? Ryan, are you crazy?" By now, the gym has pretty much emptied out. My team has headed off en masse to Vinny's, so there's no one left to hear me shriek. "Your parents will kill you!"

"Only if they find out."

"Ryan, you've been whining for weeks about what a short leash they've got you on."

"It's all right. They went out to eat tonight and then to a movie. If I get back in time, they'll never find out I left."

"Your eye! How will you explain that?"

Ryan's Adam's apple bobs in a hard swallow.

I let out an exasperated breath. "You can be so stupid sometimes!"

The last time Ryan snuck out, he only managed to keep it from his parents because Brett and I came to his rescue. Now I'm wondering if that was such a good idea. Maybe I should have let him hang.

"They're just beginning to trust you," I tell him. "Your mom let you go to the parade route with us, but you told me yourself that was practically a miracle."

"I know, Penny." Ryan's voice rises. "I know it was wrong. And stupid."

"Then why'd you come?"

He throws a desperate look Brett's way as if he expects him to say something in his defense, then looks back at me. "I just wanted to see you play."

I don't know why, but I can't respond to that. Literally.

"Penny, we need to go," Brett interrupts. "Ryan, I'll drop you off at home if you want."

"Thanks," says Ryan, but he refuses to meet my eyes as he hurries outside.

RYAN

TWENTY-SEVEN

BRETT AND PENNY drop me off in front of my house after the game, but I know I'm in for it. Dad's car is parked out front.

My parents are home early.

I consider lying to them. I could say that I was at Penny's house, or I was in the backyard and didn't hear them come home.

I touch the tender spot around my eye and wince. No matter what story I conjure up, I can't think of any that would explain away the swollen bruise on my face.

My hand hesitates on the front doorknob. Then I take a deep breath, preparing for the worst, and open the door.

Dad's sitting on the couch when I come in. Mom, still wearing the red dress and pearls she left in, stands beside the fireplace, arms crossed, jaw set. They both look up.

"Where the hell have you been?" Mom demands.

Dad doesn't say anything to me. Instead, he calls over his shoulder into the dining room. "Justin, go to your room."

I hadn't noticed my brother at the dining table, but he gives me a sympathetic look as he passes me on the way up the stairs.

I step into the living room. "I thought you were going to a movie after dinner."

"We left the tickets on our dresser," Mom snaps back. "And you weren't here when we came back to get them."

"I haven't been gone long. I tried to call, but you didn't answer."

"That's no excuse," says Mom. "Where were you?"

"Marissa," Dad says from the couch. "At least give him a chance to explain."

Mom takes a step closer to me, lowering her clenched hands to her sides. "All right," she says. "So, explain."

Gathering what courage I can, I meet Mom's eyes. "I went to a basketball game at the high school."

"A basketball game." She cuts a look at my dad as if asking him if he really believes the load of crap I'm giving them. Only it's not crap. It's true. "You left Justin home *alone*."

"He's ten, Mom. He can take care of himself. Penny was playing tonight, and she asked me to come—so I went."

She comes closer and takes my chin in her hand. "What is *this*?"

I consider telling her what happened, but I'm in enough trouble already without adding that I was the one who pushed that guy first. So, I say nothing.

"Unbelievable." She lets go of my face. "It's not enough that you got kicked out of school, or that you've jeopardized your future. Now you're getting into fights? I suppose none of this matters to you."

"It matters," I say without conviction.

"I guess I was the stupid one thinking you could be trusted. Your father's been telling me how well you're doing with your studies, how hard you've worked on your chores. I was beginning to think maybe I was wrong about you. Maybe I should ease up, give you a second chance."

I raise my eyes, looking for Dad. He's still on the couch, leaning forward, his hands between his knees. I can't tell if the frown on his face is because he's ashamed of me, or because he doesn't like the way Mom's handling this. He used to be the one to give the lectures. Where was that man now? I haven't seen him since he came home a limb short from overseas. When he doesn't raise his eyes to me, I finally give up and look back at Mom. She's glaring at me, the skin on her face so taut I bet it would pop like a balloon if I touched a pin to it.

"You are not to leave the house again without permission," she says. "You're going to obey my rules or else."

"Or else what?" I snap back.

I'm sick of this. Sick of being a prisoner in my own house. Sick of having to piss in a plastic cup. Sick of doing everything that's asked of me and still not being trusted. All this *sick* feels like a lit fuse burning inside me.

"Excuse me?" says Mom.

Despite all the warning bells going off in my head, I let it all out.

"You expect me to obey the rules or else *what*? Or else you'll send me to public school? Maybe that would be better. God knows anywhere would be better for me than here!"

Mom's jaw drops in shock. Dad lifts his face to finally look at us. Somehow, that gives me courage.

"What are you going to do, Mom? There's nothing left for you to take away from me. You're already working me like a slave every day. I can't go anywhere or talk to anyone unless you say so. The only person you seem to trust me with is Penny, which is why I didn't think it was such a big deal that I went to her game tonight."

For the first time since I came home, Mom is silent.

"And why is that, Mom?" I continue. "Why do you trust me with her? Is it because Penny's bald? Because you think I'm safe with her? That's it, isn't it? What trouble could Ryan get into with a bald girl?"

I know this strikes a nerve because Mom blinks and looks away.

"I went to a basketball game, and not even the whole thing! I was there for an hour tops. Yes, I snuck out, and I'm sorry I did that. But I didn't do anything wrong. Ever since I came home, I've done absolutely everything you've asked of me. I'm getting A's in my courses. I'm being responsible."

"You took drugs," Mom says. "You got kicked out of school."

"Yes, I screwed up. And I'm sorry! You talk about giving me a second chance? Well, I deserve one!"

"So, what do you expect me to do?"

"For one, stop with the drug testing. You've been testing me for more than a month. Has there been a single positive result? No. Because I'm not doing anything! And second, I feel like a prisoner here. How can I prove I'm trustworthy if you don't let me get out once in a while?"

When I finish, I run my fingers through my hair, which is longer than it's been in years, the military buzz gone. I expect Mom to slap me for mouthing off to her, but she doesn't. She doesn't do—or say—anything. Instead, her eyes get glossy, and she turns away from me.

"Go upstairs," she says.

Not knowing what else to do, I run to my room and slam my door. I go right to my bass, turn up the volume as high as I can stand it, and start in on a Chili Peppers lick. The anger churning inside of me sparks down my arms into my fingers, spilling out into the strings. The amp thrums and pulses, a sensation as physical as when that guy's fist slammed into my face.

If Dad knocks before he comes in, I don't hear it. I don't notice him until he sits on the edge of my bed, his elbows braced against his knees. I ignore him and finish the song. When it's over, I feel spent, like I've just run a marathon. Totally wiped out.

I turn off the amp. *Click.* Dad sits there for a while, neither of us speaking.

Finally, he says, "That sounded pretty good. Did I ever tell you I used to play?"

I set the bass in its stand. "You played bass?"

"Ukulele." He chuckles. "I got it in my head when I was your age that I wanted to move to Hawaii and become a surfer. Of course, I'd never been on a surfboard in my life, but my walls were covered with posters of professional surfers. I'd seen this movie, *Point Break*, and I thought, man, I'd love to live like that. Anyway, I lived in the middle of Idaho, a thousand miles from the nearest ocean. So, I did the next best thing: I dreamed of Hawaii and bought a ukulele."

I have a hard time imagining my father at my age at all, let alone wanting to surf or play music. Before his accident, all I ever knew him as was a soldier.

"That's why I joined the Marines," he adds, "to see the world."

"Maybe you should have joined the Navy instead," I tell him, "since you liked the ocean so much."

"Yeah. There are a lot of things I should have done, but life has a way of taking you places you don't really plan on going." He pauses for a second to study my face. "Where'd you get the shiner?"

"Some jerkoff was messing with Penny. I told him to back off, and he hit me."

"Did you hit him back?"

"I was gonna, but another kid stopped the whole thing."

Dad gives a slow nod. "You stuck up for Penny. I would have done the same in your place. Only I wouldn't have let him walk away."

That's probably true, though from the way he acted downstairs tonight, I'm not a hundred percent sure.

"You're a better man than I am," he says.

My mattress squeaks as Dad shifts his weight. Sometimes the prosthetic bothers him, like it does now. I can see the discomfort in his face. He notices me looking at him, gives an apologetic smile. Pats his fake knee with his hand.

"Don't know if I'll ever get used to it," he says. He sits there for a while longer. I can tell he's got something on his mind, but maybe he's not sure how to say it. His eyes are focused on my bass guitar. After a minute or so, he gets up from the bed with a grunt.

"I'd better let you get back to what you were doing. It's good to hear you playing again. And don't worry about your mom," he says. "She's not as angry as she comes off. Just concerned about you, is all."

I scoff. "She doesn't act like she's concerned about me."

"Well, she is. She loves you, wants what is best for you."

"How can she know what's best for me, Dad? She's at work half the time, and when she is home, she's always yelling at me."

"I've noticed that it goes both ways. You two have real chips on your shoulders. Been going on for a while, long before the problems at school. Want to talk about it?"

Dad's right, of course. Mom and I have been at each other's throats for a long time now. It started the night we got the call about Dad, but I don't want to talk about it. Especially not with him.

"It's fine," I tell him. "I just wish she'd back off."

"I'll talk to her," Dad says. "But in the meantime, you gotta cut her some slack too, all right? Your mom's had a whole load of crap dumped on her these past few years that she never saw coming. Neither of us saw coming. It's been—" he takes a deep, noisy breath, lets it out in a tired whoosh of air "—it's been tough."

He limps across the room and pulls open my bedroom door. Then he turns back and just looks at me for a second, all nostalgic like. "I was pretty good, you know."

"At surfing?" I ask.

"The ukulele. I never did learn to surf."

He steps out of my room, quietly shutting the door behind him. I stare at it for a long time, the image of him imprinted in my mind. Then I pick up my bass and turn it on again. As I strum the first chords, I smile, imagining my dad with a ukulele in his hands.

PENNY

TWENTY-EIGHT

AFTER THE GAME Monday night, Brett heads straight to his room and locks the door, all pretense of ordering Chinese and enjoying a movie gone. Obviously, our run-in with Jake upset him. So, I decide to let him be. But in the morning, there's still no sign of him. I wait until seven-thirty before I finally gather my courage and knock on his door.

"It's open," says Brett.

I go in and find Brett still in bed wearing the same clothes he wore yesterday, and he looks like he didn't get much sleep. He's just tucking something under his pillow, something he obviously doesn't want me to see, but I catch a glimpse of his red notebook anyway.

"What's the matter?" I ask. "We have to leave for the bus in five minutes."

"I'm not going."

"To school?"

"The moon. Of course, school." He shoves a fist into his pillow, adjusting it, and then rolls to his side to face me.

"You're not sick, are you?"

"No."

I already know he's not, and I know what he's upset about. I just don't want to say it, but I have to.

"Brett, if this is about yesterday—"

"I don't want to talk about it."

"You shouldn't care what Jake says. He's an idiot."

But I've said the wrong thing. I can tell. Brett blinks back tears, something I rarely see from him.

"Jake was my friend," he says at last. "I ruined everything."

No. No, we cannot go there. Not another spiral. Christmas was bad enough. But this is really bothering him, and I can't just brush it off. I know Brett. If I ignore how he's feeling, it'll just fester and then explode when I least expect it.

I cross the room and sit on the side of his bed. "Whatever happened between you two, you can't take all the blame. It wasn't your fault."

"Yes, it was, Penny."

"How could it be? I mean, one day you two are tight as twins. The next, Jake is a total butthole."

"You don't know what happened."

"I assume it has something to do with Celine, with you two breaking up last month. But you never told me what happened."

Brett's eyes connect with mine. They're filled with hurt, with self-loathing. He rolls to his other side and faces the wall. "I don't want to talk about it."

I glance at my cell phone. Time is ticking away. I almost don't have enough of it left to get to the bus stop, which means I'd have to walk to school, which means I'll miss half of first period. But I can't leave Brett like this. So, I draw in a breath and dive in.

"Brett?" I say, touching his shoulder. He's not angry, not yet anyway. And I have to be careful not to tip the scales in that direction. "Brett, it's okay. You can tell me. You have to tell someone, or you'll bust like a balloon. So, it might as well be me."

At first, I think he's just going to ignore me until I go away. But I wait anyway, and after several minutes, I feel him shifting under my palm.

"I hit her," he says in almost a whisper, like it's a struggle to get the words out.

"What?"

He answers louder this time, but his voice shakes. "I hit her, Pen."

I can't help it, but I let my hand slide off his shoulder to the mattress. "What happened? How?"

He turns onto his back and stares at the ceiling. "I don't know. I can't even remember what we were arguing about. I was having a bad day, trying to keep myself together and not doing a very good job of it. We argued about something. And I slapped her. The moment I did, I knew I'd messed up. I apologized, begged her to forgive me. You should have seen the look on her face, Pen. She was so…so scared of me. I drove her home, but we didn't say anything else about it. I felt horrible and swore I'd make it up to her somehow, but when Jake got wind of what I'd done, it was over. Jake told me if I came anywhere near Celine again, he'd tell everyone. So, I've stayed away."

When Brett stops talking, all I can hear is his breathing and my own blood pulsing through my ears. Brett slapped Celine. No wonder Jake's been such a jerk lately, but would Brett have behaved any different if someone did that to me? Still, that doesn't give Jake an excuse to say what he did after the game, calling my brother a future school shooter. What the hell was he thinking?

"It's okay, Brett," I tell him because it's all I can think of to say. "You made a mistake, and Jake's overreacting, that's all. He's defending his sister. At least it wasn't Celine who dumped you."

"She's tried to talk to me," says Brett, "but I can't let her near me. Not just because of Jake, but what if I—? I can't trust myself anymore, Pen. Not around her. Not even around you."

"That's absurd, and you know it." But something he says triggers a deep-seated emotion in me, one I always push so deep down inside that I can pretend it's not there: fear.

Brett sits up and sets his feet on the floor. He swipes a hand over his face. "You've probably missed the bus. I'll drive you to school."

He stands and reaches for his hoodie draped on the corner of his bed. I follow him to his car, and we drive the couple miles in silence. I'm hoping he'll park in the lot and walk in with me, but instead, he pulls to the curb.

"You're not coming?" I ask, but I know the answer.

"I've got some things I need to take care of," he says.

I think of that red notebook of his. What's he been writing in it?

"I just—" He hesitates. "I just need a day off."

A day off. Just one day. I can live with that. I just hope it's enough.

TWENTY-NINE

VACATION IS OFFICIALLY OVER.

Not that I really had much of a vacation at all. Except for Christmas Day and New Year's, I was still required to put in my three to four hours of schoolwork each day and do my chores. And what made it worse was that Mom *was* on vacation, which meant she was home watching every move I made. After our fight last night, Mom hasn't said a word to me. She went to work today—hallelujah—and Justin is back in school—double hallelujah! Dad's gone to his physical therapy appointment and actually left me home alone, but not before lecturing me about not getting into any more trouble.

At nine am Tuesday, I dutifully plop into the chair at my desk and turn on my computer. My main task at hand is to take an online science quiz. I log onto the homeschool website and update my progress on it. My class scores so far have been pretty good. My GPA is holding steady at 4.0.

Eat that, Norton.

I start on the quiz, but after a while, my mind starts to drift. I try to stay focused, but the house is too quiet.

I get up from the computer and head downstairs to the kitchen. I grab a Coke from the fridge, then return to my room, but I can't bring myself to study anymore. Instead, I log on to the internet. Just for kicks, I visit the website on the BandMasterz flier Penny gave me. The home page is nothing fancy, pretty much just the details from the flier and a link to request more information.

Five weeks of rehearsals. I could learn to play a few songs well enough to perform in five weeks, couldn't I?

I stare at the screen. Fred said they're short a player, and they'll have to cancel one of the bands. But with all this schoolwork and volunteering with Penny, I don't have time for anything else right now. I have to stay focused on getting back into Middleton. And except for the past couple of weeks, I haven't touched an instrument in two years. So, it's not like I'm the ideal choice for a band.

I crumple the flier and chuck it into my trash can. Then I lean back in my chair and put my hands behind my head. Penny's friend pendant still hangs on the wall over my desk. Penny thought I should sign up for BandMasterz. The more I think about it, the more I can't get it out of my head.

I fish the wadded-up flier from the trash and smooth it out on my bed. Then I message Penny before I remember she's at school, but she responds almost immediately anyway.

Me: I'm thinking about doing something really dumb.

Penny: Dumber than getting date drugged at the park?

Me: Ha ha. BandMasterz. Maybe.

Penny: That would be awesome. Talk to Fred this afternoon.

I tell her I'm scared out of my wits, that I'm no good, and Fred would never want me anyway. But then Penny threatens to blackmail me if I don't go through with it by telling my parents about the park thing. It's not a serious threat, I know, but it gets my attention.

Me: You really think I should do this? Or is this just a stupid idea? Tell me I'm being an idiot.

Penny: You're an idiot.

Me: Thanks.

Penny: I'm kidding! Hang on a sec.

There's a long pause before Penny finally starts typing again.

Penny: Gotta run. See you later?

Me: Yeah.

Penny: BTW - I'm having something delivered to your door. Bye.

Something delivered to my door? Did she order me a pizza or something? I drift back to my homework, trying to focus on the exam I'm taking, but it's useless. Fortunately, a few minutes later, the doorbell rings. That was fast. Too fast for pizza.

"Just a minute!" I call, bounding down the stairs two at a time. I open the door and find Brett standing there holding the most beautiful electric bass guitar I've ever seen—deep blue with rich, dark ripples of natural wood grain. I think I actually gasp when I see it, which makes Brett smile.

"Penny just texted me to get over here and help you out," he says, "like pronto."

"She did?" I can almost hear her laughing on the other end of the internet connection. "I mean, how…? We just barely…"

"Yeah, well, that's Penny. So, uh, can I come in?"

"Sure."

Brett follows me inside, and I shut the door.

"Wait," I say, "aren't you supposed to be at school?"

Brett pushes air through his teeth. "That's the thing. Yes, I'm supposed to be there, but I'm not." He shrugs. "Didn't feel like going today. Guess you lucked out. Got an amp?"

When I take him upstairs to my room, he crosses to the window, leans his guitar against the wall, and picks up my bass and checks it out.

"How's the eye?" he asks.

I touch a finger to the tender skin. "Still swollen."

"Yeah, you look like a prize fighter."

Brett starts playing my bass and picks out a sad, bluesy lick. "Not bad," he says when he finishes. "I'd get some new strings if I were you. These have got to be a decade old." He wipes his fingertips on his jeans to emphasize the point.

"New strings," I say, making a mental note. "Right."

He jiggles the pick-up at the bottom of the bass. "Loose," he says, then brushes his fingers over the various scuffs and scratches on the body. "It's okay for a starter."

"I'm going to save up for a new one," I reply, though I hadn't even considered that. I don't have a job and have no hope of earning any allowance in the near future.

Brett hands me my bass. "Penny says you're going to help with BandMasterz."

"I'm thinking about it."

"What can you play?"

I almost tell him not much, but instead I slip my guitar strap over my shoulder, plug into the amp, and start in on "Fly by Night" by Rush. Back when I was taking lessons, this was the song I was working on. Since Christmas, I've played at it a few times. But having someone actually watching me makes me nervous. I screw up one chord after another. Halfway through, I throw my hands up in frustration.

"It's been a long time."

"So, you're rusty. Don't get all worked up about it," says Brett. "It actually sounded pretty good. You played piano too, right?"

"Six years. And three years of bass—before I quit."

"Well, it shows. But there are a few techniques that'll improve your playing immediately."

Brett slips the strap of his own bass over his shoulder and adjusts it on his lap. "Ryan, meet Geraldine."

"Geraldine?" I can't help but laugh.

Brett runs a finger along the guitar's curves, the way he would if she was a real woman. "You have something against naming an instrument?"

"No. I mean, I've heard of guys naming their cars, but…"

"It just so happens that lots of famous players name their guitars. Haven't you heard of B.B. King's Lucille? Or Jimmy Hendrix's Betty Jean?"

"No, actually, I haven't."

"Eddie Van Halen named his guitar Frankenstein."

"Frankenstein. Really?"

"Yeah, really. He called it that because his guitar was pieced together from a bunch of other guitars."

"And you named yours Geraldine because…?"

Brett throws a long glance down the bass's neck. "She looks like a Geraldine, don't you think?"

I don't think it looks like anything at all, except a bass. I look at my own with its scratched finish and loose workings. If I were to name it, I'd probably call it The Junker or something like that.

Brett proceeds to show me step-by-step some fundamentals, things I hadn't noticed while watching the YouTube videos and probably would never notice unless I was taking lessons again. He's very comfortable behind his bass, moves with it like it's a part of him. And the music flows out of him like it's his first language. I do my best to replicate what he does on the strings. He laughs when I mess up, not in a mean way, but like he understands.

He plays this one song I've never heard before. Bass is usually the backup instrument, keeping rhythm for the rest of the band. The notes are so low and deep that you have to really pay attention to pick them out from the rest of the music. But what Brett plays now is no backup; it's a full-on song of its own with a deep resonating melody that sends waves of melancholy through me. I set my own bass against the wall and settle onto the floor, leaning back against my bed. And I think to myself, *I wish I could play like that.*

PENNY

THIRTY

BALL PRACTICE DOESN'T go so well today. I get two fouls and miss several shots. When I blow my first free throw, Tali gives me a look like "What's going on?" I ignore her and take the second shot—and miss again.

Coach Anderson blows her whistle. Practice is over. As my teammates exit the gym, some of the girls shoot me scathing looks, while a few others pat my shoulder in support.

Tali walks up and hands me my water bottle. "You're so off your game today, it's like aliens have invaded your body."

"Thanks," I say, unscrewing the cap and chugging half the bottle.

I feel a hard shove against my shoulder and see Lea "bump" past me. She spins back to give me the finger. I don't have the energy or interest to return the favor. Instead, Tali thrusts hers in the air at least six times, and her face morphs into one of the scariest expressions I've ever seen, like she's half-crazed with vengeance.

Lea backs off and jogs away toward the lockers.

"Yeah, you'd better be afraid of me, you pissanny little white girl who doesn't know her finger from her big toe!"

I can't help it. I burst out laughing. "Big toe? So intimidating, Tali."

Tali laughs too.

I finish off my water bottle and chuck it into the recycle container as Tali and I enter the locker room. I undress and step into the shower. As the warm water sprays over my body, all the stress I've been feeling just melts away. I let the water cascade over my face and scalp, just enjoying the moment.

Tali steps into the next shower over.

"I'm worried about you," she says. "Tell me what's going on."

I reach for my shower gel and squeeze some into my palm.

"It's nothing, really. I'm just not feeling great today."

"If that's true, fine, but this is me. Tali? *Soy tu mejor amigo?*"

"It's amiga. You really need to practice your genders."

Tali huffs. "Just tell me what the heck is wrong, Penny. Okay? I'm not going to ask again."

I turn off the shower and reach for my towel. "I'm worried about my brother, that's all."

Tali and I both step out of our stalls to dry off and dress. The final bell rings, but I'm in no mood to rush.

"Brett's having some issues with Jake Dillinger."

"Who isn't having issues with Jake Dillinger?"

"Ever since Brett and Celine broke up, Jake's had it out for Brett. I guess I've just let it get to me, that's all."

Tali slams her locker shut and swings her backpack onto her shoulder. "Listen, Penny, I know Jake's a total jerk. But you've gotta stop letting him bully you. Stand up for yourself, okay? Next time he touches you, give him an elbow to his package. Right there."

She juts her elbow hard toward an invisible target.

"And just for good measure, do it again." She repeats the gesture, which makes me laugh.

"See?" she says. "That's all it takes to bring Jake Dillinger to his knees. Oh, and once he's there?"

She jabs another elbow into Jake's imagined face. Then she gloats as if she's just won the biggest game of the year and takes a bow to silent applause.

"Thanks, Tali," I tell her. "You'd better head out."

"Aren't you coming?"

"Yeah, I just need a few minutes."

Tali gives me a quick hug and scurries out of the locker room. Once she's gone, I sit on a bench and set my backpack between my feet. I'm about to message Ryan to ask how it went with Brett when Coach Anderson comes in to pick up the towels the other girls left on the floor.

When she sees me, she says, "Tate, don't you have a bus to catch?"

"Yes, Coach."

"Then what are you waiting for?"

"Right, Coach."

I slide my phone into my pocket and grab my backpack.

"Tate," Coach says. "You were off today. It's not like you. Anything you want to talk about?"

I stand up. "I'm fine, but thanks."

I head for the door, but then Coach says, "Don't tell the other girls, but there was a recruiter from UCLA in the stands Monday night. A friend of mine. He's scouting some of our players. He was really interested in you, in particular."

She's got to be joking, but she looks completely serious.

"I'm just a sophomore."

"I know. I told him that, and he was more than a little disappointed. Just thought you'd want to know, is all. Keep up with your skills, and he just might come around looking for you in a couple of years. Though I suspect he'll have to get in line behind every other major university in the country to get to you."

Coach Anderson drops the towels into a laundry bin and heads for her office. "I'll see you tomorrow."

As she disappears down the hall, I almost start to hyperventilate. A recruiter from UCLA, the top school in the state, one of the best in the nation, is interested in *me*? If only I could go to IMG Academy, even for a year. Half a year. I really could have my pick of colleges.

Stop it, Penny. Just stop it now.

My enthusiasm deflates. Why do I keep torturing myself? I'm never going to IMG. I'm never going anywhere. Not as long as Brett needs me.

Brett.

Suddenly, I'm angry. Angry at Brett—for his depression, for being so unstable, for putting Mom and me through hell every time he goes off the deep end, and for making us walk on eggshells all the time because any little thing we say or do might set him off. I can't help thinking that all this—the crap with Jake, IMG, even Dad leaving—really *is* Brett's fault.

But how could I be so selfish? Brett can't help who he is. It's not his fault. None of this is. I've got to put IMG and UCLA and anywhere else out of my head for good because I love him so much, and I'm scared he'll do something stupid, and I won't be there to stop him when he does.

RYAN

THIRTY-ONE

TUESDAY AFTERNOON, I arrive at the community center early carrying my new/old bass. Brett suggested I be prepared to show Fred what I can do, if he asks. I find him fiddling with one of the video game consoles.

"Stupid piece of crap," he says. "Kids go through these like crazy. How's it going, uh—" He snaps his fingers, trying to remember my name.

"Ryan."

"Yeah, Ryan. You've been helping out with the special needs kids, right? How's that working out for you?"

"Fine. The kids are great, but I was wondering if I could talk to you about BandMasterz."

"What about it?"

"You still need a bass player?"

He stops what he's doing and looks at me. "Yeah, still short one. I was going to have to cancel band six today."

"Well, I'm not very good, but I'd like to volunteer."

His face lights up, and he smacks the broken console. "Absolutely! The gang'll be thrilled to have you. When can you start? First practices are today, you know."

"Today?"

"Yeah. Four o'clock. It's nearly four now. You available?"

I'm about to say sure, okay, but then it hits me. "I help Penny at four."

Fred looks dejected. "That's a shame," he says. "The kids could really use you."

"I can manage without him." Penny's voice startles me. I hadn't realized anyone had come through the door. But there she is, standing just behind me, basketball tucked under her arm. "Let Ryan in the band, Fred, and count it as volunteer hours. Brett sends his stamp of approval."

Fred considers this and then crosses to the desk to grab his clipboard. "Your group's in room two," Fred says, pointing a thumb toward one of the doors off the lobby. "I'll introduce you."

I look to Penny, hoping for some words of encouragement or advice. What am I doing? These kids are going to expect me to actually know how to play. But Penny's already lugging her ball bag out of the closet. When she notices me watching her, she gives me a wink. "Go on. You've got this."

I swallow down a lump of nerves. Then I follow Fred through the door.

The room is bigger than I expected, with a cherry red and chrome drum set in one corner and a keyboard in another. There are also some guitar stands and a mic. There are three kids in here, one at the drums, another behind the keyboard, and a third holding a glossy white electric guitar. I recognize the kid with the guitar as the guy who gave me a dirty look the first day at the center. They all glance up when I come in, their eyes flicking between Fred and me.

"Hey, gang," says Fred, "like y'all to meet your bass player, Ryan. Ryan, this here's your band for the next five weeks. You got Khiem on drums."

Khiem, a plump Korean boy who looks about my age, points the tip of a drumstick at me.

The girl at the keyboard is wearing skin-tight jeans and a black razored T-shirt and has cropped hair with pink tips.

"Dana's got vocals and keyboard," says Fred. "And on guitar is William."

William, who can't be more than thirteen, wears glasses and a green plaid shirt buttoned to his chin. "Welcome aboard," he says flatly while plucking at his strings and adjusting the volume on the amp.

"The first order of business is to choose your songs," says Fred. "You'll have time to perform a set of three. Any suggestions?"

Dana speaks first. "You promised I could do Queen."

"Right, right," says Fred. "So, guys, Dana has her heart set on, what was it?"

"'Under Pressure,'" says Dana. "I've always wanted to play that."

"That all right with the rest of you?"

I'm not big on Queen, but as the new kid on the block, I'm not about to protest. Of course, I haven't a clue how to play any of their songs. Guess I'll have to figure it out.

William crosses his arms over the body of his guitar. He's young, but he's got attitude. "Maybe we should find out what Ryan can handle. How long have you been playing, Ryan?"

Again, all eyes are on me. I haven't even taken my bass out of its case yet, and I'm already beyond nervous. "It's, uh, been a while. But I've got a couple songs down pretty good."

William and Dana exchange doubtful looks. Khiem seems preoccupied with his cymbals.

I unzip my case and slide out the ancient black bass. Compared to William's guitar, mine looks like something dragged out of a trash heap. I can't help feeling embarrassed. Swallowing my fear, I cross the room and plug into the amp. "I've been working on some Red Hot Chili Peppers and Arctic Monkeys songs."

"Let's hear 'em," says Dana.

"What? You mean now?"

Dana attacks the keyboard with a harsh minor chord. "We've only got two hours today, so let's get going. I'm not very familiar with Arctic Monkeys, but I know the Chili Peppers, and so does William. Khiem can play just about anything. So, go on."

"Um, all right." So, I play for them. I'm so nervous, I completely screw it up, but I don't stop. About a minute into the song, William and Dana both join in. They're good. Really good. And a lot of my mistakes are thankfully covered up by their playing.

"It'll do," says William once I've finished.

"So that's 'Under Pressure' by Queen and 'Can't Stop' by the Peppers," says Fred, jotting something down on his clipboard. "One more?"

William immediately starts in on 'No Surprises' by Radiohead. The notes sizzle; it's obviously something he knows well. How long has this guy been playing?

Fred adds the last song to his list. "So, basically, you three know the routine. Ryan, this is your first gig with us, but these guys will show you what to do. I'll go print your sheet music off the computer. I'm here to help wherever I can. But this is your band, guys. Your show."

Fred slips out of the room. William, who seems to be the one in charge, suggests we start with Dana's song. We wait until Fred comes back and passes around the music. Once we're all settled, Fred leaves us to it. William and I spend about half an hour plunking through our parts, while Khiem and Dana work on rhythm. Turns out William is beyond talented. He's done two BandMasterz before. Dana and Khiem have both done three. By the end of our first hour together, we're ready to tackle this.

Dana's expression is serious as she begins the melody on keyboard. Khiem, I've realized, is as quiet a guy as they come. We dive into 'Under Pressure,' and despite the previous hour's practicing, it's a train wreck from the first note. With the exception of Dana's vocals, it sounds terrible, but we keep on playing. Halfway through, I notice Khiem struggling to keep a straight face. William's got his bottom lip clenched between his teeth, and I can't tell if he's focused on his music or on not losing control. My bass is past all help. I keep trying to find the right notes, but it's hopeless.

We finish the song, barely. As soon as the last note trails off, William and Khiem burst out laughing. I join in. The whole thing was so awful—not just me, but all of us—that I can't help but laugh. Dana is not so amused. She stands with her hands firmly planted on her hips, her jaw set.

"C'mon, guys," she says. "Seriously?"

I hate to admit it, but I'm relieved that I'm not the only one who's got something to learn over the next month or so.

The two-hour practice is over in a blink. Fred congratulates us on a job well done, hands each of us a printed schedule of practices and the final performance. We'll be meeting each Tuesday for the next four weeks, which still allows for me to help Penny on Thursdays. The final dress rehearsal is on the Friday before the 2:00 p.m. Saturday concert, which will be held at the park's amphitheater. Six bands will be playing, with ours slated first.

Seeing everything in print drives home the reality of it all. Four weeks to practice, a concert, and then a week later my meeting with the school board. It's overwhelming to think about, but exciting too.

"What'dya think?" William zips his guitar into a nylon case and hefts the strap onto his shoulder. "Is this gonna work for you?"

We head out of the practice room together with Khiem and Dana. The community center is alive with kids hanging out at the video consoles and playing ping pong. It's more kids than I've ever seen at one time in here.

"I think so," I say. "It was fun, actually."

Khiem twirls his drumsticks, then taps them against my head. "We need a name for the band," he says, the first words I've heard from him all afternoon.

Dana groans. "God, not that again."

"What?" I ask.

William leans his guitar case against the wall. "Dana hates picking names."

"Why?"

"Because," Dana says with overdramatic emphasis, "boys always pick such stupid names."

"I still think we should use The Blaster Balls," says William, and then rattles off a string of the dumbest band names I've ever heard.

"See what I mean?" says Dana. "Anyway, let's see what some of the others have come up with." She takes a few steps toward a group of kids clustered around the pool table, but then she stops and looks back at me.

"Are you coming?"

My confusion must show on my face.

"It's tradition," she says. "After practice, we all hang out for a while. You know, to talk about music, the upcoming gig and all. Sometimes we pitch in and order pizza. Wanna join us?"

I'm tempted, I really am. I scan the kids' faces, hoping to find Penny among them. But she isn't here. Basketball practice ended an hour ago.

"I can't," I tell Dana. "Maybe next time?"

"Sure," she says.

I watch as Dana, Khiem, and William blend into the mass of student musicians. I feel a pull to follow them, like a magnet drawing me in. Instead, I head out the lobby doors. Hoping Penny's still on the courts, I walk around to the side of the building. The disappointment I feel at finding the court empty surprises me. What do I need to talk to Penny for anyway? To tell her about the practice? Thank her for encouraging me to sign up?

I stare at my house across the street. Dad's car isn't in the driveway yet, so I've got some time. He knows I'm volunteering at the center, so if I'm late, it's no big deal. But he doesn't know about BandMasterz. I wonder what my parents will think when they find out.

But they don't need to know, at least not yet. I'll find my own way of telling them—eventually. I just need to make sure Penny and I are on the same page about this. So, instead of going home, I head for Penny's house.

When I knock on her door, it's Brett who answers.

He leans against the jamb, an open can of Coke in his hand. His hair is wet and moppy, like he just got out of the shower.

"Hi, Brett. I, uh, just finished my first practice with BandMasterz." I sound like a dweeb.

"Awesome." Brett chugs down some of his Coke. "I probably know the kids in your band. Unless they're new, I know 'em all."

"I'll tell you about it next time we get together. But I was wondering, is Penny here?"

He shakes his head and combs his hair back with his fingers. "She went shopping with Mom."

I'll have to message her later, I guess, ask her not to spill the beans to my parents until I'm ready. I'm sure she'll understand.

I thank Brett and start to leave, but he steps out onto the porch.

"Wanna pick up where we left off this morning? Play some more music?" I'd forgotten I was holding my bass until he points at it with his can.

"Yeah, sure," I tell him. "Do you have time?"

He answers by opening the door wide and waving me in. I follow him into the living room where Geraldine is already plugged into an amp. I take out my bass and plug in too. We go over the songs the band picked and hammer out several of the rough spots. Before we know it, half an hour's gone by. Brett announces it's time for a break. He fetches two cold cans of Coke from his fridge and tosses me one.

"So, what's your band's name?" he asks after downing half his can in a single breath.

"We don't have one yet. I mean, we only talked about it for ten seconds. This one kid named William kept throwing out ideas, but they were all stupid, like Burning Buttocks and Scruffy Scrotum."

"William Hall? Yeah, he acts like a dick sometimes, but he's a killer guitarist." He finishes his drink and tosses the can to the end of the couch. "You'll come up with a name eventually. You'll hear something and be like, 'Ah, that's perfect.' And it'll just stick."

"What were your band names, the ones when you did BandMasterz?"

"They were dumb names too," he says. "They weren't my ideas, in any case. But if I ever had a real band, I know what I would call it."

"What?"

"I'd call it Tyger, Tyger, with 'y's instead of 'i's."

"Tyger, Tyger? That's a weird name for a band."

Brett gives me a questioning glare. "Aren't all band names weird?"

"Good point," I say. "Where'd you come up with it?"

"It's from a poem by William Blake. Tyger, Tyger burning bright, in the forests of the night; What immortal hand or eye could frame thy fearful symmetry?"

"That doesn't rhyme."

Brett laughs and shakes his head. "Doesn't have to," he says. "But it's cool. You see, the poem asks how God could have created such a magnificent yet destructive beast. I imagine Blake must have had the same questions I have, like why there's so much suffering in the world mixed up with the good."

This makes sense—I think.

"My favorite part," he continues, "goes like this: When the stars threw down their spears and water'd heaven with their tears, did he smile his work to see? Did he who made the lamb make thee?"

Brett closes his eyes when he says this last line, and then pauses almost prayer-like. I don't say anything for fear of disturbing him. But Brett opens his eyes again, peering at me expectantly.

"It's a nice poem," I offer.

"Yeah," he replies, laughing again. "It's a nice poem."

We play through a few more songs, but the energy we had earlier peters out. Brett seems lost in his own thoughts, not focusing on the music at all. I'm thinking maybe I'll just thank him for the session and head home. But just then, the front door opens and Penny dashes in, all out of breath. She stops short when she sees me.

"Ryan! What're you doing here?" Her eyes shift from me to Brett to the basses. "Right," she says. "I'd love to hang with you guys, but Mom's waiting in the car. I'm just grabbing her sweater, and then we're running to Tommy's for burgers. Double cheese for you, right, Brett? Ryan, can we bring you something?"

Penny's glowing, like the skin on her arms, her head, her face is lit up somehow. And her eyes are impossibly bright. I realize that in this moment, she looks happy.

"I'm good," I tell her, though I wish I could find some excuse to stick around a bit longer. I need to talk to her, but I'm pretty sure Mom's home from work by now and wondering where I am. I'll just have to talk to Penny later.

She disappears into a back bedroom and returns two seconds later with a blue sweater in her hands.

"Bye!" she says, and she's gone again.

I don't realize that I'm staring at the door until Brett asks me a question.

"What do you think of my sister?"

The spell is broken by my surprise. Did I hear him right?

"Penny," he continues. "Do you like her?"

Do I like Penny? Why would he ask me that? Did I do something wrong? What did she tell him about me? I wrack my brains trying to remember everything I've said or done to or about Penny in the past few weeks. I think of the parade floats, the 'Friends' pendant, the chili dog. I groan. Somehow, she found out I didn't like the chili dog?

Brett leans toward me, his eyes narrowing. "It's because she's bald, isn't it?"

"What?" I say. "No, I mean…"

Penny. He just asked me if I like Penny. If I *like* Penny.

"I, uh, hadn't really thought about it… *her*… that way."

Crap. That did not sound right.

Brett's eyes study mine for what feels like an entire minute. I try not to look away, like a guilty man during an interrogation. But I can't help it.

"She used to be really pretty," says Brett after a while. "She had long, coppery hair. Wavy. And these killer eyelashes. You don't normally pay much attention to people's eyelashes, unless they don't have any."

I want to say that I think Penny looks pretty the way she is now, but something tells me to just listen.

Brett looks away from me, his gaze turning to the window where, outside, a slice of sunlight has found its way through the clouds.

"It started about four years ago. She was almost twelve when her hair started coming out in clumps. Mom thought she was sick or something. It was nuts." He turns back to me and smiles, but it doesn't reach his eyes. "Girls that age are so self-conscious, you know? They're always worried about their weight, their clothes, their hair. Every little zit is a natural disaster." He shakes his head, as if remembering something fondly, but then his smile fades. His voice cracks. "No girl should ever have to go through what Penny has."

I think of the pendant Penny gave me and wonder if it had anything to do with her illness. Did the girl who had the other half change her mind? I need to know.

"She gave me a pendant with the word 'friends' on it," I tell Brett. "Do you know anything about that?"

"I didn't know the girls she hung around with too well," he says. "I was already in high school when all that started happening. I just know that before she lost her hair, she had friends over here all the time—laughing, doing their nails, stuff like that. After…Well, after—no one came at all."

Silence slides into the space between us, as present as another human being. I feel it all around us, heavy and solid as a brick. I can't deal with it—the silence, so I find my voice.

"What happened to her?"

Brett's eyes flick up to mine and down again. He leans forward on his knees, his fingers weaving in and out of each other.

"The doctor diagnosed her with alopecia," says Brett, "told us there was nothing we could do to stop the hair loss. At first, she covered it up pretty good, styling her hair in different ways. But pretty soon all that was left were a few sparse tufts. She had these hats she'd wear, felt with rolled brims, flowers. But it didn't help. Some days she wouldn't even get out of bed or go to school. At night, I'd listen to her cry herself to sleep. She didn't know it, but sometimes

I'd cry too. I know my mom cried, but never in front of Penny."

"What about your father?"

Brett picks up his empty Coke can, rolling it between his palms. "He was fine about it, I guess. He's the one who usually brought home those hats for Penny. Anyway, one day Penny announced that she wanted the rest of it off. Said she was sick of looking like a freak. So, Mom drove us to the salon, and Penny had her head shaved."

Brett's eyes are moist, but no tears fall because he pinches them away.

"Anyway," Brett continues, "Penny's cool with it now. Comfortable with herself. She doesn't wear those hats anymore. And she thinks it's funny when people avoid her or look at her strangely. But it gets to me, you know? Sometimes I wanna just punch them for being so ignorant."

"Why don't you?"

"Because Penny'd kill me if I did something like that. She'd say, 'I can take care of myself.' And you know what? She can."

PENNY

THIRTY-TWO

BRETT'S MISSED THREE days of school. Mom doesn't know because Brett calls the automated attendance line pretending to be Dad. I guess the school's too stupid to realize Dad lives in Florida.

Other than a searing look or two, Jake Dillinger leaves me alone. And I manage to avoid Lea as well. Tali is too preoccupied with Connor to hang out with me, but she promises we'll go shopping soon.

By the time Thursday afternoon rolls around, my anxiety levels are bumping the red zone. As the center kids arrive with their hugs and smiling faces, the stress starts to ease off. Then, when I see Ryan step out of his house and start jogging toward me, everything that's been bothering me all week seems to melt away like magic. He lifts a hand and waves. I wave back.

Julia, one of the girls in the class, pokes me in the arm. "Oooh," she says, "Coach Penny has a boyfriend."

The other kids giggle. There's no point arguing with them. I've learned from experience that paying too much attention to comments like that only serves to fuel the flame. So, I just laugh with them and roll my eyes.

Ryan reaches us and greets the kids with high fives. He greets me with a smile. His eye is looking better. Swelling's about gone, and it's just a little discolored.

"So," he says, snatching up a ball and fake passing it to Jared, which sends the kid into a fit of laughter, "let's get started."

Class is over too soon. Parents pick up their kids, the kids say goodbye. In minutes, the court is quiet. Ryan and I start gathering up the stray balls and stuffing them into the bag.

"I didn't get a chance to thank you," he says, taking a shot at one of the hoops. The ball hits the backboard and cuts to the left. Ryan snatches the rebound.

"For what?" I ask.

"Not telling my parents about BandMasterz."

"Like I messaged you yesterday, I think *you* should tell them."

"I will. Just—not yet."

He passes me the ball. I drop the bag to catch it.

"Then when?" I ask.

"When I'm ready, I guess."

I shoot. The ball goes in smoothly. Ryan takes it and starts dribbling, passing it under a knee.

"Are you trying to impress me?" I ask, laughing as the ball escapes him and bounces down the court. "You're failing miserably, you know that?"

"Really?" He scurries after the ball and manages to halt its retreat with a kick, sending it rolling toward me. "I could've sworn you were completely enamored by my mind-blowing skills."

"Enamored? Did you look that up in the dictionary?"

He laughs. "Well, actually, it's on this week's vocab list for English. Thought I'd try it out."

"I see."

"I also wanted to say thanks for connecting me with Brett."

Even though Brett hasn't been at school all week, at least he's been hanging out with Ryan.

"I probably should be thanking *you*," I tell Ryan, picking up the last ball and cinching the bag shut.

"What for?"

"For getting Brett interested in music again. It's been a long time."

"For me too," he says, brushing the bottoms of his sneakers across the asphalt.

"That's right. You quit because you got too busy with school."

"Yeah, well, that's part of it."

"What do you mean?"

Ryan hooks his thumbs through his belt loops. "I actually played a lot my freshman year. Started my own band and everything. Mom didn't approve, of course, said it was distracting me from my schoolwork. She and Dad had pulled some strings to get me into Middleton, but it was what *they* wanted. Not me. I wanted to go somewhere I could study music."

"What changed?"

Ryan's silent for a moment. "My dad," he says finally. "I quit when he came home from Afghanistan. Like Mom says, I guess I finally got my priorities straight."

He averts his eyes when he says this. I don't know why, but his words don't ring completely true. Maybe it's the fake nonchalance in his voice or the off-handed shrug.

"Anyway," he continues, "it's great playing again. And it's for a good cause, right?"

I don't know if he means helping out the other kids in BandMasterz or getting his required volunteer hours. I can't help but think his good cause is my brother.

We carry the ball bag inside, get Ryan's paper signed, and head back out. I'm about to invite him to my house when my cell phone buzzes. I pull it out of my pocket and check the screen.

"It's a text from my friend, Tali," I explain. "We've been meaning to get together all week. She's inviting me to go bowling."

"You should go," says Ryan. "Sounds like fun."

"I wish you could go with us. Any chance your mom—"

"Nah," he says. "She's still pissed about my going to your game the other night. It'll be weeks before she lets up again. I'd better not push my luck."

The phone vibrates again.

Tali: Are we on?

Me: Just a sec.

I feel bad about abandoning Ryan like this. But how can I tell him I'd rather be with him than Tali, than with anyone? I could never say that. He'd think I was insane.

"Are you sure?" I ask Ryan, almost hoping he'll change his mind and suggest we stay here and play basketball, or eat Girl Scout cookies, or just talk about music. Instead, he slides a hand through his hair, which I now realize is about an inch longer than when we first met in December.

"Thanks for the invite," he says, "but bowling's not really my thing."

I shoot Tali a text that I'll go with her. She replies that she'll pick me up in twenty. Then Ryan and I say goodbye and turn toward our separate houses. When I reach mine, I try to resist the urge to look back. But it's too strong. I glance over my shoulder, and when I see Ryan standing at his gate watching me, my breath catches. Like earlier, when he was heading to the court, he waves, and I wave back.

THIRTY-THREE

AFTER SPENDING THE weekend working on my music and the next two days on homework, I'm the last one to show up for practice today. William is tuning his guitar when I come in. Khiem pokes him with a drumstick to get his attention.

"You're late," says William.

"It's not even four yet," I reply.

William brushes me off and flips on the amp.

I plug in and slip my bass over my shoulder. "Ready?"

Our second practice goes a lot like the first, only better. Meaning we've had a week to work on our parts, so when we put it all together, it sounds pretty good—rough, but good. I'd be lying if I didn't admit I'm scared as hell to perform, but I'm also excited.

After practice, I follow the others out of the room and join the rest of the band kids, ranging in age from about twelve to maybe eighteen or even nineteen. No one seems to care. Everyone mingles, talking and laughing like there's no difference. Some kids have guitar cases, others have drumsticks. The singers and keyboardists carry folders of music. All of them have soda cans in their hands.

"What's your poison?" asks Dana, stepping up to the center's lone vending machine.

"I'm fine," I tell her. I don't want to admit I don't have any money. I notice the stack of pizza boxes on the pool table, kids helping themselves to slices. Beside the boxes is a pile of cash. I'll have to remember to ask Dad for some money next week. Maybe he'll feel sorry for me and give me some.

"You can't *not* get anything," Dana says. Then she turns to William. "Will, you got an extra buck on you?"

He pulls a dollar from his wallet and hands it over. "Perfect," says Dana. She slips the bill into the machine and selects a Sprite. Then she adds a second dollar and selects a Coke. She holds up both to me.

"I don't have a preference," I tell her. So, she hands me the Sprite. Next, we move to the pizza. When I hesitate, Dana glares at William. He rolls his eyes and digs out his wallet again.

"Oh, all right," he says. "But you owe me, man."

We carry our pizza and drinks to a dumpy couch by the TV. The four of us barely fit, but it's cool.

"You do this every week?" I ask.

William pops open his Mountain Dew and swirls the can around. "Sure. Where else can we socialize with like-minded musical geniuses?"

Dana snorts. "Not at school, that's for goddamned sure. Imagine me trying to blend with the uptights in the marching band."

"Can't," says Khiem. Khiem, I've learned, is spare with his words.

"You all go to Kennedy?" I take a long swallow of my Sprite.

William shakes his head. "Some of the kids here do. Dana and Khiem go to Brooks on the other side of town. I'm homeschooled."

"Really?" My remark comes out as a mixture of surprise and disbelief.

"What?" snaps William. "Did you think homeschoolers have horns or something?"

"No, sorry," I stammer. "It's just that I'm being homeschooled right now—but just temporarily."

"Temporarily?"

"Just for this semester. I'm going back to Middleton Academy in the spring, if I can swing it."

William looks at me like I'm crazy. "Why would you ever *want* to go back?"

His question throws me off guard. I'm not sure how to reply. Luckily, Dana chimes in.

"William, believe it or not, some people like existing in a totalitarian, mucked-up social order. Why do you think Communism was so successful?"

"It wasn't," says William, smugly.

"My point exactly," says Dana. "I, for one, would gladly trade the drudgery of school for that kind of freedom."

"Me too," says Khiem.

William bites into his pizza. "Not this again," he says, his mouth full. "It's not like I lounge by the pool or make finger paintings all day. I have schoolwork too, you know."

"But you don't spend seven hours a day, five days a week sitting behind a desk," Dana counters. "You have what neither Khiem nor I have—*time*. Time to play that guitar of yours as much as you want. You're living my dream, William."

A sly grin pulls at the corners of William's lips. "Sucks to be you, Dana."

The three of them laugh.

I finish off my drink and my pizza, then I thank William and promise to pay him back when I can. As I walk home from the community center, I think about what Dana said about time, and I wonder—what would I trade for that kind of freedom?

PENNY

THIRTY-FOUR

AFTER AN ENTIRE WEEK absent, I finally convince Brett to return to school. How long can he keep convincing them that he's got the flu?

The next couple weeks pass without incident. Brett heads to Ryan's just about every afternoon to play music, Ryan seems to be doing fine in BandMasterz, and the kids in my basketball class love him more than ever. The only person not spending enough time with Ryan is me. With all my after-school practices and games, the best we can do outside of the community center is message each other.

But today is Saturday.

I find Ryan and his little brother out front of his house, lathering a fresh coat of paint on their gate.

"Ryan," I say as I approach. I guess he's deep in thought because his paintbrush slips, resulting in a swath of black across his arm.

"Hi, Penny," says Justin, a matching black smear of paint across his cheek. I can tell by the missed patches on his side of the fence that he's having fun, but Ryan's probably going to have to go over it again later.

Ryan chucks his brush into the can of paint at his feet, and a tiny tidal wave of it sloshes over the side onto the grass. "Damn," he says.

"Having issues?" I ask.

"You could say that. It's Saturday, and I'm out here working as usual. You'd think my mom would let up already."

"Well, it looks pretty good." I pick up the brush and touch up a spot on the gate. "You wanna go out?"

Ryan blinks and draws his eyebrows together, like maybe he didn't hear me right. Or maybe he thinks I meant something else by the phrase *go out*.

"No need to look all paranoid," I tell him. "Brett, Tali, and I are going to grab an early dinner at the mall and then see a movie."

Ryan looks relieved. "I can't, Penny. Not only do I have all this work to do—"

Justin cuts in. "*We* have work to do."

"We—right," Ryan corrects. "But you know I'm still on lockdown. But thanks for asking."

"C'mon, Ryan. I've been drowning in basketball practice, and you've been completely absorbed with BandMasterz. Plus, it's been three weeks since you last ticked off your parents. I'm hoping maybe they'll show you some mercy and set you free for a few hours. Besides, Tali needs the diversion. Seems Connor finally asked her on a real date tomorrow. She's wigging out."

Ryan glances uncertainly at the house. "If my dad were here, maybe he'd say yes, but he's at therapy, and—"

"Do I need to go in there and talk your mom, Ryan?" I make a move for the door. "You know I will."

He steps in front of me, laughing. "All right. All right. Tell you what. If you help me *and Justin* finish this fence, I'll gather what little courage I have to ask my mom if I can go. But it's a million to one she'll say yes."

I dab my finger against the wet bristles of the paintbrush and touch my blackened finger to the tip of Ryan's nose. "Then you've got nothing to lose."

THIRTY-FIVE

WITH PENNY'S HELP, I wrap up the painting, rinse the brushes, and put away the paint cans. Then, against my better judgment, I head upstairs. Mom's in her room, folding laundry. A woman's voice chirps from the radio clock on the nightstand, something about El Niño.

Mom looks up when I come in. "The news says there's a storm coming. Seems winter has finally arrived in California."

"About time," I reply. "January's nearly over."

Mom picks up a pair of Justin's jeans and shakes them out. "You need something?"

I consider just slinking out of my parents' room and pretending this never happened. Who am I kidding anyway? So, she let me go see the floats—with Penny's mother—and sort of forgave me about the basketball game. What makes me think she'd actually let me go to the mall?

I'm about to leave, hoping Mom will ignore me, when she looks right at me with the intensity of a hawk eyeing its prey.

"Ryan, what's up?"

I step over to the bed, pick up a sock from the pile, and start rummaging for its mate.

"Penny's here," I begin hesitantly.

"Oh? I haven't seen her for a while. How is she?"

"Fine. She and Brett are going to the mall, maybe catch a movie or something. They invited me to go."

Mom sets the jeans aside and picks up one of Dad's T-shirts. She's got this rhythm to the way she folds laundry. Lift, bend, fold, set aside. It's like she's on autopilot.

"You finish painting the gate like I asked?"

Asked? More like commanded.

"Just finished."

"And you rinsed out the brushes?"

"Yep."

Mom continues folding. I find the match to the sock I'm holding and roll them together in a ball. I pick up another sock. We continue with the laundry for another minute or two. The woman on the radio has moved on to local traffic.

Finally, I dare to speak again. "Mom? Penny's actually waiting downstairs."

The silence that follows is painfully long. But then Mom says, "All right."

And that's it.

Did she just say *yes?* Yes to hanging out with my friends—without adult supervision?

Rather than jinx my good fortune, I offer a quick "Thanks, Mom!" and bolt from the room before she can change her mind or tack on some insanely unfair chore for me to finish before I can go, like Cinderella trying to get to the ball.

But I don't even reach the door.

"Ryan," says Mom.

I stop and turn around. Mom is leaning over the bed, her hands pressed into the comforter. She's looking at me with a stern, urgent expression.

"I know I've been hard on you," she says, "but it's for your own good. You're a smart boy with so much potential. You could go anywhere, do anything. I just don't want you to throw away your future."

I say nothing. Mom straightens, snatches up another pair of pants and folds them like she's wreaking vengeance against them. Then she looks at me again. Her eyes are softer this time. "You can go to the mall, but..." she adds with emphasis... "Be home by eight, all right? Not a minute later."

"Great," I say, trying not to sound too eager. "Thanks."

Yes!

I leave Mom's room and start for the stairs, excited to tell Penny I can go, but then it hits me. I'm going to the mall. Mall means buying things.

I have no money—none. Nada. But I know where I can get some.

Grabbing a bundle of paper coin wrappers from Mom's junk drawer in the hall closet, I dive into Justin's room and pour the contents of our change jar onto his bed. In no time flat, I've packed half a dozen rolls of assorted coins, a total of seventeen bucks, enough for a matinee ticket and popcorn. I set the now nearly empty jar back on the windowsill and hoist the heavy rolls into both hands. Downstairs, I drop them all into a gallon Ziploc bag, then I hurry outside. Brett has driven up to the house. He, Penny, and a girl I recognize from Penny's basketball game are waiting in it. I'm afraid I'll find Justin still in the yard and have to explain the bundle in my hands, but he's gone. Probably went inside for a snack.

Penny opens the car door for me, and I climb into the backseat. "Would you guys mind if we stop at the bank on the way?"

"What is that?" asks Penny, spotting the wad of paper cylinders.

I open the Ziploc and take a whiff. "Freedom."

The mall is crowded, even for a Saturday afternoon. The brisk winter weather drives people indoors, and the mall is the most likely place to go. The theater occupies one end of it, and the food court occupies the other. According to the Fandango website, we have an hour before the show starts, so we decide to have dinner first.

Claiming I already ate, I indulge in a dollar order of fries in an effort to hoard the few bills the bank gave me for the coin rolls. I nibble at my fries while Penny and her friend, Tali, chatter about a boy named Connor between bites of pepperoni pizza. Apparently, Penny's supposed to help her pick out shoes for her date tomorrow.

Brett's in an unusually cheerful mood tonight. After talking practically non-stop all the way here, now he's going on and on about how delicious his pizza is. After most of it's been eaten, he sticks the crust in his ear and makes a face. Tali and I laugh, but Penny isn't amused.

When the conversation begins to lull, Brett pipes up, "Why don't we play 5 in 5?"

Penny seems to know exactly what he's talking about because she groans as if in agony.

"Oh, come on, Penny," Brett says, playfully squeezing her shoulder. "You love to play, and you know it."

"What's 5 in 5?" asks Tali, finishing off her strawberry shake with a loud slurp.

"It's where we set a timer for five minutes," explains Brett, brimming with excitement. I haven't seen him this animated in—well, ever. "We go our own ways and come back with the biggest bang for five bucks. Whoever buys the most creative item wins, majority vote. How 'bout it?"

"Brett, why don't we just go to the movie, okay?" says Penny. She casts an anxious glance between Brett and the theater entrance. I wonder what she's worried about. It's not like we're short on time.

Brett pulls his wallet out of his back pocket. "Just one round. It'll be fun."

"Fine," Penny relents. "If it makes you happy, Brett."

"Yes, it does. Tali?"

"Sure. Why not?"

"What about you, Ryan?"

I've got three fives and a one. The movie ticket costs nine-fifty, which leaves just enough for popcorn. But hey, I can live without popcorn.

"Yeah, sure," I say.

Penny pulls a fiver from her back pocket and waves it in the air.

"We'll meet back here in five minutes," Brett says. "Synchronize watches—or cell phones."

"Wait—how does this—" I stammer, but Brett's too quick.

"Ready. Set. Go!"

With a war cry loud enough to draw attention from the other mall-goers, Brett speeds away like he's in the Grand Prix. Tali and Penny dart off in the opposite direction, and for a moment, I'm left standing there in the food court feeling like a complete idiot. Then I shift into high gear.

Exploding with speed, I sprint through the mall, trying not to run anyone down. I don't even take the time to look back to see where Penny and Brett have gone. I get about thirty feet before the panic hits me. What do I get? And worse, where do I get it?

I come up short, my sneakers squeaking against the floor. I am out of breath and laughing. I spin, scanning every storefront: Footlocker, Picture People, Perfume Corner. I glance down at the wadded five-dollar bill in my hand. And then I spot Nonnie's Nook, a trinket shop with a big sign in the window: EVERYTHING $10 OR LESS. I make a mad dash for it.

"What can I buy for $5, with tax?"

The lady at the register is ancient, with fluffy white hair and thick glasses. I wait for her to answer, wheezing for breath. Time comes to a standstill as she ever so slowly raises her arm and points a neon pink fingernail toward the back corner of the store: CLEARANCE.

A rack of off-colored T-shirts: $7.99

Another rack of leggings, also $7.99

Piles of assorted decorations ranging in price from $2.99 and up. I pick up a ceramic bloodhound, hand-painted apparently, with a chip on its ear. $1.50. Its eyes are lopsided, and I think if I give this to Penny, it will give her nightmares.

Penny.

I hadn't realized what I was doing. This was just a game, right? Buy the best bang for my five bucks. But deep down, I know what I want. I want something for Penny, that gift I have yet to give her.

In the back corner of the store, on the floor, sits a plastic laundry basket overflowing with things like scarves, fuzzy socks, and hats. With just two minutes left, I start rummaging through the pile. When my hand fishes it out, I know right away I've found my prize—and it's $3.99, which, with taxes, brings the cost to somewhere around $4.40.

"Keep the change," I say when the lady starts ringing me up. I don't even wait for my receipt before I'm running full speed back to the food court. I spot Penny jogging toward me from the opposite direction, dangling a brown paper bag from her hand. We nearly collide in front of Cinnabon.

"Whoa there!" I grab her by the shoulders and laugh. She sways, gasping for breath between giggles. So, she finally got into the game.

"I found the perfect thing," she says. "I am so going to win!"

"What did you find?"

She tears into her bag like a kid ripping open a birthday present. She holds up a rectangular piece of cardboard wrapped in cellophane. At first, I'm not sure what I'm looking at, but then she shoves it right in my face. I see now what's inside the plastic: a set of six bright green guitar picks in the shape of a ram's skull.

"They're for you, silly," she says. "For BandMasterz."

For me. Penny bought them *for me.*

She hands them to me, and I gaze at them with awe. "Where did you find these?"

"The music shop at the south end. I thought you could use some picks for your bass."

"These aren't just any picks," I tell her. "They're the *Pick of Destiny* from Tenacious D., one of my favorite bands."

"I know," she replies. "Brett told me."

Penny is smiling, which isn't unusual for her, but there's something different this time. It's not the same one she was wearing five minutes ago when we all took off on our treasure hunts. Or the one she wore on Christmas, looking at the lights. This one looks pleased, like she's relieved that I like—no—that I *accept* her gift. And there's something else in her eyes, something that, when I see it, sends a sudden rush of heat through me.

"I, uh, bought you something too," I say. It sounds stupid, but Penny lights up.

"Really?" she squeals. The something I saw a moment before is gone now, swallowed up with a childlike glee. "What is it?"

I reach into my bag and wrap my fingers around the soft, velvety fabric. "Ta da!" I say, holding up the blue crusher hat like a trophy.

Penny blinks. The smile on her face takes on a strange, forced appearance.

"It's your favorite color," I tell her. "And look. It's got this really cool pink flower." I flick the flower petals with my finger.

But something's not right. She folds her arms, rubs her hands across them.

"Do you...do you like it?" I ask. I can hear the uncertainty in my voice. I've done something wrong, but what?

"I wonder what Brett and Tali found?" Penny turns away from me, scanning the crowd. But I see it, for just a split second—the quick lift of her arm, the single sweep of a finger beneath her eye.

"What's taking them so long?" she asks.

And then I know what I've done. I've made Penny cry.

PENNY

THIRTY-SIX

THERE'S NO SIGN of Tali, but I spot Brett in the food court. He must have finished before either me or Ryan and has been waiting for us. He's been off all afternoon, his mood growing increasingly—for lack of a better word—happy. But I know from experience that for him, what goes up inevitably comes crashing down.

Right away, I see that his mood has already started to nosedive. Also, he's not alone. Several kids from school are standing near him, including Jake Dillinger.

Ryan and I head toward him, our prizes forgotten, thank goodness. I see Jake stab Brett in the chest with his finger.

"You stay away from my sister, got it, freak?" says Jake. Behind him are three girls, including Lea and Celine, and a couple of guys from Jake's team. None of them is bigger than Brett, but he isn't doing anything about it. Just standing there, looking at the floor.

Ryan and I arrive on the scene.

"What's going on?" I ask, touching Brett's shoulder.

Jake answers for him. "Your crazy brother was bothering my sister."

Brett shrugs off my hand, but he doesn't look up. "Celine asked me how I am," he says. "I answered."

Celine stands apart from the other kids, clutching a pink plastic shopping bag to her chest like a shield. Lea and the other girl look like they're trying to comfort her.

"It's true, Jake," says Celine. "I started it. I saw him and just thought I'd—"

Jake snaps at his sister. "I told you I don't want you anywhere near him! Not after what he did to you."

"But—"

"No, Celine!"

She clams up and allows Lea to slide an arm around her shoulders.

"Let's go," I tell Brett. I try to take his hand to lead him away, but he twists his hand out of mine.

Jake laughs. "Yeah, nut job. Go home with your little bald sister."

Brett bristles, his gaze rising from the floor until it meets Jake's. He glares at him with a cool intensity I know all too well.

"Back off, Jake," I warn. "He wasn't trying to cause trouble."

"He *talked* to her," says Jake, "and I don't want you talking to her. Not ever again."

Ryan steps up beside me. "Is everything all right, Penny?"

Jake casts an angry glare at Ryan. "You again? Want me to bust your other eye?"

Fortunately, Ryan says nothing in response, but I can see the muscles in Brett's jaw tense. Once again, I take hold of Brett's hand, urging him to follow me. "C'mon, Brett. Let's get out of here."

To my relief, Brett's eyes shift from Jake to me. He nods, turns, and together with Ryan, we start for the sliding doors leading out of the food court into the parking lot while I text Tali to meet us at the car. I have a feeling Brett's no longer in the mood to watch a movie.

But Jake won't let it go. "Yeah, run away, coward," he shouts behind us. "Better yet, come back here and show me the real Brett Tate, the one that beats up girls."

Brett stops. His hand grips mine, but it's shaking.

"Brett?" I look into his face. He's struggling. He moves again, taking one step forward, and I think we're in the clear. We're getting out. But then Jake rushes at us from behind.

"Where you going, freak?" He shoves Brett so hard his hand rips out of mine. He falls forward onto his knees and collides face-first with a cement column.

"Brett!" Celine screams, darting forward as if to get between them, but Jake shoves her back. Then he glares down at Brett with intense hatred.

I reach for Brett to help him up, but he ignores my hand, instead getting to his feet on his own. His bottom lip is split, and there's a line of blood down his chin.

"You know what you are?" says Jake.

Celine is crying now. "Stop it, Jake!"

"Shut up!" he shouts at her before refocusing on Brett.

"You're a schizoid. A psychopath. For all we know," Jake says, grinning back at his friends, "this guy's another Jeffrey Dahmer. Hiding body parts in his basement and eating them for dinner."

Jake bursts out laughing. But in a sudden rage, Brett roars like an animal and lunges for Jake. He tackles Jake with the force of a wrecking ball, and they both go down. Brett's on top of him, swinging both his fists at Jake's torso and head.

Celine cries out for them to stop. Lea shouts for help. The two other boys who are with them try to pull Brett off Jake, but he takes a swing at each of them, leaving them both with bloody noses. They back off, not daring to interfere again. Ryan steps in, grabbing at Brett's shoulders, but it's no use.

"Brett!" I shout. "Brett, stop! Stop it!"

People have started to gather around us, macabre spectators carrying shopping bags and plates of food. Through them, I spot Tali, a look of astonishment on her face. She manages to squeeze through, a blue shopping bag swinging freely on her wrist.

"What's going—?"

"Don't ask!" I tell her. "We need to leave... now."

Then I see the security guard. He's pushing toward us through the crowd, talking into a two-way radio. After that will come the Sheriff's station, the hospital, and days, if not weeks, in the mental health ward.

Brett's fists are still flying. He grunts with the effort. Blood and spit drip from his lips. It's been a long time since I've seen that much rage in him. If I don't stop him, he really could kill Jake. But if I get too close, I could get hurt. I decide to take the risk and grab Brett's arm. "Run, Brett! We've got to run!"

Thankfully, the familiar touch of my hand seems to reach him. Dazed and blinking, he awkwardly gets to his feet. He's breathing hard and fast. His face is covered with sweat and splatters of Jake's blood. He glances fearfully at the crowd, the approaching security guard, Celine. Then he turns and runs for the doors. Ryan, Tali, and I follow, but not before I see Jake lying motionless on the floor, his face so bloody I hardly recognize him.

RYAN

THIRTY-SEVEN

AFTER DROPPING PENNY'S friend off at her house, we drive the rest of the way home in uncomfortable silence. I keep glancing behind us, expecting red lights and sirens, but nothing happens. Brett stares straight ahead, both hands gripping the steering wheel. Beside him in the front, Penny stares out the window. She looks scared.

When we pull into Penny's driveway, the engine barely has time to cut off before Brett is out the door.

"Brett!" Penny shouts, scrambling out of the car after him. She reaches for his arm. "Brett, wait—"

I get out of the car, worried about Brett—and about what he might do to Penny. He spins toward her and jerks his arm free of her grasp. "Leave me alone!" There's a mix of fury and fear in his eyes.

"I just want to make sure you're all right," Penny tells him.

"All right?" He laughs in a sad, ironic sort of way. "You want to know if *I'm* all right? I just beat a guy half to death, Penny! Or didn't you see that?"

"He started it, Brett. You didn't mean to—"

"I *did!* Don't you get it? I wanted to hurt him! I wanted to kill him!" His expression tightens like he's fighting back tears. "I'm a monster."

I step in closer. Maybe I can talk some reason into him. Maybe I can help.

"Brett, it's okay—"

"It is not okay!" He pushes past me and tramps down the driveway.

"Where are you going?" Penny calls after him, choking back tears. She runs after him, grabbing his shirt. Pleading. "I'll come with you!"

Without warning, Brett shoves Penny hard into the side of the car. She bends over, grabbing her hip where it collided with the door handle, but she doesn't cry out. Brett takes a step toward her, instant regret in his face. But I've seen enough. I can't let him hurt her, so I step in front of him, blocking his path. Brett's eyes cut to mine. They burn with hurt, like I've betrayed him. He turns and sprints across the park toward the hills. And I let him go.

Once he's out of sight, I turn to Penny. "Are you okay?"

"I'm fine."

But she's crying now, and her hand protectively cups her hip. She's not okay. She's in pain, and she's worried about her brother. She wipes her face dry with her free hand, which is shaking badly, then slides down the side of the car to the pavement. I kneel beside her. I want to help, but how?

"What happened?" I ask her. "Back at the mall. What was all that?"

Penny wraps her arms tightly around herself, like she's fending off some unseen threat. "That boy," she says, her voice constricted, "the one that hit you after the game and was harassing Brett—that was Jake. The girl with the blond hair was Celine, his sister, Brett's ex-girlfriend. Just before Christmas, she and Brett had an argument, over what I don't know. But Brett got angry. He had an episode. That's what we call it when he loses control like that. He slapped her."

I say nothing. This doesn't sound like the Brett I've come to know over the past few weeks.

Penny continues, agitated. "When Jake found out, he went ballistic. Hasn't let Celine near him since, and he'll never let Brett forget what happened."

"These episodes, do they happen a lot?" I ask, wondering if he's ever done anything like that to Penny.

"Sometimes," she says. "He takes medication to keep his mood stable, but once in a while, something will set him off. He gets in these rages, and it's like it's not even him anymore. Then, when it's over, he gets really depressed. He feels bad about the way he acts. He doesn't mean to get violent, but sometimes he can't help it, as if there's a monster raging inside of him that he can't control. Like when our parents first split, Brett punched a hole in his bedroom wall and busted his finger.

"He's always had—issues," Penny continues. "Mom says even as a kid, he was either extremely happy or uncontrollably angry, like Jekyll and Hyde. After he tried to hang himself when he was fifteen, he was diagnosed as bipolar. The doctor actually called it a 'mood disorder' because supposedly only adults are bipolar. That's what finally drove my dad away. At least that's what Brett believes."

She stops talking, waiting for me to say something, but I have no idea what to say. Brett has problems, serious problems. How didn't I see it?

I look in the direction he ran off. "Will he be all right?"

Penny rubs her arms as if trying to stay warm or to comfort herself. She seems to be calming down now, not like things are any better than they were a few minutes ago. More like she's resigned to the fact there's little she can do about it.

"I hope so. He just needs some time to cool off."

I take her hand and help her to her feet. "Are *you* going to be all right?"

She glances warily at her front door. "Mind if I walk you home?"

We head across the park to my house. The silence between us feels heavy, like being in a room where the heat's up too high.

When we reach my gate, Penny asks, "Why did you buy that?"

I'd forgotten all about the hat I bought at the mall. I'm still holding it, twisting the fabric in my hands. "This?" I twirl it on a finger. "I dunno. It was on clearance. And I didn't know what else to buy."

"You bought it for *me*."

I don't say anything at first. I remember how, when I showed it to her earlier, she looked like she was going to cry.

"Would you be mad if I said yes?" I finally reply.

I don't know how I expect Penny to respond, but not with the anger that explodes out of her.

"Why?" she asks, not quite shouting. "Why did you think I'd want a hat? That I *need* a hat, Ryan?"

"I didn't—" I answer, but she cuts me off.

"Because I don't want your stupid hat. If you haven't noticed, I never wear one. Do you wanna know why? Ask me why, Ryan!"

"Why?"

"Because when I was twelve, I lost most of my hair. The other kids at school didn't make fun of me. No. They shunned me completely, like I had some disease they might catch if they talked to me or touched me. But that wasn't the worst of it. When all I had left were a few straggly patches, I had my head shaved."

Penny clenches her fists at her sides, rage building in her. I suspect it's the first time she's ever really talked about her hair loss this way to anyone.

"That night my mom thought it would be fun to get ice cream," she continues, "to take my mind off everything. So, we went to the frozen yogurt shop where I'd been more times than I could count. There was another family there with a girl about my age. A total stranger. I was holding my cardboard cup under the mango yogurt dispenser, really happy to have a treat like that, when this girl walked right up to me and said, 'Do you have cancer?' I couldn't meet her gaze, I was so embarrassed. But I managed to say, 'No, I don't have cancer.' Then she cocked her head to one side and said, 'You mean you did that on purpose?' Then she just walked away."

Penny swipes away the tears with her fists. "I had a choice to make right then and there: to feel ashamed of the way I looked, or to accept myself for who I was, bald or not. I vowed I would never let anyone make me feel ashamed again, and I'd never wear a wig or a hat to hide the real me. So, you may not like me this way, but I like me just fine."

I stare at Penny, my mouth open in shock. She blinks away the rest of her tears and clenches her jaw, waiting I'm sure for what she expects to be some ridiculous comment about how bald is beautiful or some other stupid nonsense.

I close my mouth, weighing my next words carefully. Then I open it again. "It's just a hat."

Then I fling it, like a Frisbee, and it soars over my neighbor's front yard and lands in an ungraceful clump on their roof.

Penny and I stand there, gaping at the hat. And then we both burst out laughing. It feels good to laugh. It's good to see Penny laugh. We look at each other, laughing and smiling. God, she is so beautiful.

I know I'm staring into Penny's eyes, but she's staring right back. Our laughter fades as I step close to her, so close I can feel the warmth radiating off her body.

"I like you just fine too," I tell her. And then I lean in and kiss her.

I've kissed other girls before. This is way different. I press my lips against Penny's, and it feels like someone lit a fire inside me, hot and all-consuming, like I could burn up on the spot.

When the kiss ends, I don't wait for her reaction. I've already felt it. I wrap my arms around her and draw her close against me. I want to protect her, to keep her safe. She lays her head on my shoulder, and for some reason, she starts crying again. So, I just hold her, and we stand like that for a long, long time.

PENNY

THIRTY-EIGHT

I SLEEP IN UNTIL almost noon today. I feel like crap when I finally drag myself out of bed and into the shower. It's not surprising since I spent most of the night feeling sick to my stomach, my mind churning with thoughts of what happened at the mall last night. I think I finally conked out around three or four a.m.

Once he came home, Brett had a hard time sleeping too. I could hear him through the paper-thin wall dividing our rooms, the sound of a pen scratching furiously on paper, probably writing in that red notebook of his.

I also can't stop thinking about Ryan. Kissing him was amazing. I never dreamed he'd ever think of me that way. Although with everything that happened with Brett last night, maybe it wasn't that at all. Maybe he was just trying to comfort me. I don't know. It's all so confusing.

After my shower, I dry off and dress in a pair of jeans and a T-shirt. I'm beyond starving at this point and seriously craving my mom's chocolate chip pancakes. I can already taste the fresh strawberries and whipped cream she was planning to pick up at the store last night.

I head down the hall toward the kitchen but stop abruptly at the entryway where Mom's standing at the open front door. I take a cautious step forward, and when I see who's on the other side, I nearly run back to my room, but before I can, the uniformed officer spots me.

"Morning," he says. He's tall and burly-looking, with hair cut military style. A pair of aviator sunglasses is tucked in his breast pocket. This isn't the first time he's been to our house. "I understand you were at the mall with your brother last night."

Too stunned to speak, I just nod.

"I was explaining to your mother what happened. A boy was taken to emergency after being beaten in a fist fight. Several eyewitnesses named Brett as the one responsible."

Mom clutches her bathrobe in a white-knuckled fist. "You were there?" she asks me. "Did you see what happened?"

I don't answer. What am I supposed to say? I think of that line I've heard a hundred times in the movies—anything you say can and will be used against you. I don't want to get Brett in trouble.

The officer pulls a ballpoint pen from his pocket and scribbles something on a pad of paper.

"The victim's sister and several other witnesses stated that Brett acted in self-defense, so the kid's parents aren't pressing charges. But I still need to take Brett's statement." He glances at me and adds, "Have him call me at this number when he's available."

He tears off the sheet of paper and hands it to Mom. "I know Brett's a good kid, Mrs. Tate, but this isn't the first time something like this has happened. If there's any more trouble, I'll have no choice but to take him into custody. Do you understand? Get the boy some help."

The officer says goodbye and heads back to his car. Mom shuts the door. She stares at the paper with a vacant look and then stuffs it into her robe pocket.

"What happened?" she asks in a shaky voice.

"Jake started it," I begin earnestly. "He was calling Brett names. He shoved him—"

Mom holds up a hand to stop me. "I know what the witnesses said. Everyone there agrees that kid was harassing Brett. But Brett hurt him—badly. The boy's nose is broken, Penny. The deputy says he was unconscious, and Brett was still hitting him."

"I know. I know! But—"

"Do you realize what would happen to Brett if he's ever arrested? Convicted? What would happen to *us*?"

I turn an icy glare on Mom. "I can't believe you just said that. What would happen to *us*? Who gives a crap what happens to us?"

"That's not what I meant—"

"Yes, it is," I tell her, disgusted.

"I only meant—" She sighs, trying to find the right words. "Brett's already difficult as it is. I know he's the reason you're not applying to IMG, which your father and I have actually been discussing."

"You talked to Dad about me?" Now I'm really pissed.

"He wants to pay for it. I think you should go, Penny."

"No."

"You could stay with your father on the weekends. He lives so close to the school."

"I said no!"

"Penny, you can't keep living your life around your brother."

I can't stand what I'm hearing. Go away to school? Leave Brett behind? How could she even suggest it? I'm so angry, I just need to get away. So, I turn for my room.

"Penny—" Mom calls after me, but then I stop short.

I don't know how we didn't hear it, Brett's bedroom door opening. But somewhere in the middle of me and Mom hissing at each other, Brett has come into the room. We both notice him at the same time, standing at the end of the hall, watching us. Mom's face goes white, and I feel as though someone just slugged me in the gut.

"Brett, I—" Mom starts, but she doesn't finish.

I'm not sure how much he's heard. Maybe everything, maybe nothing. I suspect he knew the cop was here and was listening from the very beginning. But either way, as if nothing has happened at all, he says, "Good morning, Mom. Morning, Penny."

He crosses the living room to the kitchen, takes a glass from the cupboard, and fills it at the sink. Then he swallows the whole thing in half a dozen gulps and heads back to his room.

Once his door is closed again, I let out a long, agitated breath. Mom lowers herself onto the sofa and drops her face into her hands while I just stand here. I don't know what disturbs me more—Mom's careless words about Brett, or the resolved look in his eyes when he pretended not to care about them.

RYAN

THIRTY-NINE

I KISSED PENNY TATE.

I *kissed* Penny!

I don't know what came over me at that moment. She just looked so—beautiful. And the kiss was incredible. Her lips were warm and soft like velvet. But she cried, not because I kissed her—I hope—but because of what happened with her brother. He comes home eventually. I know because Penny and I are still standing outside my house when he does, and then Penny says goodbye and goes home.

I'm so dazed when I walk into the house, I hardly notice Mom and Dad in the kitchen. They're standing at the counter making a salad for dinner.

"You're back sooner than I thought," Mom says. "Didn't you see the movie?"

I'm already halfway up the stairs when I answer. "Decided not to. Nothing good playing."

I don't feel like explaining. I just want to be alone to savor the moment with Penny. I can't stop thinking about her.

Once upstairs, I make a beeline for my room, but then I decide to continue down the hall to Justin's room. His door is open, and through it I spot him sitting on the floor by his window, the empty penny jar in his lap.

A lump the size of Indiana forms in my throat.

I step into the room. "Hey, Pipsqueak," I say, nudging him gently with my foot, but he doesn't respond. "How was your afternoon?"

"Fine," he says with no enthusiasm at all.

"I, uh, borrowed the money. Hope you don't mind."

His little shoulders give a slow, sad shrug.

"There's still eleven dollars left." I reach into the back pocket of my jeans and pull out the remaining bills. I stuff them into the jar.

I feel bad. I knew how much that money meant to him. I think of the stale fries I ate and that stupid blue hat. It so wasn't worth it.

"I'm sorry, bro," I tell him, but the words feel empty.

He looks up at me with teary brown eyes, and seeing him like that cuts me deep, but not as deep as what comes next.

"You can keep the money," he says. "The wishes are gone."

I stay up late that night, going over and over my songs, trying to work out the kinks. The truth is, Justin's response to my taking the money hit me hard. So I throw myself into the music until I finally fall asleep.

Sunday morning, I do it all over again. I want to make sure I've gotten everything down before I go to practice on Tuesday. A few times, I glance out my window at Penny's house. She's not home. I know because she messaged me earlier that she was going shopping again with Tali. They hadn't found those shoes she wanted for tonight's date.

I think of the kiss Penny and I shared, the one good thing to happen yesterday. Had she wanted me to kiss her? Should I have asked her first? What if I go over to Penny's house and she doesn't want to talk to me? The hat is still on my neighbor's roof. Maybe I should get it down.

A million thoughts spin inside my brain. I try to keep playing, but between Penny, and Brett, and Justin—it's hard to concentrate. Finally, I put my bass away, tucking a Pick of Destiny into the strings, and step to my desk. Might as well get some more homework done.

I've just turned on my computer when I hear the doorbell ring.

"Ryan?" Dad says from downstairs. "Brett's here. Can I send him up?"

"Sure," I say, a twinge of hope flaring inside me. Maybe he's brought Penny with him. But then I think maybe she told him what happened between us after the mall. Maybe he's angry.

When he steps into my room, the first thing I notice is how normal he seems, like last night never happened. I decide it's best not to bring it up.

I greet him with a fist bump. "You brought Geraldine. Wanna jam?"

"Not today," he says. "I just came over to say goodbye."

"What are you talking about?"

"I'm leaving." He says this without hesitation, as if the news were as trivial as telling me he's going to the store for some milk. But the words knock me completely off balance.

"I don't understand. Where are you going?"

"Camp Pendleton. I'm joining the Marines."

This news hits me like a sucker punch to the gut. I have to sit on the edge of my bed. "Why? Is this about yesterday? Because if it is, I'm sure—"

"No, man," says Brett with a shake of his head. "Not that. At least not only that. I, uh, I've been thinking about it for a long time. My mind's made up."

"What about high school? It's still five months to your graduation."

"I'm eighteen. And I've had it with school." He sits on his usual chair by the window, his arms draped around Geraldine. "Besides, in the Marines I can still get my GED *and* see the world, right?"

Something's up. This doesn't feel right. Can someone with Brett's mental history just join up like that? Penny says he takes medication. I didn't think that was allowed, but what do I know?

"What about your mom?" I ask. "What about Penny?"

He looks at his hands. "I'll tell them in my own way. Anyway, I can't take much with me, so I came to give this to you."

He holds his bass out to me.

"You want to give me Geraldine? But I can't—"

"There's no one else I'd trust her with, Ryan. And besides, you need something better than that piece of garbage you've been playing." He gives my shoulder a playful shove. "C'mon. She needs someone to love her as much as I do. Please take her."

I reach for her, grasping her by the neck. Brett lets go, and something strange and wonderful flows into me. I hold her close, stroking her glossy finish. "I don't know what to say."

"Just promise you'll take good care of her." Brett raises his fist, and I meet it with my own. Then he heads for the door.

"You'll keep in touch, right?" I ask.

"Of course," he replies. "I'll call you as soon as I get settled. And I'll come back for a few weeks after boot camp. You won't even have time to miss me."

Then Brett leaves. A few moments later, I hear the front door close downstairs. I look out my window and watch Brett make his way across the park to his own house. I stay at my window for a long time. I don't know why. Maybe I'm waiting for Penny to show up. But that's nuts, right?

After a while, I let my curtains fall back into place. Then I plug in Geraldine, and pretty soon I'm ripping into Led Zeppelin's 'Stairway to Heaven,' a song Dad says was one of his favorites growing up. The music sounds smooth coming from Geraldine, and playing her feels like I'm driving a Lamborghini.

This is surreal. I can't believe Brett gave her to *me*.

PENNY

FORTY

I HEAR NOISES COMING from Brett's room all Sunday morning. Mom has to go in to work tonight, so she's sleeping in, trying to catch up for the twelve-hour shift. I don't know how she's managed to sleep through the *bangs* and *thuds* and curses.

What is he doing in there?

At noon, Tali picks me up for a quick trip to the mall. She's got her first real "date" with Connor tonight and is absolutely convinced that nothing in her closet is acceptable first date material.

We bum around Macy's and Abercrombie for a while and finally find a periwinkle blouse with a matching sweater in Forever 21.

"This would look better on you," she says, holding the sweater up to me. "It makes your eyes look even bluer, if that's possible."

"I'm not the one with the big date." I snatch the blouse away, giggling. "We're not here for me. Remember?"

It takes some effort, but I finally convince her that the black leggings I know she owns will go perfectly with the outfit. But she *must* have shoes. So, we scour every shoe store in the mall until she finally settles on a pair of black suede heels.

"So, it's finally official between the two of you?" I hold up the new blouse to a rack of nail polish, searching for just the right shade.

"I guess so," says Tali. "At least we have an understanding."

"Which translated means…?"

Tali pops open a lipstick and swipes it across the back of her hand. "Too pink," she says. "It means we're together—for the most part."

I choose a different lipstick from the display and pick a polish to match. "From what I saw after the game a few weeks back, things seemed pretty serious."

Tali grins like a little girl with a secret. "It is. I mean, we are serious. Except. . ."

"Oh, here it comes."

"Except if his parents are around, which they hardly ever are. They're always off on business trips, so it should be fine. It's just until he's ready to tell him, which he will soon. He promised."

She sounds so certain, I hate to say anything to burst her bubble, even if I have serious doubts about Connor's sincerity.

Tali pays for the outfit and accessories with cash, and we drive back to her place to get her all spruced up. First, I help straighten her hair. Then we tackle make-up.

When we're done, Tali steps up to her full-length mirror and gives a model's turn. "What do you think?"

"I think you're a goddess." I hand her the new purse, which goes great with the shoes. "I also think Connor's an idiot."

"Why?"

"For being ashamed of you."

The expression on Tali's face sags. I immediately regret what I said. What's it to me if Connor's too afraid of his parents' disapproval to show off the prettiest girl in school?

"I'm sorry," I sputter. "That was lame of me."

"No, it's all right." Tali reaches for the open nail polish on her dresser and twists on the lid. "But you've got it wrong about Connor. All wrong."

I can't believe I almost screwed up Tali's night. Me and my big mouth.

She reaches for a pair of silver dangle earrings and puts them on. "What about you?" she asks, tucking a strand of hair behind her ear. "Despite all the insanity at the mall, you and Ryan seemed pretty cozy."

"We were not *cozy*!"

"Really? Then why did your face turn five shades redder when I mentioned his name just now?"

I sit on the corner of Tali's bed. How did the topic of conversation shift so quickly?

"C'mon," she presses. "Something happened between the two of you. Spill it, or I'll call Connor right now and make him bring a blind date for you."

"All right. Fine!" I throw up my hands, defeated. There's no use hiding anything from Tali. She's like a bloodhound on the trail of truth.

"After we got home, we talked in his driveway for a while."

"And...?"

"And—he kissed me."

Tali casts a giddy glance at me in the mirror, an 'I-just-knew-it' smirk on her face.

"It was nothing!" But I'm laughing now. "Just a teensy-weensy kiss."

"And do you expect there to be more teensy-weensy kisses in the near future?"

I can't keep my lips from curving into one of those cheesy, hopeful smiles. "I'm not sure. I think, maybe, it was just a thing, you know?"

"A thing?"

"Yeah, a one-time thing." I turn my gaze out Tali's bedroom window, my thoughts now focused on Ryan. What if he regrets kissing me? He might have been grossed out, or worse, maybe he just felt sorry for me. That possibility is too painful to even consider. It might have been a one-time kiss, but I sure hope it wasn't.

Tali drops me off at home just after six, giving her plenty of time to get back to her place before Connor shows up. I tell her to break a leg and that I want to hear all about the date tomorrow at school.

In the kitchen, Mom's making dinner, beef and vegetable stew.

"You're home," she says. "Grab some bowls from the cupboard, will you?"

I take down three bowls and set them on the table, followed by a round of spoons and napkins.

"I have to get some grocery shopping done before work tonight," says Mom. "So, I'll be heading out early. I'll be home in the morning around nine. If there's anything you or Brett need from Wal-Mart, just text me." She turns off the stove and tastes the soup. "Perfect. Go get your brother."

I knock on Brett's door, but I don't bother waiting for an answer. I just turn the knob and walk in. "Dinner's ready. What the—?"

Brett's room looks like an archeological dig, with piles of artifacts inches deep scattered across his floor and bed. One pile is nothing but folded T-shirts. Another is shoes. Another is books. There are piles of sports stuff, photographs, and music CDs.

"What are you doing?" I ask, nudging the pile of baseball caps with my toe.

"Spring cleaning," he says, and then adds quietly. "Close the door."

There are half a dozen boxes stacked in the corner, each one labeled with black Sharpie.

"You do know that spring is two months away, right?" I say. "And since when do you ever clean anything, let alone your bedroom?"

Brett lifts a CD from the top of his pile and holds it out to me. "You like Foster the People, don't you?"

"You know I do." I take the CD, one I've coveted for a long time. Brett transferred some of the songs onto my phone last year but would never let me borrow the actual disc. He keeps his CDs in pristine condition, like works of art.

"Keep it," he says. "In fact, why don't you dig through these and take what you want."

"Really? But why? You love these."

He pulls out another and taps it on his knee. "I figured it would be easier for Mom if I clean out my stuff on my own. Whatever you don't want goes to Goodwill."

"Why?"

"Don't tell Mom, okay?" Brett's voice drops to a whisper. "I'm going away."

"You're what?"

"Shhh. Some friends and I are going on a pre-graduation road trip."

"Where?"

"I dunno. Canada maybe."

"You can't just take off! What about school? And Mom. Mom-will-totally-kill-you!"

Brett avoids looking at me, like he knows I'm right.

"Just promise you won't tell Mom," he says.

"I won't make any promise because what you're doing is stupid!"

His expression hardens. "It's done, Penny! I've made up my mind, and there's no going back."

I let out an exasperated breath. Brett is eighteen, so I guess he can do what he wants. It just seems so irresponsible, so not like Brett.

"When are you leaving?"

"Tomorrow."

"But you can't just leave without telling Mom. It's not fair to her."

He exhales forcefully. "All right. I'll tell her—in my own way. Privately. Just let me handle it. Promise?"

I don't like these conditions, but I agree.

"Take a look through this stuff and see what you want."

"Sure. I guess."

I run my fingers along the top of his dresser as he turns his attention to stacking books into a cardboard box. The top drawer is open a crack, and inside I spot something red—Brett's notebook, the one he's been scribbling in for weeks now. Curiosity gets the better of me, and I slide my hand inside to pull open the drawer. I reach in for the notebook and am surprised when, instead of feeling paper, my skin connects with cold, hard metal.

I yank my hand back as Brett slams the drawer shut.

"Is that a gun?" I ask, feeling both curious and a little freaked. "Where the heck did you get a gun?"

Brett presses his palm against the drawer front. "You can have what's in here *after* I leave," he says tersely, but then he relaxes. "It's not what you think, okay? Now, how about we eat Mom's dinner? Nothing like a last meal, right?"

I don't laugh at his stupid joke. And I don't follow him out to the kitchen, at least not right away. I stand in the middle of my brother's room, taking in the boxes and piles, and even the smell of him—Axe cologne and just the overall scent of 'boy.'

What is my brother doing with a gun? Or maybe I was mistaken? I didn't actually see anything, just touched something that felt an awful lot like one. But Brett said it isn't what I think.

I'm tempted to open his drawer again to convince myself that my brain was just playing tricks on me, but Brett pops his head back into the room.

"Coming?" he asks.

"Yeah. I'm coming."

As I step out of his room, I feel a jumble of emotions I'm not exactly sure how to sort through. There's only one, really, that stands out, that seems to encompass all the others.

I feel lost.

RYAN

FORTY-ONE

I'M ON MY LONG BOARD riding down the street, which goes on and on for miles. The sky is thick with rain clouds, but the cold wind on my face makes me feel alive. I could ride forever. Up ahead, I see Penny, just standing there on the sidewalk. I stop, and she steps onto my board in front of me. I wrap my arms around her, and we sail ahead.

Suddenly, we hit a crack in the asphalt, and Penny and I both take to the air. I look down and see that the crack is widening. Its sides pull apart, leaving behind a wide, gaping canyon so deep all I can see is blackness. A fear sharper than I've ever known explodes through me, but it's not me I'm afraid for: it's Penny. I have to save Penny.

I reach out to grab her hand, and when my fingers slide around hers, I'm so happy. But she's still falling, and I realize I can't save her. I can't save her because I'm falling too.

The moment before we both dive into the depths, I jerk awake, gasping.

Dad is watching me from the foot of my bed.

"God, you scared me," I tell him, though it wasn't him that scared me but that wacky dream.

He smacks the end of my mattress with his hands, sending a jolt through the bed frame. It's obvious he's done this a couple times already.

"Get up," he says. "It's a beautiful Monday morning, and we've got work to do."

"C'mon. I just woke up." I groan with a voice still raspy from sleep. "What time is it?"

"Six-thirty, but Mom's got a new task for you, and I want to get you started before I drive your brother to school. So, be down in five. Breakfast is already on the table."

As he pivots and limps out of my room, I scowl at his back, but then I dutifully roll out of bed—my warm, cozy, soft bed. Sliding my hand longingly over the sheets, I say, "So long, bed."

Breakfast is a bowl of lukewarm instant oatmeal and a glass of grapefruit juice. I hate grapefruit juice. Dad downs his in a single gulp. "It'll put hair on your chest," he says. I think of my own chest, still relatively smooth, and choke mine down as well. Then I follow Dad outside.

"Am I in trouble?" I ask, blinking against the bright early morning sun.

Dad turns a pointed look in my direction. "Should you be?"

I think of the pills and the marijuana still stashed in my drawer, and of my vow to Penny to never touch the stuff again, which means more to me now than it ever did before.

I shake my head. "No," and I mean it. "It's just you don't usually get me up in the morning."

Dad's eyes linger on me, then I feel a wave of relief as he turns his gaze to the yard. My stash is still safe.

"Your mom wants the rose bushes trimmed," he says. "And if you're planning to trick your brother into helping you this time, you're too late. He and your mom already did the ones in back Saturday while you were out with your friends." He hands me a pair of gloves and a pruner. "You know what to do. Put the branches in the green recycle bin over there. And, son?"

"Yeah?"

"Be careful. Those rose bushes bite."

He laughs at his own joke, then disappears into the house to get Justin up and ready for school. I can't help but feel sorry for myself. Glancing up at my bedroom window, I try to imagine what it would feel like right now if I were still rolled up in my blankets or jamming away on Geraldine. That makes me think of Brett. What possessed him to join the military? I wonder if Penny knows yet and how she'll take it. I wonder if she'll be sad. Maybe she'll need a shoulder to cry on. I close my eyes, remembering our kiss. I haven't seen her since Saturday night. I messaged her yesterday asking how the shopping trip went, but she never replied. Maybe I should go over after she gets home today from school, find some way to tell her how I feel.

Mom's rose bushes are nothing but dead and fragile blossoms. I could go to the florist and buy some roses for Penny. Is that too much? Roses for just a kiss? Maybe carnations would be better. Mom always likes carnations, says they're perfect for any occasion. But Penny isn't just any occasion.

This is going to be difficult.

I step up to the first rose bush, which has grown chest-high this year, and snip off several spindly-looking branches. The thorns claw at my gloves. A particularly nasty one gouges my wrist right through my shirt sleeve, and I yank my arm back in pain. I roll up my sleeve and see the small bead of red on my skin.

I want to attack the stupid plant, but if I do, I'll only get hurt more. I have to tackle this job with tenderness, like my mom taught me to do when I was young. "Rose bushes are like people," she'd tell me. "On the outside, they put forth their best faces, like the blossoms, but underneath, they're vulnerable. If you handle them too roughly or without compassion, they'll fight to protect themselves."

I roll my sleeve back down and gingerly approach the bush again, taking care not to move too fast. *Snip.* A branch falls. *Snip. Snip.* Brittle blossoms collapse. *Snip.*

"Hi, Ryan."

Startled, I look up into Penny's blue eyes. "Hi. I didn't see you walk over."

She leans on the gate. "You were so intent on hacking those plants, I guess you didn't notice me."

She looks great today in a yellow T-shirt and jeans. I want to kiss her all over again.

"Yeah, my mom always manages to find something to keep me busy."

"Can I help?"

"Don't you have school?"

"Yeah, but I've got a few minutes before the bus gets here."

"So, you were just wandering aimlessly around the park until you found yourself standing in front of my house?"

She smiles at my teasing, but it's off, like something's bothering her.

"You okay?" I ask.

"Actually, I came over to talk to you."

Oh no. Here it comes. How does a guy acknowledge a first kiss with a girl? Do I say something like 'Hey, that was some kiss, wasn't it?' or 'I liked feeling your lips on mine. Can we do it again sometime?' It's all so stupid. What if I say something wrong?

"Sure," I tell her. "See that green bin? Roll it over here, and I'll stuff these branches in it while you talk."

Penny opens the gate and crosses the yard to the plastic bin, then hauls it across the lawn. I scoop up a handful of dried leaves and twigs and drop them in, grateful for the gloves.

"How's your day going so far?" Penny asks.

"Fine," I reply. "You?"

This is beyond awkward. Maybe she's here to tell me it was all a mistake, that she really doesn't like me that way. I start trying to think of something offhanded to say, so that she doesn't see how much her brush-off will hurt.

"I'm fine," she says, but she's chewing her lip. Looks worried. "Well, mostly fine. Brett's being weird, but otherwise. . ."

So, she's not here about the kiss. It's about Brett. I wonder if he's told her about his plans to join the military yet. I feel like I should say something, but I promised I wouldn't.

"Weird how?" I ask.

Penny plucks a dead rose from the bush, crinkling it between her fingers so the broken petals drift to the ground.

"I don't know. He says he's going away on some trip, but he's boxing everything up like he's moving halfway across the country or something."

I snap off a few more branches with the clippers. "Huh."

Penny stiffens. "Huh? That's a snappy reply." She folds her arms across her chest, annoyed.

"Sorry," I tell her, "I just don't exactly know what to say. I mean, maybe he *is* moving away—or something."

I focus harder on the rose bush, snipping furiously at the stupid thing.

"What's going on, Ryan?" Penny asks. "What did Brett tell you?"

"Nothing."

She snorts. "Really. Then why won't you look at me?"

I look at her.

"C'mon, Ryan," she says, not mad but like she sincerely needs to know, and that she trusts me to tell her the truth.

"Okay," I start, "but Brett'll kill me if he knows I told you."

"Out with it."

"He told me he's enlisting in the Marines."

The skin between Penny's eyes wrinkles, taking in what I said. "What? That's not true! It can't be."

"I don't know, Penny. That's what he told me."

She goes quiet, and she fingers the edge of the recycle bin. "I found a gun in his drawer," she says.

"A gun? Are you sure?"

"At least I think it was a gun. I didn't see it for certain. Do you think the Marines gave it to him?"

I consider this for a moment, then shake my head. "I don't think so."

Penny scratches agitatedly at the spot above her left ear. "What does he want with a gun?" She stops, and her eyes grow wider. "Jake? Do you think maybe Brett's—?"

Suddenly, the air all around us ruptures with an explosive *CRACK!* Penny ducks, an instinctive reaction. Just like in my dream, adrenaline bursts all through me, and I drop the clippers. What idiot is setting off fireworks, I think. But then—

Wait.

Was that a—a gunshot?

"Oh my God." Penny's face goes white. She stares across the park at her house. And then she's running full speed through our gate and down the steps.

"Penny!" I shout after her.

"Brett! Brett!" she screams, racing across the grass.

The thoughts that run through my head are impossible. This can't be happening. God, make it not true.

I shout as loud as I can, "Dad! Dad!"

Dad throws open the front door. "Ryan, what's going on?"

"Call 9-1-1!"

And then I take off after Penny.

FORTY-TWO

I BURST INTO MY house, sprinting through the living room and down the hall to Brett's room. I try the doorknob. Locked! So I pound on the door.

"Brett, open up!"

Keep it together. Keep it together, Penny.

All I can think of is that gun in his drawer. Where the hell did he get a gun?

I keep pounding. "Brett!"

Then Ryan appears beside me. I'd forgotten about him.

"Move aside," he says. "I'm going to kick it in."

The hall is narrow, but Ryan steps back with his spine nearly against the wall. The whole house shakes when he kicks the door. *Boom!* He kicks again. *Boom!*

Despite all the noise we're making, I hear nothing inside the room. This has got to be some horrible mistake. Maybe Brett really did join the Marines like Ryan said, and he's already gone.

Another kick. *Boom!*

But what if Brett lied to him? To both of us? They don't just hand out guns at recruiting offices.

Boom!

How did he find a gun—if it was a gun? Did someone give it to him? Did he steal it?

One more kick—*Boom!*—and the door frame splinters. The door swings open, hanging lopsided on a broken hinge. For a moment, there is silence. Ryan freezes there, gaping. As I shove past him into the room, the smell of copper hits me, and my stomach instantly feels sick.

Brett is lying on his back on the bed, an arm flung out over the side, a pistol on the floor. Blood is everywhere.

"Brett!"

I lunge for him, clutching at his shirt. His eyes are closed, his face smothered in red. Blood oozes from under his chin and his head, where a chunk of flesh and bone is missing.

Cries burn in my throat, threatening to shatter me into pieces. But Mom would tell me to keep it together. Keep it together for Brett.

But Brett's dead. He's got to be—

But then his arm twitches.

"Brett?"

His fingers shift on the blanket. His chest rises and falls.

"Oh my God, you're alive!" My cries turn to a deranged laugh. "Ryan, he's alive! He's still alive!"

I hover my hands over the wound as if I could somehow heal him. But I have no idea what to do.

Ryan snatches a dirty towel from the floor, pressing it to the bloody crater on the side of Brett's skull.

I touch Brett's cheek. "It's okay, Brett," I murmur, tears and snot waterfalling down my face. "Hold on. Just—just hold on."

Under the blood, Brett's skin is white as paper. He's breathing, though, so there's hope—isn't there?

The towel in Ryan's hand quickly soaks through with blood. "Oh, God," he mutters. "Oh God. Please, God. Please."

I hear a siren somewhere in the distance, coming closer. Closer.

Then Mr. Rojas is there, next to us.

"Dad— Dad—?" Ryan says over and over, like a broken record. I'm no better. I've lost control, weeping hysterically. But this isn't really happening. It couldn't be.

Mr. Rojas pulls off his jacket and pushes it down on top of the towel. "Hold this in place," he tells Ryan.

Mr. Rojas puts his hands on my shoulders and pulls me away from Brett.

"No! No!" I scream, trying to hold on, but Ryan's dad is gentle, his voice calm.

"The ambulance is on the way. The paramedics need space to work in here."

"I'm not leaving! I have to stay with Brett!"

His eyes lock on mine. "Penny."

The siren is so close now, screaming like the screams inside my head. I let go of Brett. Mr. Rojas gathers me into his arms the way my dad used to when I was little. I bury my face against his chest and sob.

RYAN

FORTY-THREE

FROM THE MOMENT I hear the gunshot, time slows down. Reaching Penny's house takes forever. And now that I'm here, I'm floating, suspended in a dream. Dad's talking to me, but I can't make out what he's saying. All I can hear is Brett's breathing and his heart pulsing, or is that mine?

And then I'm being pushed back by a man in a blue uniform. And Dad has his arm around me. We're walking down the hall. I see Penny. A cop is telling her he's called her mom, and that she's already at the hospital and will meet them there.

Brett's on a stretcher, rolling through the living room and out the front door. Dad and I follow. We stand on the porch as Penny climbs into the front seat of the ambulance. The doors shut. The ambulance drives away. The sirens fade.

A police officer is talking to my dad. I hear them, but it's hard to process what they're saying, like their words are coming from far away.

"I've known this kid a while now," the officer says. "He's had a lot of problems. Honestly, I'm surprised this didn't happen sooner."

"Will you be investigating?" Dad asks. "A crime scene?"

The officer shakes his head. "Nothing to investigate here. Clearly self-inflicted. Such a shame." He tucks his notepad and pen into his shirt pocket. "We could send someone out later to clean up if you'd like, for the family's sake. I'd hate to be that boy's mother and come home to this."

"Would you mind calling me when you get there?" Dad asks.

The cop agrees and jots down Dad's number.

I hold my hands in front of my face. They're red and sticky with blood. Brett's blood. Dad's arms are still around me. His voice becomes clearer now, directed at me.

"Ryan, you did good. It's all right, son. It's all right."

I want to believe him more than I've wanted anything in my life, but how could anything ever be all right again?

Sometime later, maybe minutes or maybe years, Dad guides me back inside the Tate house. I think the officer confiscated the gun, and I think he's left, but I really don't know for sure.

I stand, zombie-like, in the living room while Dad rummages in the kitchen. He appears beside me with a plastic bucket and a bottle of cleanser, some dish rags, and a roll of paper towels.

"I told them not to send anyone. I'll clean up," he says grimly. "Why don't you head home? Check on Justin. I told him not to leave the house, but I'm sure he saw the ambulance and is wondering what's going on."

When I make no move to leave, he lets out a hard breath. Then he heads down the hall to the bathroom. I hear the water turn on in the tub. Dad's filling the bucket. I hear it slosh as he carries it into Brett's room, followed by the sound of a spray bottle and Dad vigorously scrubbing something.

I don't know how I manage to finally get my limbs to move, but after a while, I go to the bathroom, turn on the faucet, and pump some liquid soap onto my palms. I massage it across my skin, holding my hands under the warm water. I watch Brett go down the drain. It takes several washes to get him off me, and the whole time I'm feeling guilty because of the sick feeling inside me, the feeling that wants to go home, to check on Justin, to leave Dad here to clean up alone. But I'm stronger than that, aren't I?

After drying my hands on a towel, I return to Brett's room. Dad has already stripped the quilt and sheets off the bed and rolled them up into a ball in the corner, but some of the blood has soaked through to the mattress.

"I'll take these to the laundromat," Dad says, "or the trash. We'll buy new ones."

His sleeves are rolled up to his elbows, and he holds a wet, brown rag in his hand. The rags were all white when he brought them in. "I don't know what to do about the mattress. Scrub it, I guess." He glances at me with an apologetic expression. "Your mother would know what to do. She can clean just about anything."

He attacks the mattress with the rag. I watch for a minute, but then he stops. He just freezes there, his muscles tense. In front of him, just above the bed, the wall is splattered with blood. I can see where he's wiped most of it off, but there's still a persistent stain of red.

"It happened so fast," says Dad, his eyes fixed on the smear on the wall. I wonder what he means, if he's talking about Brett. He seems to sense my question and adds, "The explosion."

Dad sits on the side of the bed. The hem of his jeans rides up his artificial leg, revealing the metal pylon.

"We were in Kabul, deep in combat. I remember waking up that morning thinking what a beautiful day it was. An hour later—gunfire, bombs erupting everywhere. One of my buddies dropped just eight, nine yards ahead of me. Bullet sliced right through him. I'd seen battle before, but when he went down, something in me snapped. I ran toward him, screaming his name."

He pauses, takes a slow, deep breath.

"Stepped on an IED. Simple as that."

I knew Dad had his leg blown off stepping on a buried explosive device, but he's never talked about it before. Not like this.

I say nothing and let him continue.

"The blast blew my foot apart, shattered everything up to my knee. My boot was the only thing holding it all together. I was a mess, but all I could think of was my friend. One bullet, and he was gone. I came home in a wheelchair. He came home in box."

Dad sits there for a minute longer, staring at the bloody rag in his hand. Then he starts on the mattress again.

"I want to help," I tell him.

He looks at me. "Go home, Ryan," he says. "You need to go home."

I'm about to refuse, about to tell him I have to help—for Penny—when his cell phone rings. Dad drops the rag into the bucket of water, now a sickly shade of brown. He dries his hands on his pants and pulls the phone from his back pocket.

"Officer? Brett, is he—?" he asks. Then he goes quiet. I watch as his expression collapses. His eyes grow glossy, and his lips start to tremble. "Yeah," he whispers. "Yeah. Thank you."

He ends the call and lowers the phone. Then he does something I've never seen him do before.

He cries.

PENNY

FORTY-FOUR

PEOPLE COME AND GO.

Doctors, nurses, friends of my mother's. They touch my shoulder. Embrace me. Tell me they're so sorry.

They move around me like shadows flitting in and out of my line of sight.

Someone in uniform asks me questions. I don't look at him. I don't answer.

A woman with a name badge sits beside me. She's here to listen, she says. Eventually, she leaves. They all leave.

The paramedics worked on Brett all the way here, putting in an IV, using a respirator, the works. I couldn't stop crying—or praying, if you can call it that. Pleading? Begging? But even though they rushed him into the ER, before the ambulance even came to a stop, I knew. I just... knew.

Mom takes the empty chair beside me, her arm sliding across my shoulders. Her voice is hoarse from hours of crying. Her mascara is smeared, but she doesn't care.

"It's time to go," she says softly. "Penny, it's time to go home."

But we just sit there together for a long time while the shadows move around us as if we aren't here at all.

He's gone—

I can't believe Brett is gone.

RYAN

FORTY-FIVE

I STAY IN BED for the rest of the day—and for all the next day too.

Dad calls the community center to let them know I'm not coming in for a few days. Mom arranges to take the week off work. She brings me food, but I don't eat it. She sits beside me and rubs my back. She hasn't done that since I was a kid.

"I'm so sorry," she says. "Is there anything I can bring you? Anything at all?"

But I just lay here and stare at the wall—and at Geraldine. She leans in the stand as casually as someone might lean against the side of a building, waiting for a ride. Waiting for Brett.

Every few hours, Dad comes to check on me. I know because I hear his uneven footsteps creaking along the hall outside my room. He pauses at my door and then moves on. We haven't said much to each other since Monday. I think finding Brett like that was as hard on him as it was on me.

Tuesday night—I think it's Tuesday—Mom tells me she's made dinner for the Tates and asks if I would like to go with her to take it over.

"You could see Penny," she says. "She could probably use a friend right now."

But just thinking about her—about what we saw—makes me sick all over again. I *can't* see Penny. I just can't. I don't have the courage to face her.

PENNY

FORTY-SIX

TUESDAY MORNING, Dad flies in from Florida. Mom waited to call him until we got home from the hospital late Monday night. She stared at the phone in her hand for nearly an hour before dialing the number, started crying before he even answered.

Dad rents a car at the airport and drives the hour and a half to our house. It's the first time he's been to California in two years.

He looks good. Trim. Tan.

His hair is turning gray.

Serves him right.

"Joelle," he says when Mom invites him in. He takes her in his arms and holds her. Mom curls her arms around him too. I guess this is no time to hold grudges.

At least for them.

Dad lets go of Mom and takes a step toward me. I pivot and strut down the hall, past Brett's room with its broken door and into my room. Then I slam the door shut behind me.

I spend the next couple days in my room—crying, sleeping, looking at pictures of Brett on my computer, crying some more. Mom sleeps with me so we don't have to cry ourselves to sleep alone. Dad stays on the fold-out sofa.

There's a hole in my gut the size of Jupiter. It opened up the moment Brett died, and it will never close again. I don't want it to.

After Mom calls Fred, letting him know I won't be in this week, the phone rings a hundred times. Most of the time Dad answers. "Thank you," he says. "We appreciate it very much."

A few times, I hear him say, "Penny's occupied at the moment. You can try again tomorrow if you'd like."

Maybe it's Tali, or Fred, or Ryan. I don't know. And I really don't care.

Wednesday afternoon, there's a knock on my bedroom door.

"Honey?" says Mom. "Tali's here to see you. Can I bring her in?"

I roll off my bed and put my feet on the floor. I haven't showered today or even bothered to get dressed.

Tali appears in my doorway, her face streaked with tears. She hurries over and throws her arms around me.

"I tried to call, lots of times," she says. "Your dad told me you weren't up to visitors, but I had to see you. Please don't hate me for coming over."

She relaxes her hold on me but doesn't let go.

"You okay?" she asks, then answers before I can. "Of course you're not okay. Dumb question. I just want you to know I care."

"Thank you," I say, and I mean it. It's been a long three days. Feels more like three centuries. "It's just hard, you know? Brett. . ."

Saying his name calls up a fresh wave of tears. I can't help it.

"Sorry." I reach for a tissue from the box on my nightstand.

"Don't be." Tali squeezes me again.

We sit quietly for a few minutes—me blowing my nose into the tissue and dabbing at my eyes, Tali rubbing circles on my back. I hadn't wanted to talk to anyone, but now that she's here, I don't feel quite so alone.

"So, the school held a moment of silence today," Tali says after a while. "The teams are taking up a collection for your family, and they're offering counseling to anyone who wants it."

"Did you see a counselor?" I ask.

Tali bites her bottom lip. I can see she's fighting back tears. "I've been to the office a couple of times. It's all right, actually. Not as New-Age-all-feel-good as I expected." She pinches a tear from her eye and then takes my hand. "I should be asking you that question. Have you talked to anyone?"

"What do I need with a shrink when I've got you?" I try to laugh, but it comes out wilted. "Trust me, I've seen enough shrinks about my parents' divorce to last me a hundred lifetimes. Maybe the best thing for me right now is to think about anything else. Like your date with Connor." I try to sound really interested when I say it, as if I've actually been thinking about it. "I never got a chance to ask you how it went."

Tali gives an exaggerated eye roll and an angry cluck of the tongue.

"What?" I ask. "Did something happen?"

"Oh, something happened, all right. He picked me up at eight, and we had a nice ride over to the restaurant. We were going to catch whatever movie was playing afterwards."

Tali shifts on the bed like she's gearing up for something important. "So," she continues, "we're waiting to be called to our table, right? And all of a sudden, Connor moves away from me, like ten feet! The other side of the room! And I'm like, 'Connor, what's wrong?' And you know what he said? 'My parents.' He'd spotted his mom and dad coming out of the frozen yogurt shop next door. He was afraid they'd see us together."

"Are you kidding?"

Tali shakes her head, and she starts to look sad.

"What did he say? What did you say?"

"He tried to apologize, but I told him to screw dinner. Then I called my mom to come get me."

Tali plucks a tissue from the box for herself. "What about you?" she asks, dabbing the corner of her eye. "Has Ryan been over?"

"I don't think so."

"Called?"

I shake my head. "Mom would have told me if he had. But I'm not sure I could handle talking to him anyway."

"Of course. I understand," she says. But I don't think she does. No one does, except Ryan, because he was there. I can't help but wonder if he's all right—and if he's thought about me at all. Why hasn't he called?

"He was with me," I tell Tali, "when I found Brett. Maybe he's not ready to see me yet. And in truth, Tali, I'm not sure I'm ready to see him either."

"He'll be at the funeral Friday. Right?" she asks.

"I guess. Mom told his parents about it." I reach for another tissue. I just can't seem to keep it together, no matter how hard I try. "I just—I don't know how I'll get through this."

Tali hugs me. "No one expects you to get through it, Penny."

I collapse against her and cry some more.

RYAN

FORTY-SEVEN

THURSDAY, I START to feel almost normal again—almost, meaning I wake up hungry and actually eat the scrambled eggs and bacon Mom leaves on my dresser. Then I take a shower and get dressed. Justin says good morning on his way out the door for school. Mom's doing laundry. Life seems to be back to usual, but none of it seems real—more like I'm moving through a weird dream or a movie. I don't feel sad. I don't feel anything.

I watch the Tate's house through my bedroom window. People I don't know come and go like bees in and out of a hive. Mom told me they've had lots of family and friends stopping by. I'll bet Penny wishes they'd all just leave her alone.

"I'm glad to see you up and around," Mom says when she comes to collect my plate. "I thought maybe you'd like to watch TV or play some video games. Or maybe we could go to the store later."

"Sure, Mom." But I don't really want to go to any store, and I don't feel like playing games or watching some dumb show on TV. Mom's eyes dart to Geraldine. Just for a split second, but it's enough to send a cold chill through me.

"I'll just read," I say, indicating the stack of textbooks on the floor.

"All right," she says. "I'll be back later with lunch. Any requests?"

I think about it for a moment, but then shake my head.

She comes to the bed and leans over to kiss the top of my head and gently ruffles my hair. Her way of saying 'I love you.' Then she leaves.

Once alone, I get up and sit in my desk chair, pushing it side to side the way Penny did on New Year's Day.

Penny.

I turn on my computer. I could at least message her, tell her how sorry I am about Brett. I start to type.

Me: Hi Penny. I know this is really hard right now—this is—(my fingers twitch over the keys)—terrible. I know you miss him. I miss him too. I just—(I blink hard)—I just can't—

I stop typing. Words are so stupid. Everything is so stupid!

I hold the BACKSPACE button down, and the words vanish one letter at a time until the line is blank again. Then I turn off the computer and slam it shut.

PENNY

FORTY-EIGHT

THURSDAY AFTERNOON, Dad opens Brett's bedroom door. It's the first time any of us has been inside since Brett died. Mom waits at the kitchen table. She doesn't want to see, and I don't blame her. But Dad says there might be something important inside, like a letter. He has to check.

Dad and I step into the room. It's just as Brett left it, boxes still stacked in the corner, his clothes hanging neatly in his closet. The bed has been stripped, and most of the blood has been cleaned up. I imagine Ryan's family or the police did it while we were in the hospital. But there are still places on the wall and the mattress where the bloodstains, impossible to clean, have dried to a deep brown.

"Look around," Dad tells me. "See what you can find."

I try to think where Brett might have left a note, anything that might explain why he did what he did. The boxes are all taped shut, the contents marked with Sharpie. Dad starts sorting through Brett's clothes, checking every pocket. But I know what I'm looking for.

The top drawer in Brett's dresser is pulled halfway out. It contains a bunch of assorted items: a couple of broken baseball trophies with his name on them, a playbill from a BandMasterz performance three years ago, a half-eaten bag of Red Vines, and a stack of postcards from Florida, all addressed to him and signed *Dad*. I find what I'm looking for at the very bottom of the drawer—Brett's red spiral notebook, the one he'd been so secretive about.

As the metal spine brushes my finger, I remember the gun that had been in the drawer and shudder. Then I open the notebook cover, expecting to find journal entries or song lyrics or even school assignments. But there are none of those. Just a list of random things that goes on for pages and pages, things like book titles, music albums, and descriptions of clothing like 'Blue Abercrombie Hoodie' and 'Muse Concert Tee.' And there are other things, like:

Xbox 360 + Games – *Frankie*
Coin Collection – *Uncle Travis*
Skateboard – *Austin*
Sketchpad + oil paints + brushes – *Heather*
Class Ring – *Celine*

I flip through seven or eight pages filled back and front. Most of the names are people I know—relatives and Brett's friends from BandMasterz and school. A few names are unfamiliar, but I see 'Penny' and 'Mom' a lot. Then I get to the end of the list:

Geraldine – *Ryan Rojas*

This isn't just a list. It's a will. Brett had been deciding who to leave all his belongings to.

I hand Dad the notebook, and he skims over the pages. Then he takes it into the kitchen. Mom cries when she sees it. She brushes her hand over the cover the way she used to smooth back Brett's hair.

"It's what he wanted," Dad tells her, "to share his life with those he loved the most."

"No," Mom says, sniffing. "It's too soon."

She marches down the hall and shuts Brett's door. With its busted hinge, it doesn't close properly. So she turns the inside lock and forces the door into place.

After Mom retreats to her room, Dad drops onto the sofa with a heavy sigh. I sit in the corner loveseat, watching him in his perfectly matched shirt and slacks, his perfectly combed hair, his perfectly groomed nails.

"This is difficult for your mother," Dad says. He slides his thick hand across his face, then drops his arm over the side of the sofa like he's just laid down a heavy burden and is taking a break. "It's difficult for all of us."

Who is this man who used to make pancakes for us every Sunday morning, who taught me and Brett to ride our bicycles, who read stories to us every night until we were too old to admit we still enjoyed it? I stare at him and wonder how often he thought of us after he left, how many women he slept with, how much money he spent on them. Marriages fall apart. People get divorced. But this was different. Brett was different, even before. He *needed* more, hurt more. Dad knew that, and he still left.

"Where were you?" I ask, disgust and rage filling me.

He raises his eyes to me but doesn't respond.

"Where were you, Dad, when Brett cried himself to sleep night after night for a month after you left?"

The rage begins to boil over.

"Where were you when he was in the hospital after slicing open his wrists? When Mom held his hand and told him everything would be fine?"

Dad opens his palms to me. "Penny, I—"

"Where were you when he needed a father? When he needed someone to look after him and love him and protect him?"

The tears burn so hot in my eyes that I can hardly see.

"Don't you dare say it's difficult! You don't have the right to say that!"

When he finally answers, Dad's voice is weak and uncertain. "You're right, Penny," he says, which is not what I expect to hear. "You're right. I've made mistakes."

He shifts forward, resting his elbows on his knees, his hands twisting into knots. For the first time since he arrived here, his perfect shell begins to crack.

"I should have been here for him," he says, "but I didn't know how. I'll have to live with that—if I can."

He clenches his fists together, presses them against his forehead. The muscles in his face tighten, fighting to keep his emotions at bay. Soon despair wins, and his shoulders shake from his sobbing. Despite my anger, I feel sorry for him. Part of me wants to comfort him, to be comforted by him, like when I was small. But instead, I pull my knees up to my chest and stare out the living room window.

FORTY-NINE

IT RAINS THE NIGHT before Brett's funeral. Friday morning, the ground is soft and mucky. My shoes slip on the wet grass as I tromp uphill to the gravesite. Dad, Mom, and Justin walk ahead while I follow behind. We're all dressed in black. I don't own a suit, so yesterday Mom insisted on taking me to the mall to find one. It's uncomfortable as hell.

There are a lot of people, most of them standing behind a row of chairs where Mrs. Tate sits with a man I don't recognize. She looks down at her hands and, every so often, dabs at her eyes with a tissue. I wonder if the man is Brett's father. Penny sits on the other side of her mom. Tali, who sits behind her, reaches out to squeeze Penny's shoulder.

Penny and I haven't spoken all week. I picked up the phone and started to dial a dozen times at least, but I always hung up before it started to ring. And there have been people going in and out of her house. I figured they didn't need me around anyway.

Penny stares straight ahead at the casket, which rests atop a metal contraption draped in a blanket of fake grass.

There are white roses on top. Penny's wearing a black knee-length dress with long sleeves. Her ankles are crossed, and her hands are in her lap, clutching a tissue. She glances up at me as I walk by. Our eyes connect briefly before she looks back to the casket.

The service isn't very long. A pastor reads a passage from the Bible, and a woman sings a song about grace, accompanied by someone on a portable electric keyboard. A prayer is said, and the man I think might be Brett's father approaches the casket and kisses it. Then, with tears in his eyes, he plucks the flower from his lapel and adds it to the bouquet of flowers draped over the top. Mrs. Tate gets up next. She has a red rose in her hand, which she lays with the others. Her cheeks are wet, her mascara slightly smudged. Several people, her family probably, gather around her, embrace her, console her.

One by one, the guests say their goodbyes and make their way to their cars.

"Are you ready to go?" Mom asks.

"Can I have a few minutes?"

"Of course." She glances toward Penny, who's sitting alone with Tali now. "Take your time." She kisses my forehead before walking off to join Dad and Justin.

On my way to the casket, I see Fred from the community center. He stops and offers a hand. I shake it.

"He'll be missed," he says sincerely.

I politely agree. "Hey Fred," I tell him, "thanks for covering for me this week."

He pats my shoulder. "No prob. The kids understand. I hope you'll still be there tomorrow, though. Show starts at two. They're counting on you."

I promise him I'll be there, but the truth is, it's the last place I want to be right now.

Once Fred walks away, I approach Brett's casket. Reaching into my jacket pocket, I remove a small triangle of green plastic—one of the Tenacious D guitar picks Penny gave me that night at the mall. I tuck it into the seam between the lid and base of Brett's coffin so that no one can see or remove it.

"Something to remember me by," I say, laying my palm against the cool metal in a parting touch.

I walk past the row of chairs to where Penny and Tali are sitting.

"Hi, Tali," I say.

Even though we don't know each other well, Tali stands to give me a hug. Then she hugs Penny. "I'll see you at the church," she tells her, then leaves.

Penny and I are the last ones.

There's a damp, musty smell in the air and a faint hint of roses. A wind has picked up, biting cold. Looks like it's going to rain again.

I should say something, like it'll be all right or Brett is in a better place, things I've been hearing people say to one another for the past hour. But all those words ring hollow for me. It isn't going to be all right, and how do they know if he's in a better place? Better than what? Than living in a world where people care about you? Where you have a mother and sister who love you? Where there is music, and laughter, and sunsets, and oceans?

Even if Brett is in a better place, the rest of us have been left behind with gashes in our hearts that will never heal. Not ever.

So, I don't say anything. And Penny doesn't say anything. Instead, I reach for her hand, and when our fingers touch, she grasps mine tightly in hers. We hold onto each other like that for a long time, as if by letting go we might die.

PENNY

FIFTY

TOO MANY PEOPLE.

There are just too many people here, all heaping piles of pasta salad and store-bought lasagna onto Styrofoam plates and talking to each other about their kids' latest sports victories or how their bosses suck or the weird lump they found in the shower that turned out to be benign, thank God. I know because I make my way around the church gymnasium, orbiting each cluster of conversation like a gnat or a ghost. No one seems to notice I'm there. They've paid their respects to my brother, offered their condolences to me and my parents. Now they've moved on to something more important—lunch.

Tali was here for a while. I wish I could have gone with her when she left.

At a table in the corner, Mr. and Mrs. Rojas and Justin are eating from plates of cookies. I spoke to them earlier, and they apologized that Ryan didn't come with them. I hadn't expected him to. In fact, I'm jealous that he had the choice and I didn't.

I can't take it anymore.

"Mom? Can we go?" I ask, pulling on Mom's arm. She's been sucked into a monologue with the priest, who's telling her about what Christ really meant when he told Peter to feed his sheep. I say monologue, because my mom isn't getting a word in edgewise, and her eyes are opened wide in the universal symbol of "Someone save me, please!" So, I do.

"Mom?" I say again, interrupting the priest. "I'm not feeling well. Would you drive me home?"

The priest has drawn a breath and is just starting another sentence when Mom politely cuts him off. "I'm sorry, Father, if you'll excuse me." Then she follows me to a quiet corner of the room.

"What's wrong?" she asks, pressing a palm to my forehead. "Are you sick? I knew I shouldn't have let you stay out in that damp weather too long."

"Mom, I'm fine," I tell her. "I thought maybe you needed to be rescued."

"God, yes. I mean, he was incredibly thoughtful for officiating the service today, but the man just goes on and on."

"I'm really done here. Could we just go home?"

Mom glances around the room with a look of longing. "I wish I could, Honey," she says, her eyes finally resting on me. "Really, I don't want to be here any more than you do. But they're our family and friends. I can't just *leave*."

"What about Dad? No one here knows him, except for some of the relatives who hate his guts for divorcing you. Look at him." I point out my father, who's standing alone against the far wall, making his way through a small stack of cheese rolls. "Put him out of his misery and let him drive me home."

Mom thinks about this for a moment. "Actually, maybe that will work out. There's something we need to talk to you about anyway."

"What?"

"Not here. But talk to your dad, and we'll discuss it later when I get home."

I try to pry more information out of her, but Mom refuses to say anything more. Instead, she passes me off to Dad, who practically melts with gratitude for the chance to leave.

Outside, the sky is crowded with black clouds, and rain has started to fall. Once in Dad's car, I don't waste time.

"Mom said you wanted to talk to me?"

He starts the engine, and we turn onto the street.

"Boy, you don't mince words, do you?" he says.

I stare at him intently, waiting.

"All right. I'll just say it. I want to pay your tuition to IMG Academy."

This is not what I was expecting to hear. "I already told Mom, I'm not going to IMG."

"But that was before—" Dad's voice breaks, then he continues cautiously. "I know how you felt about going, and you had a very good reason. It was selfless of you to put your dreams on hold for your brother, but now—"

"Don't say it." I want him to shut up. Why is he talking about this with me now? Doesn't he know this is the last thing in the world I want to hear?

"Penny, you have an amazing talent. You deserve to go as far as it can take you."

"I don't care!" I shout at him. "I don't care about me! Don't you get it? Brett is dead, or haven't you noticed?"

"I know that—"

"Tomorrow, you fly home and go back to your non-Brett life, but my whole world is destroyed! Everything! I don't care about basketball. I don't care about anything except getting my brother back!"

The signal ahead of us turns red. The car idles at the intersection. Dad rests his elbow against his window and rubs his face.

"Let me try this another way," he says. "Your mom and I have been talking. She wants what's best for you, and so do I. And we both feel that it's time for you to at least consider IMG. You don't have to go if you don't want to. Just apply and see what happens. If they accept you, then you can decide what to do."

The light turns green. We move forward.

Apply to IMG? It's almost funny, all the letters I've torn up, the scholarship offers that Dad doesn't have a clue about. I remember what Coach Anderson told me in the locker room a few weeks back. I could have my pick of universities, and going to IMG would all but guarantee it. All I have to do is say yes.

We drive the rest of the way listening to the window wipers. When we pull up in front of the house, Dad doesn't turn off the engine, and I realize he's got to go back for Mom.

"Penny," he says, "think about Brett."

"I'm always thinking about Brett."

"Then think about what he'd want you to do. Would he want you to keep putting your life on hold for him when it won't do any good? Or would he want to see you thrive and live your dreams?"

Dad's words drill into me. As painful as it is to admit, he's right. Maybe that's one reason why Brett took his life. Maybe he believed he was holding me back. He wasn't, and I'd never think that in a million years, but did he? I wish so much I could talk to him, tell him that he was never a burden. Not to me. He was the best part of me. But now that he's gone, he's still a part of me, and maybe living, really living, is one way to keep him alive.

"Penny," Dad continues, his voice softening, "Let me do this for you. Let me at least try to be the father to you that I should have been to Brett."

I wrap my fingers around the door handle. The rain is really coming down now.

"I'll think about it," I finally say. "I still have to consider Mom. I don't know how I'd feel being that far from her, especially now."

"Actually," says Dad, "your mom and I discussed that as well."

My hand slides off the handle into my lap. I have a feeling we're going to be sitting here for a while. Sure enough, Dad turns off the engine.

"Penny, we need to talk."

RYAN

FIFTY-ONE

AFTER THE FUNERAL, I lie on my bed staring at the ceiling. There's a circle of brown up there, water damage from years ago. Dad fixed the roof then, but the stain is still there. I've been here all afternoon. Mom, Dad, and Justin went to the church for the after-funeral luncheon, but I didn't want to go. The thought of all that food makes me feel nauseous. I keep thinking about BandMasterz, how I probably should have made it to practice, and how Dana, William, and Khiem are counting on me for the performance. But tomorrow is too far away for me to think about right now.

I can't shut off my brain. I keep seeing it, over and over—the hole in Brett's head, the blood on my hands. For five days now, it's all I've thought about—that and Dad's accident.

Mom hasn't made me do any homework this week, but I wonder if that's made it all worse, not having anything to occupy my mind. I keep waking up in the middle of the night in cold sweats, harassed by nightmares of gun shots and explosions. Then during the day, I wander around like a zombie from lack of sleep. Guilt eats at me—

Guilt at knowing I have nothing on Penny and her mom.

Guilt about everything Dad's been through.

Guilt that I haven't been honest with Mom.

After a while, the sky outside my window starts to darken. It's barely five o'clock, but it's the first week of February, and days are short and cold.

Down the hall, the phone in my parents' bedroom rings—three rings, four. The answering machine clicks on. Dad's voice tells whoever's calling to leave a message. The next thing I hear is a familiar male voice.

"Ryan? This is Commander Norton calling from Middleton..."

I don't wait for the rest of the message. I roll out of bed and sprint down the hall. Fumbling with the phone, I press the answer button.

"Hello?" I'm out of breath from running and nearly drop the phone, but I manage to tighten my grip on it and press it to my ear. "This is Ryan."

"Ryan, glad to find you at home. How are things going?"

Couldn't be worse. Thanks for asking.

"Fine," I tell him.

"Yes, I think they are going fine. I've been monitoring your progress with independent study. You're turning in top-notch work. And I got your most recent volunteer hour sheets. Seems you're going over and beyond."

My lungs actually stop functioning for a few seconds while Norton speaks.

"I'm really pleased," says Norton, and I can hear in his voice that he means it. "I am optimistic about your meeting with the school board."

"That's good news," I tell him. "I'll definitely be ready for them next weekend."

"Actually, that's why I'm calling," says Norton. "They were scheduled to meet next Saturday, as you're already aware, but one of the members will be out of town on business. So, they've bumped it up to tomorrow."

Tomorrow? The same day as the BandMasterz concert?

"What time?" I ask.

"One-thirty."

The concert starts at two.

"Is there any other time I could come? I have a conflict tomorrow."

I can just imagine Norton shaking his head on the other end of the line.

"I'm afraid not," he says. "As it is, I've had to call more than twenty students to come in for their scholarship interviews. The board has a full slate, but I managed to schedule extra time for them to hear your case. Plan to be there at least an hour—and be prepared. This is your one shot to get back into Middleton."

Norton congratulates me again on my progress. I tell him thanks and hang up the phone. Tomorrow. I'm supposed to meet with the school board tomorrow.

The concert is tomorrow.

I go back to my room and sit on my bed facing the two things that have become most important to me lately. The first is my bass guitar. The second is Brett's. A wave of sadness washes through me as I snake my fingers around Geraldine's neck and lift her from the stand. She feels sleek and comfortable in my arms, like a well-loved lady. And that's what she is because Brett loved her.

I start playing one of the songs Brett and I worked on together. The notes are smooth and natural, like it was made for me. I start to get into the music, but again Brett is in my brain. My fingers go numb. I can't play anymore.

I replace Geraldine in her stand and step over to my dresser. I open my top drawer and slide my hand along the underside of the dresser top and carefully detach the lighter and plastic baggie stuck on with duct tape.

Then I see Penny's pendant, and I'm filled with even more guilt. I've hardly even thought about this stuff since Penny made me swear to lay off it. I've kept my promise, but between Brett and now the board review, this is more than I can take. I need to escape. I need to feel whole again, if even for an hour or two.

I stuff the baggie into my jacket pocket. Then I flick the lighter to make sure it still works. I won't be gone long. If all goes well, I'll be passed out in my bed by the time my parents get home. Maybe, if I'm lucky, I'll sleep right through the board meeting and BandMasterz.

It's pouring rain when I step out of my house. I wish I'd run into Andrew or even Chris. It would be easier to get high if I wasn't alone. But no one's here. I stand at the street curb for a while, staring through the rain at nothing in particular. I will my feet to move forward across the grass to the play gym. It's got a plastic roof, so I'll be able to light up out of the rain.

I pass the table and bench where I met my friends that night in December. I haven't seen or heard from a single one of them since. So much for friends. I remember how I woke up in my own living room because Penny and Brett found me here and took me home. I think about all the times Brett jammed with me and taught me stuff on the bass, and how Penny and I taught the kids at the center how to play basketball. But they're not why I'm here.

Why *am* I here?

I remove the baggie from my pocket and take out one of the joints. Penny would be pissed if she knew what I was doing. She'd call me a coward for resorting to this. I wonder if she'll forgive me. But why should she? I promised her I would never do this again. She made me swear.

But she's got to understand how I feel—about Brett. How I can't get the picture of him, all the blood, even the smell of it, out of my head.

I take the packet of Xanax and pour all four bars into my palm. I clench them in my fist and then press my hands against my skull.

I want Brett gone. Gone out of my head. Gone.

Brett's gone.

Brett's *gone.*

Then it all bursts out of me—the emptiness, the guilt, the loss, the tears. I can't control it. A flood of grief overwhelms me. But I can't do this. Not to Penny. Not to my parents. Not to me. As horrible as this feeling is, I have to face it. I have to live with it. That's what my dad would do.

I fling the pills away, and they fly into the gray rain to dissolve somewhere into nothingness. I break open the joints and drop them into the mud.

That's when I see someone, standing not far off. At first, I could swear it's Brett, still alive, come to tell me what an idiot I am and to get the hell out of the rain. But I blink. It's not Brett. It's Penny.

"What are you doing out here?" I call to her.

She's still wearing her dress from the funeral, now limp and sagging with moisture. She comes closer. "I should ask you the same question."

"I thought you were at the luncheon."

"I was, but my dad brought me home early. I got tired of everyone telling me how sorry they are and to call them if I need anything, as if I'd ever call any of *them*."

Penny rubs her arms. She's shivering.

"You shouldn't be out in this," I tell her. "You'll get sick."

"And you won't?"

I know I should say something, do something. I should get down from the play gym, offer my coat to her, and be the hero. But I don't move.

"I should have stopped him," I shout into the rain. "I should have known what he was planning to do."

I wait for Penny to say something. She says nothing.

The tears start up again. And I can't stop crying. "The signs were there—giving away his stuff, lying about joining the military—but I didn't see them. I didn't see—"

Penny takes a couple steps toward me. "Ryan?"

I leap from the play gym and run to her, my sneakers slapping against the wet sand and concrete sidewalk. "I'm sorry, Penny," I say. "I'm so sorry."

I reach for her, and she coils her arms around me. We pull each other close, sobbing. Rain be damned.

PENNY

FIFTY-TWO

RYAN AND I STAND for a while, just the two of us crying on each other in the rain. I'm shaking with the cold, so Ryan takes my hand and leads me across the park to his house. We go inside and take off our wet shoes. Ryan grabs a towel from a closet, wraps it around me. Then he lights a fire in the fireplace and makes us each a cup of hot cocoa.

By now, the sun has set, and the sky outside is ink black. This is the end of Brett's last day on the surface of the planet. I'm sure his casket has been lowered into the grave by now and covered with dirt. Such an unceremonious thing compared to a funeral and a luncheon. I wonder what it must be like to be the man who drives the little tractor that pushes the heaps of earth into each new grave. Does he say a private prayer over every stranger? Or is it just a job to him, something to do to earn a paycheck?

If I had been the one to bury Brett, I would have used a shovel like in the old days. I'd have said goodbye one shovelful of soil at a time. And I would have done it slowly so that it took all day and night. And when I was done, I'd have put smooth stones around it, the way pioneers used to mark their loved ones' graves along the side of the trail, knowing they would never be back that way again. There's something to be said about the way we bury our dead, as if it really doesn't matter anymore. But it does matter. At least it matters to me.

Ryan and I sit in silence, drinking our cocoa, gazing into the fire. I finally stop shivering. My dress starts to dry. I set my empty mug on the coffee table.

"It stopped raining," I say, sensing the growing awkwardness. I wonder if things between us will ever be the same. "I guess I should get back." I get up from the couch and hand Ryan the towel. I don't know what else to say, so I start for the door.

"Wait a sec," Ryan says. So, I stop.

Ryan runs upstairs. He's gone for only a minute before he returns, a familiar blue bass guitar in his hands. When I see it, tears threaten to fall all over again.

"It's Brett's," Ryan says, though he doesn't have to tell me. "He gave it to me the day before he…" His voice comes to a cliff. He swallows. "I thought I should return it, that you'd want it."

I sit back down on the couch, overwhelmed. "He really liked you, you know," I tell Ryan. "Brett didn't have many friends. He used to, but he changed after my dad left. I mean, he still had Jake, but then the thing with Celine changed that too. Jake and some of the other kids called him freak and crazy and a whole slew of other things. The sad thing was that he believed them. I sometimes wonder, if they really *knew* him, understood what he'd been through and how every day was a struggle to just get out of bed, to function, to exist—would they have treated him that way?"

My eyes well with tears, and I swipe them away. "All this time, I've been telling myself that they're complete pricks. Jackasses who don't know a decent human being from a cockroach. But the crazy thing is they're not. I've hated them, dreamed of getting back at them, but the reason they treated Brett the way they did is because they were afraid."

Ryan sits beside me on the couch, Geraldine braced between his knees. "Afraid of Brett?"

"A little. But I think more so, they're afraid of anyone who's different than them, of things they don't understand. And because they were afraid, Brett felt like there was no place for him in this world, no place where he could be accepted for who he was. But he was wrong." I shake my head, and the tears start to fall.

"Anyway," I continue. "Mom and I know Brett gave you the guitar, and we want you to keep it."

"What?" says Ryan, surprised. "No, I can't."

"Yes, you can. Besides, he meant for you to play it in BandMasterz."

He grows quiet, gazing into the fire. "I won't need Geraldine for BandMasterz because I'm not doing it. I can't play, not after what's happened."

"But, Ryan, they need you."

"They can find another bass guitarist to fill in, someone from one of the other bands, maybe. Besides, I got a call from my school. The board's review has been moved to tomorrow. My parents and I have been waiting for this. I have to go."

I don't know what he expects me to say—that I understand, that I'm disappointed, that I wish things could be different. But I don't say anything at all. Instead, I look out the living room window where it's started raining again, heavy now. Sheets of gray slam down from the sky, assaulting the house like typhoon-driven waves. The sky lights up for one brief, brilliant moment. I hold my breath, waiting for the inevitable roll of thunder to follow. The sound explodes—too much like the sound of a gunshot.

I grab Ryan's hand, and I'm sure my pulse is racing so fast he can feel it.

"When I was a kid, I mean really little, like four or five," I tell him, "I was terrified of storms. The lightning and thunder were like some horrible monster clawing at the windows. I tried to tell my father that I was scared, but he'd have none of that. He'd tell me to go back to bed, but I couldn't. So, I'd sneak into Brett's room and crawl into bed with him. He never sent me away. He was only a few years older than me, but I felt safer when I was with him. Every time lightning struck, we'd hide under the blankets. And he'd sing to me. Dozens of songs. Some of them two or three times, until I finally fell asleep."

Another flash of light illuminates the sky, and with it the entire living room, as if a flare has been lit and then goes out.

"After my dad left," I continue, "it was Brett who was afraid. Or maybe not afraid. Angry? Hurt? I don't know. There were many nights I could hear him crying through the bedroom wall. Sometimes I'd go in and try to comfort him the way he comforted me when I was young. We'd sing some of those old songs until we either ended up laughing or falling asleep. But the truth is, nothing I did really made much of a difference."

Ryan gives my hand a squeeze.

"I tried to save him," I continue, "but I just couldn't. I failed, Ryan. I let him die."

A warm tear slides down my face, getting lost in the corner of my mouth. After all the crying I've done, I can hardly believe there are any more tears left in me.

"You didn't let him die, Penny," Ryan whispers. "You loved him—and when we love someone, really love someone, we can never fail them."

Ryan reaches up and traces the path of my tear. I close my eyes, and he kisses me. His lips are soft and gentle, and I press into them with my own. Ryan wraps his arms around my waist. I slide mine over his shoulders, and we pull each other close.

When our kiss ends, I peer into Ryan's face, searching for any evidence that this is a misunderstanding, but all I see is warmth.

"What?" he asks when I look away.

"I—nothing. It's just that I thought, maybe what happened before, that night after the mall. I thought you changed your mind about me."

"Changed my mind?"

"I thought you regretted kissing me."

"Why would I do that?"

"Because I wasn't—pretty enough."

Ryan slips a finger under my chin and lifts my face until my eyes meet his. "That's impossible. You're the most beautiful girl I've ever known."

And then he kisses me again. For a long time.

When it's over, I rest my head against Ryan's chest, and we lean back against the couch, holding each other. We sit like that for a while, watching the lightning strike.

A few minutes pass, and I know I have to tell him what my father and I discussed. Not telling him would be cruel, so I whisper, "I'm going away, Ryan."

My news must hit him like a sledgehammer, because I can feel his muscles tense up.

"I'm moving to Florida. There's a school there, a private school for student athletes. They've offered me a scholarship, and I've decided to take it."

Ryan shifts so that we are sitting facing each other. "You're leaving?" he asks.

"I'm going to stay with my dad until I get everything arranged. The school's just an hour from where he lives."

"I thought you're not close to your dad."

"I'm not. I mean, I wasn't, but—" This is harder than I thought it would be. "I can't stay here, Ryan. After everything that's happened—it's just too hard."

Ryan leans back into the couch, his expression blank.

"I know my dad has been a total dick," I continue. "But he *is* my dad."

"But you'll come back this summer, right?" Ryan asks. "You'll come home between semesters, and for holidays."

"No, Ryan. I'm not coming back—ever."

There's a long silence between us, filled only by the sound of the fire and the storm outside. Ryan looks at me, stunned. I take his hand in mine again. I need him to understand why I'm doing this.

"I couldn't leave my mom behind. She knows that, which is why she's decided to find a position in Florida, near the school. She says she doesn't want to stand in my way, that I've spent enough time thinking about everyone else. It's time to follow my dream."

Even as I say it, I still feel unsure about my decision. It feels wrong somehow, to do what I want to do. But my parents were insistent, and deep down, I know it is the right choice. I just have to get used to it.

Ryan rubs the side of my hand with his thumb. "I think what you're doing takes courage. I'm proud of you."

He kisses me, and I savor the feel of him. In the fireplace, a spark pops and a log settles.

"When are you leaving?" asks Ryan, our kiss ended.

This is the toughest part of all. "Mom's staying an extra week to pack and sort through Brett's things, but Dad flies back to Tampa tomorrow." I draw a deliberate breath. "I'm going with him."

Ryan presses his lips together and nods. "I guess that means no Rose Parade next year?" He tries to laugh, but it doesn't hide the anguish in his voice. I lay my head on his shoulder, and we listen to another crack of thunder.

"I can't believe it," he says after a while. "All this time I've had you here, and I'm only now realizing how wonderful you are, how I want to be with you."

Geraldine, Brett's bass, is still between Ryan's knees. I'm going to IMG, doing what I am meant to do. But Ryan—is he doing what he's meant to do?

"You need to perform tomorrow," I tell him.

"I can't, Penny."

"I know what you said about the meeting and about Brett—but you still *want* to play, don't you?"

He grows silent again. The storm outside rages on. Ryan squeezes his hands together and looks at the floor.

"There's something I haven't told you," he says. "I haven't told anyone."

I move my hand to Ryan's knee, but I don't say anything. I just want him to know I'm listening.

"The night my dad was injured in Afghanistan," he begins cautiously, "my mom and I had a fight. I wanted to go out with my friends. We'd started a band, and we wanted to get together and jam. Mom suspected we did more than play music. And she was right. We drank, got high. She told me I couldn't go. I got pissed, said some things I've regretted ever since."

Ryan pauses and swipes a hand across his eyes.

"The thing is, I snuck out after she went to bed. Took my bass with me, headed to my buddy's house, and got stoned. I was only gone for a couple hours and thought she'd never know. But when I got home, I found her sitting at the dining table, crying her eyes out, her cell phone in her hands. She'd just gotten the call about my dad."

So, that's why Ryan quit playing music. It wasn't because of school. He quit because of what happened to his father, and he felt ashamed.

"Is that why you've fought so hard to get back into Middleton?"

"I thought maybe," he says, his voice hoarse with tears, "if I throw myself into school, go into the military like Dad did, he'd be proud of me, and maybe Mom would forgive me. But no matter how many A's I get, or how many scholarships I earn, I can't forgive myself."

I notice how suddenly quiet it's gotten. There's no more thunder, no more lightning. The storm's over. I slip my arm around Ryan and kiss his cheek. How didn't I see how wonderful he is from the very beginning?

"Ryan, I'm going to ask you again. Do you want to play music?"

Ryan dries his face with the edge of his shirt then lifts Geraldine into his lap. He touches her with such tenderness it surprises me. "Yes," he answers, "more than anything."

He cradles her against him, the way Brett would hold me when I was a scared little girl.

"If you want to play," I tell him, "then do it."

"Will you come if I play?"

My heart sinks. "I want to," and I can't believe I have to say this, "but Dad plans to leave early for the airport. I'm sorry." I turn Ryan's face so that he's looking at me, and what I say next is urgent. "Swear to me you'll play Geraldine in the concert," I whisper, "that you'll find some way to be there."

"I promise," Ryan replies just as quietly.

"No," I say, more desperately. "Don't promise. *Swear.*"

I want to tell Ryan how much I care about him and that I can't stand the idea of leaving him. But I can't say anymore tonight, not without completely falling apart. And I have to be strong now. I have to face whatever comes next.

I press my lips against Ryan's, kissing him like it's the last thing I'll ever do. When we stop and look at each other, tears trail down my cheeks. Ryan gently brushes one away with his thumb.

He whispers back to me, "I swear."

RYAN

FIFTY-THREE

AFTER I WALK PENNY home, my parents return from the luncheon. I tell them about Norton's call, how the meeting with the school board has been moved to tomorrow afternoon. Mom is thrilled and goes right to my closet, choosing a blue long-sleeved Oxford for me to wear.

"Make sure you explain to the board that you've learned your lesson, that you'll follow school rules no matter what," she says while ironing the shirt. "And be prepared to tell them all about your volunteer work at the community center."

I almost tell her then what I've really been doing at the center—about BandMasterz—but I chicken out.

When I finally go to bed, what little sleep I get is tormented with bottomless black pits and me trying to claw my way out of them. When I wake up Saturday morning, it's still dark outside. The house is quiet. All I can hear is my own breathing, ragged and on edge.

I look at my clock. It's just past five a.m. After using the bathroom, I head back to my room and turn on my computer. I figure I might as well work on my presentation to the school board. I'm supposed to tell them what a good student I am, how I'm an asset to Middleton and should be given a second chance. I open a blank document, but even with Mom's suggestions, I have no idea what to say.

I stare at the screen for a while. Then I look at the pendant Penny gave me. She made me swear to play in BandMasterz today, but how can I? Norton can't change the board's schedule just for me. I haven't even told my parents about the band, let alone about the concert. And despite what I told Penny, I have serious doubts about whether I could handle it right now.

In the corner of my room, Geraldine sleeps quietly in her stand. Seeing her stirs an ache in my gut. What would Brett tell me to do? But that's just it. He wouldn't tell me what to do. He'd just play his music and let me decide. Either choice would have been fine with him.

My computer hums on the desk. Insistent. Impatient.

Someone knocks lightly on my bedroom door. It opens, and both my parents are there in their pajamas, looking through the gap with worried expressions on their faces.

"Can we come in?" Dad asks. He's leaning on a pair of crutches, his pant leg tied in a knot over his stump. He doesn't sleep with his prosthetic.

I put the computer into sleep mode. "Sure."

"I was up early," says Mom. "I saw your light on."

"I couldn't sleep."

They step into the room and close the door behind them. I guess they don't want to wake Justin. Dad hobbles to the edge of my bed and sits. Mom stays standing.

"Anything we can help with?" Dad asks.

I shake my head. "I was just trying to think of what to say to the school board today."

Mom squeezes my shoulder. "I don't think you need to worry too much about what you say. Your grades speak for themselves. They'll have to let you back in."

She's probably right. Even Norton sounded surprisingly optimistic on the phone when he called, and he was the last person I imagined would want me back at Middleton. Maybe he regrets being such a hardass. He's probably hoping I'll pin a gold medal on Middleton's lapel by getting accepted to Kings Point. Make the school proud, and all. They might as well polish me like a trophy and prop me up in their display case.

"I'm not sure about this," I say.

Mom tightens her bathrobe belt and then folds her arms. "What do you mean you're not sure?"

"I mean, I'm not sure I want to do this."

"You really don't have a choice, Ryan. The school board won't meet again for another—"

"Mom, could you stop...and just listen? Please?"

Mom looks shocked and annoyed at my request, but to her credit, she takes a seat beside my dad and says nothing more.

The courage I felt a minute ago starts to wilt. Then I think of Penny and Brett. I take a deep breath.

"There's something I need to tell you." I pause, but then keep going. "I haven't been completely honest with you. When I volunteer at the community center—"

Mom levels her eyes at me, expecting something bad, I'm sure. Dad slides his hand over hers. *Patience, Marissa.*

"—I've been helping Penny teach a basketball class to disabled kids—"

Mom relaxes.

"—and I've been playing bass guitar with a band."

I stop talking. I can see the irritation in my mom's expression and confusion in my dad's. But before either of them can make a comment, I jump right back in, telling them about how Fred needed an extra player or a band would get cut, and how I get volunteer hours for my time. I finish by telling them about the concert this afternoon.

When I'm done, Mom looks frozen next to my dad. After an awkward minute, she finally speaks.

"You've been lying to us all this time." She shakes her head. "Why doesn't this surprise me?"

Seeing her disappointment hurts. "I'm sorry about everything I've done in the past," I tell her. "I've made a lot of mistakes, but I've been trying hard to make it up to you and to Dad. You might not believe me, but helping with Bandmasters was the right thing to do. And for the first time in a long time, I've felt really good about something."

My parents are silent, taking in everything I've said. Finally, Dad says, "So, the interview today conflicts with your concert."

"Yeah," I reply.

"But if you don't go to the interview, you might not get a second chance at school."

"Then the answer is obvious," Mom says. "You have to go to the interview. Getting back to Middleton is what you've wanted, what you've worked for."

And that's the key to everything, I realize, why I was so stressed at school these past couple of years, why I resorted to pot and pills to relax.

"It's what *you* wanted, Mom," I tell her. "My going to Middleton and Kings Point is your dream, not mine."

Mom looks dumbstruck. "What are you saying?"

"I don't know what I'm saying exactly. I just—" I glance at Penny's pendant hanging over my computer. "I just want to make up my own mind about things. Maybe I'll go back to Middleton like we've planned. Maybe I want to go back to playing music. I just need to decide for myself."

Mom stares at me, mouth open. Then she turns to Dad. "Juan, do something," she says. "Talk some sense into our son."

Dad wedges his crutches beneath his armpits and hauls himself off the bed. He looks at me for a second, then turns to Mom. "Let the boy do what he needs to do," he tells her. "He'll be all right."

Mom glares at both of us, conspirators.

"Please, Mom," I say. "Just trust me."

Mom looks like I've just committed high treason, but she doesn't argue with me. Instead, she turns sharply and leaves the room. Dad starts to follow but stops when he reaches the door.

"Remember when I told you about my leg? The funny thing is, I don't regret it. Not any of it. I made a choice to be there, to fight. I knew the risks, but the risks were worth it because I knew what I wanted, and I didn't let anything or anyone get in my way. Once I made that commitment to myself, I stuck to it. Maybe it's time you did the same."

I stare at the door for a long time after Dad leaves. What did he mean, telling me to stick to my commitment? Which commitment? To Norton and the school board? To Mom? To BandMasterz? Or Penny? I can't keep them all.

Through my window, the sky starts to lighten. I can make out the distant silhouette of the mountains against the rising sun. The first spears of light creep into my room, glinting off Penny's pendant. I lift it off its thumbtack and lay it across my palm. I still want to give her something, but what?

The metal pendant is about half the size of my guitar pick with a small hole near the top for the chain. Simple really. I could even make something like this.

Wait a sec.

I open my desk drawer and grab the package of green guitar picks Penny gave me (minus the one I've been using and the one I slipped into Brett's coffin). I remove a third pick from the plastic wrap and study it. It's sturdy but not too thick. I could punch a hole through it with a small drill bit.

I look up at the sunrise, how it spills across the mountains like liquid gold, chasing away all the shadows. I grip the pendant and pick tightly in my fist.

I know what I need to do.

PENNY

FIFTY-FOUR

AFTER I LEAVE RYAN'S house Friday night, I think about him for hours. Mom and Dad spend those hours packing up boxes and making plans. I do my best to pack up my stuff as well, filling a suitcase with what I'll need for the next couple of weeks until Mom can ship the rest. But my thoughts aren't on the move. Instead, I'm thinking about what I have to do before I leave.

On Saturday morning, Tali picks me up around eight-thirty. I don't even bother telling Mom I'm going out. She understands, and besides, I'm not in the mood to explain anything. I consider asking Ryan to come along, but he's getting ready for his big day. And besides, I don't think I can handle saying goodbye again.

Tali and I don't talk much while we drive. We just listen to the radio, some oldies station playing a bunch of sappy love songs.

Tali pulls the mustang up to a battered apartment building on the south side of town. It's not the first time I've been here, but it's been a while. And it's not somewhere

I'd ever want to go again. But I have no choice, not if I'm going to fulfill Brett's final wish.

"Are you sure about this?" Tali asks. Only when I feel the steadiness of her hand over mine do I realize how much I'm shaking. "I'll go in with you if you want."

"It's fine." I'm really not sure if it is, but hopefully this will only take a minute.

I open the door and swivel my legs out of the car. "Keep the engine running." Then I get out and shut the door behind me.

The building is constructed of old bricks once painted a pale blue, but much of the paint has been chipped off or graffitied on. Despite the condition of the building, though, the grounds are nice, with a pine tree and trimmed hedges. I hurry up the front steps and through a set of glass doors. Inside the entry is an elevator and an old-fashioned staircase, but the apartment I want is on the ground floor just down the hall.

When I reach number 14A, I knock. Through the door, I can hear a TV sports announcer rattling off the score of some game. There's a *click* and metallic slide, and then the door opens a crack.

A woman's face appears, eyeing me suspiciously.

"Hi, Mrs. Dillinger," I say. "I'm Penny Tate, Brett's sister. Remember me?"

The door opens wider. Mrs. Dillinger, a heavy woman with thin, graying hair, clutches a house dress closed with her right hand and slips her left hand around me in an embrace. "Oh, Honey. I heard about what happened. I'm so sorry."

This takes me by surprise. After the incident at the mall, I expected to get the door slammed in my face. Jake and Celine's mom was always so nice to me when Brett would bring me over. I can't count the number of cookies she fed me over the years.

Mrs. Dillinger lets go of me and gives me a sad smile. "Before you say anything, I just want you to know that what happened between the boys—" She takes a shaky breath like she might cry. "I know your brother had problems. We don't harbor any ill will. I just can't stop thinking about your poor mother."

She's sincere when she says this, and I'm glad to hear it. If anyone would have reason to hold a grudge against Brett, it would be her.

"Why don't you come in?" she says more brightly. "I've a cobbler in the oven. Would you like some?"

Beyond her in the living room, the TV is on, and someone's sitting on the couch watching it. At first, I can't tell who it is, but then he turns and looks right at me. Jake's face is a collage of fading yellow and purple bruises. When our eyes connect, an arrow of acid burns right through me. But I don't look away, and neither does he.

"No, thank you, Mrs. Dillinger," I say, finally breaking away from Jake's gaze. "I'm actually here to see Celine. Is she home?"

Mrs. Dillinger leaves the door open while she goes to find Celine. Jake is still looking at me, which makes me feel beyond uncomfortable. His expression isn't what I expected, however. Not mean or threatening at all. Instead, he looks—numb.

"Penny?"

I turn to find Celine standing beside me. We stare at each other for a second, and then she wraps her arms tight around me. When she finally lets go, I notice that her cheeks are moist with tears.

"I'm so sorry I wasn't at the funeral yesterday. I wanted to come." She darts a nervous glance at Jake, who turns back to the TV. "But we didn't think it would be—appropriate."

I can tell she's rehearsed these lines, words Jake probably fed her. And he's right. After everything that happened, it would have been awkward had they shown up. I'm glad they didn't.

Her mom has disappeared down the hall, and Jake seems intent on the TV. Still, I speak quietly so no one but Celine will hear.

"I wanted to thank you," I tell her, "for telling the truth about what happened that night with Brett and your brother."

"Why wouldn't I? Jake shouldn't have said those things or pushed him like that."

"I appreciate it. I just needed to tell you that."

I reach into my coat pocket for Brett's class ring and hold it out on my palm. The thick band is white gold with a Topaz in the center. Before Celine and Brett broke up, she used to wear it on a chain around her neck.

"Brett wanted you to have this back. He left a list, and this was on it."

Celine's lips part in surprise, then she reaches for the ring. Clutching it in her fist, she starts to cry again. She takes a step closer to me, talking softly. "I really loved him, you know?"

I swallow down the hurt we're both feeling. "I know. He loved you too."

I start to leave but then hesitate. I don't want to do this. Every cell in my body wrestles against it, but I have to.

I step closer to Jake. He doesn't look at me.

"I can't imagine what you're thinking," I tell him, "whether you're glad he's gone or if you miss him. But either way, I want you to know that I don't blame you. I did at first. I hated you, in fact. But that was wrong of me. Brett wanted a second chance. He wanted your forgiveness, but you refused to give it. So, for him, I'm giving you mine."

I turn away then and hurry out of the apartment. I wish I could blame Brett's death on Jake, or my dad, or even myself. But that wouldn't be fair—to any of us. What Brett did wasn't even *his* fault. Maybe it was defective neurons, or emotional trauma, or a combination of things. Maybe he was just too good for this world. I don't know. I won't ever know.

I leave the building and make my way back to Tali's car. I have to get back home to finish packing. Tali offered to help, but there are some things I would rather handle on my own. Then there are other things no one can help me with, even if I want them to.

Losing Brett is one of those.

RYAN

FIFTY-FIVE

BY ONE O'CLOCK, I'm dressed and ready to go. I glance out my window at Penny's house, as if maybe, by some twist of fate, she's changed her mind about leaving. But her dad's rented silver Honda is in her driveway, the trunk open. Several suitcases are already in it.

There's a knock on my bedroom door. Mom pops her head in. "We need to be there in half an hour. Come down as soon as you're ready."

I try to get my head into the day, but it's hard. Nothing feels right. It'd be easier to stay home and do nothing at all, but I promised Penny I would do this.

No. I swore.

I still need to run a comb through my hair, so I start down the hall toward the bathroom. When I pass Justin's room, I look in. He's making his bed, smoothing his comforter over the mattress. We haven't said much to each other since that night at the mall when I "borrowed" the money from our jar. I spot the jar in its usual place on the windowsill, the leftover cash still in it.

I go back to my bedroom, grab the old bass Dad gave me for Christmas, and return to Justin's room.

"Justin? You got a minute?"

I find him sitting on the floor with a pile of clean bedsheets on his lap. He doesn't say anything when I come in. Instead, he reaches for his pillow, pulls off the case, and slips on a new one. He's doing his best to ignore me, but I've got something important to say.

"I'm sorry about the money, bro."

He sets the pillow on the floor beside him. "It doesn't matter," he says dejectedly.

"It matters to me. Will you forgive me?"

He doesn't answer at first. He's been glum all week, and I can't blame him for hating me.

I squat beside him on the floor. "I feel really terrible about what I did. You have every right to be angry with me, and if you don't want to forgive me, I'll understand. But you're my brother, and no one is more important in this world to me than you are. I love you, bro. So, I'm asking you to forgive me."

He thinks about it for a minute, his fingers fiddling with the corner of his pillow. "I guess so."

I smile, relieved. "Thank you, Justin," I say, tousling his hair. "But I want to make it up to you somehow. For starters, how 'bout I give you bass lessons?"

He notices the guitar in my hand for the first time. His face brightens, but he still looks skeptical. "Really? You'd do that?"

"Yeah," I say, holding out the bass to him. "Take this. It's yours, Pipsqueak."

He hesitates at first but then reaches for the guitar neck. The instrument is heavy, and his skinny arm drops from the weight of it. He wraps his other hand around it as well and hefts it into his lap. His eyes grow wide as he runs his fingers along the strings.

"Whoa," he says.

"Like I said, I'm really sorry about the wish jar," I tell him. "I promise to teach you to play bass, but you gotta be serious about it."

"Oh, I am. I am!"

"Great. First lesson is tonight. But first, there's something I gotta do."

I start to leave, but Justin jumps up and flings his arms around my waist. "Thanks!" he says, and I squeeze him back.

I hear him plunking away at the strings while I finish up in the bathroom. After I comb my hair, I check myself out in the mirror. I'm wearing the blue button-up dress shirt Mom picked out—blue for Penny's eyes—and a black tie. Not bad. This is supposed to be a big day, but all I feel is numb. Worse than numb. I feel non-existent.

My parents are waiting in the car with the engine running when I come out. I pause for a second in our yard. A splash of yellow has appeared in the garden I planted, daffodils blossoming in the afternoon sun. It's a little early in the season, but the warm weather coaxed them to bloom. So even Mom got what she wanted after all.

I go through the gate and put what I need in the trunk of the car. Justin appears at the front door to wave goodbye. He convinced Mom to let him stay home alone for an hour, which was a feat all on its own and resulted in a long 'To Do' list and a lecture about not opening the door for strangers, what to do if the house caught fire, and the hazards of the internet. By the time Mom finished with him, I think Justin wished he had decided to come with us instead.

I motion for Dad to roll down the car window.

"Can you hang on a sec?" I ask. "I'll be right back."

I start across the park toward Penny's house. Just as I reach the driveway, the front door opens, and Penny appears, hauling a suitcase down her front steps. I hurry and grab the suitcase, lugging it the rest of the way to her car.

Once it's loaded, I reach into my pants pocket for what I've brought with me.

"I've wanted to give you something ever since Christmas," I tell her, "but then there was that hat thing, and I couldn't think of anything better, and now you're leaving."

I hold up the necklace, and her eyes go wide. The 'Friend' pendant has been replaced with one of the green Picks of Destiny. For a second, I think she doesn't like it, but then she hugs me tight.

"Sorry about it being the same chain," I tell her, "but I don't really wear necklaces."

"I've noticed."

"But I put the pendant you gave me on my keychain."

This makes Penny laugh, and she slips the chain over her head.

"It's so you'll remember me," I tell her.

We kiss, long and desperate. I hate thinking that this is probably the last time I'll kiss her. The moisture from her cheeks rubs off on mine. Then I step back, our hands just touching.

"You'll keep in touch, right?" she asks.

"I'll message you every day."

I want to hold her again so badly, but time is running short.

"I have to go," I tell her, pointing a thumb at my family waiting in our car.

Penny places her warm palms against my cheeks. "You're going to be spectacular."

She kisses me once more, and I don't want it to end. But then she gently pulls away. It's time to say goodbye.

My dad has driven the car around to Penny's driveway. I jump in and slam the door shut. It takes every ounce of strength in me not to turn around and watch Penny disappear behind us.

The clock on the gymnasium wall ticks off the minutes to one-thirty as if each one was carrying its own impossible load. Time drags by. Right now, across town at Central Park, BandMasterz is getting ready to start. I try not to think about it, try to keep focused on the here and now.

I grasp the knot at my throat and tighten my tie, then run a finger around the back of my collar to make sure it's straight. I sit in a folding metal chair between Mom and

Dad, each looking as nervous as I feel. Dozens of other students and their parents sit in several parallel rows. Some intently study papers in their hands. Others mumble quietly to themselves, as if rehearsing lines from a script. Every few minutes, Principal Norton appears to call someone's name, and a kid and his parent or guardian follow him out into the hall.

I look at the clock. My time has come and gone. The board must be behind schedule.

Mom reaches over and squeezes my hand. "You'll do fine," she says.

Finally, at one-forty, Norton calls my name.

He shakes my hand when I come through the door, greets my parents the same way. Then he tells us to follow him. The four of us walk down the school hallway to a classroom. We go in. A tribunal of five adults, four men and one woman, are seated at one end of the room. Two of the men are in business suits, the others in dress shirts and ties. The woman is wearing dark slacks and a white blouse, a gauzy yellow scarf draped around her shoulders.

They introduce themselves and invite my parents to sit down. Mom and Dad take seats along with Norton on the side of the room, leaving me standing alone in the center.

"So, Mr. Rojas," says the woman, glancing at a clipboard on her lap, "we are aware of your circumstances. Principal Norton has explained what happened and has apprised us of your progress in independent study. We have reviewed your records. What we'd like to hear now is why you believe you should be reinstated as a full-time student at Middleton Academy."

The school board members all look at me, some expectantly, others with doubt in their faces. My hands start to shake, so I clench my fists at my sides and then relax them.

"In December, I made a big mistake," I begin, "one I wish I hadn't made. I'm not here to excuse what I did or try to convince you that it wasn't a big deal. What I *am* here to do is to ask you to give me a second chance."

One of the board members shifts in his chair. The metal squeaks. I continue.

"I've maintained a 4.0 grade point average since freshman year. I've gotten nothing but A's on my homeschool assignments. And you can see for yourself that my test scores are guaranteed to attract the attention of the best colleges around. I'm an asset to the school, and as a member of the Middleton student body, I promise to make you proud."

I glance at my parents. Mom is smiling. Norton nods approvingly. I turn back to the board, who are sitting up straighter now, paying attention.

"However," I continue.

Eyebrows raise. Curious expressions appear on their faces.

"I respectfully withdraw my request to be re-admitted to Middleton Academy."

There is an awkward pause while the board absorbs what I have said. After a moment, the woman speaks.

"Do I understand you correctly, that you do *not* want to return to school?"

I can sense my mom's reaction, as tangible as a shock wave.

"Yes," I tell the board. "I would, instead, ask that I be permitted to remain in the independent study program through my senior year."

I try not to look at my parents, but I can't resist stealing a glance in their direction. My mom looks stunned, her body stiff. She slides forward in her chair like she's about to stand up and march over here. But before she can do anything, Dad takes her by the arm. He looks at her and gives a slight shake of his head. Reluctantly, Mom slides back into her chair.

"I've spent some time researching my options," I continue. "First, universities are now accepting more homeschool students than ever before, and that includes Kings Point—*if* I decide to apply. Second, by doing my schoolwork at home, I'll have more—" I stand straighter, my confidence growing "—more time for my music."

Next to my parents, Norton sits rigidly, his left toe nervously tapping the floor.

"It is an odd request," says the woman on the board, "but not unreasonable. But may I ask what changed your mind?"

This is the hard part.

"Despite how it looks," I begin, "my decision isn't sudden. I've wanted to study music for as long as I can remember. But I've made mistakes along the way, like getting into drugs, which I swear is over. I've been clean since the day I left Middleton." I look at Mom when I say this. I want to make sure she knows I'm telling the truth.

"My other mistake was quitting music. For a long time, I beat myself up over what happened to my dad. I thought giving up what I loved and doing what I thought my parents wanted me to do would make things right. But all it did was make me miserable."

I should feel nervous, but all the tension I felt a few minutes ago is gone. I've never felt surer about anything in my life.

"So, if it's all right with you, and with my parents, I'd like to continue doing what I'm doing."

The woman turns to the other board members. They exchange quick whispers. Then she turns back to face the rest of us.

"Principal Norton, do you have any issue with allowing Mr. Rojas to remain on independent study?"

Norton slides a hand down his tie. "Well, it isn't something we normally do. There are some special cases, of course, though I can't think of any reason why—" He stops. Glances at each of the board members. "No," he says more confidently. "That would not be a problem."

"And what about you, Mr. and Mrs. Rojas?"

I glance at my parents and see them looking at each other, communicating the way they sometimes do without words. Finally, it's Mom who responds.

"If this is what Ryan really wants," she says, giving me a reassuring smile, "then it's fine with us."

"Good," says the woman. "The board will need to discuss your request in private. We'll get back to you in a few days with our final decision, but I think you can expect an affirmative response."

I let out a lungful of air in relief. I feel as though a two-ton boulder has been removed from my shoulders. My parents and I thank the board and Principal Norton, and then we leave the classroom.

Once we're in the hall, I face my Mom. "Thank you."

"For what?" she asks.

"For letting me decide."

An awkward moment passes, and for a second, I think Mom's going to let me have it. But instead, she sighs.

"I'd be lying if I said I wasn't *a little* disappointed," she begins. "But this morning after we left your room, Dad and I talked about it, and, well—" she darts an appreciative glance at my dad "—we agree you're old enough to make your own choices. Just promise me you'll make good ones."

"I will, Mom." I give her a hug. She hugs me back.

My dad clears his throat. "I don't mean to break up this touching moment, but if we don't hurry, you're going to be late."

"What time is it?" I ask while loosening my tie.

"Ten after two."

Dad leads the way to the parking lot. The car beeps as he unlocks the doors. He reaches for the door handle when Mom puts a hand on his shoulder.

"I'll drive," she says.

"Mom?" I ask, surprised she'd want to.

"Sorry, Juan, but if Ryan's going to make that concert, we'd better step on it. And let's face it," she adds, "I'm a better driver than you."

Dad slaps a hand against his chest, pretending to be wounded. I slip my tie out from under my collar, and we all climb into the car. Mom starts the engine and shoves the gearshift into drive. Then she adjusts the rear-view mirror, and our eyes connect.

"Let's do this!" she says and peels out of the parking lot.

PENNY

FIFTY-SIX

AFTER TALI AND I dropped off Brett's ring to Celine, Dad and I spend the rest of the morning helping Mom put more of our things into boxes. She'll be staying here long enough to finish her two weeks at the hospital and apply for new jobs, then she'll be driving to Florida.

Ryan came by while we were loading the car and gave me a pick on a chain, one of the best gifts he could have ever given me. I know he thinks this is a fair trade for the pendant I gave him at Christmas, but the truth is, the pendant hadn't meant anything to me. The "friend" I'd shared it with hadn't been a friend in a long time. When I gave it to Ryan, I was just saying thank you. Thank you for decorating my house for Christmas, and for caring enough about me to do it. But then, later, I came to realize that Ryan had actually given the word friend meaning again. He cared not only about me, but about Brett. And although I failed to keep Brett safe, Ryan had given Brett a reason to live, even if just for those few short weeks. I think if it wasn't for Ryan and playing music again, Brett might have left us sooner.

Outside the house, I hear the noise of a gathering crowd and the sounds of guitars tuning up. BandMasterz is getting started. I wish we could stay to listen, but Dad says we've got to get on the road.

Mom gives me a long hug goodbye and presses a kiss into my scalp, just the way Brett always did.

"Text me once you land," she says. "And I expect a call every day."

"I will, Mom."

"I should be there in three weeks tops."

Dad and I get into the car, and Mom watches from the driveway as we pull away from the curb. As we leave the cul-de-sac, I roll down my car window. All traces of yesterday's storm are gone. The sky is a brilliant blue, and the air is warm and lazy. I look at the clock. Two. The concert is set to begin any second.

We reach the end of the street and turn onto the main thoroughfare. The freeway isn't far, and from there it's an hour and a half to the airport. But we'll still be getting there two hours before our flight, since Dad says it's good to have a cushion of time.

The farther we get from home, the more my mind spins with everything that's happened. From the run-in with Jake at the mall, my first kiss with Ryan, Tali's failed date, finding Ryan in the park, Brett's suicide. My mind finally settles on that last memory of Ryan, soaked through with rain, throwing his arms around me, and holding me tight. I close my eyes, and I can still feel him pressed against me. I reach up and rub my thumb against the smooth plastic of the Pick of Destiny.

What if I never see him again? What if he doesn't really know how I feel about him? He and I have shared something that few others have. We had Brett.

"Dad?" I ask as we head up the on-ramp onto the freeway.

"Yes, Penny?"

"Do we really need to get to the airport two hours early?"

He considers my question for a moment. "I like to have plenty of time, just in case, but I guess we have some time to spare. Why? Is there somewhere you want to go first?"

I lay my forearm across the open window and lean my face into the breeze blowing into the car. I take a deep breath of the fresh afternoon air.

"Yeah, Dad," I say. "Would you mind turning around?"

RYAN

FIFTY-SEVEN

THE STAGE FOR today's show is the park's outside amphitheater up the hill from the community center. Most of the seats are already filled, and the concert is well underway by the time we arrive. Mom says she and Dad might as well park at home and walk over, but first, she drops me and Dad off at the curb.

I run around to the back of the car, pop open the trunk, and extract Geraldine from her nylon case. Then I wave to my parents and run backstage. There are six bands playing today. Ours was originally scheduled to go first, but thanks to a quick phone call to Fred, we're now second.

I spot William on the sidewalk, tuning his guitar.

"Thanks for waiting," I tell him.

He breathes out in relief when he sees me. "Man, I'm glad you showed up. I was beginning to think we'd have do this without you."

"Never. Ready for this?"

"Ready as I'll never be," he says.

"Nervous?"

"Nah." His grin gets wider. "Yeah, just a little."

He tucks his guitar pick into his strings and rests an arm over the body. "Fred told us about Brett. We're all really sorry."

"Thanks," I reply. "I appreciate it."

Khiem joins us a minute later, twirling his drumsticks like miniature batons. "Where's Dana?"

"Right here," says Dana, coming up behind him. She makes a beeline toward me and doesn't even pause before wrapping her arms around me. "You all right?"

"I'm okay," I tell her, but she gives me a look that says she knows better. "Thank you, guys," I add. "The truth is I'm not entirely okay, but I will be. Really. I can't tell you how much I appreciate this."

Khiem pushes a friendly fist into my shoulder. Dana gives my arm a squeeze. "No biggie," she says. "It's a full house out there, and word has it the mayor is here. Can you believe it? The mayor! And the local news crew."

"Great," says William. "You had to tell us that? Now I'm so nervous I'm gonna puke."

Fred joins us, rubbing his hands together. "You ready, gang? You're up in five. I'll be announcing you soon. What name do you want me to give?"

William groans. Khiem bangs his sticks together.

A name. We still don't have a name.

"Tyger, Tyger," I say. "With 'y's instead of 'i's."

Fred scribbles it down on the palm of his hand. "You got it," he says, then melts into the crowd of other performers.

"Tyger, Tyger?" asks Dana. "Where'd you come up with that?"

"It's from a poem."

"I like it."

"All right, guys," says William. "We'd better get on stage and plug in."

We head to the platform, and William and I plug into the amps. Khiem does a few warm-up drum rolls while Dana tries out some chords on the keyboard. From up here, I can see the entire audience. There's the camera crew off to the side, just like Dana said, taking pictures of an important-looking man in a blue suit.

Scattered throughout the audience, I see some faces I recognize—a few from school, and several of the kids in Penny's basketball team, including Danny and Julia. When I called Fred earlier, he asked if I knew Penny was moving. When I told him I did, he asked if I'd be interested in taking over the class for a while, since the kids know me, and it would take a while to find a replacement. I told him no replacement was needed, and that I'd be there on Tuesday.

Mom waves at me from the third row, where she's just found a seat. Justin is with her now, but where is Dad? It's great having them all here, but the fact is, it's not what I had imagined it would be because Brett and Penny *aren't*.

A wave of fear smashes into me. What if I screw this up? What if I can't remember the songs? What if—

Someone taps me on my shoulder. I turn to find Dad standing beside me, holding my cell phone.

"It's for you," he says.

I take it from him. It's fully charged and has been cleaned up. There's a call on hold.

"When you're through," he continues, "keep it. And, son?"

"Yeah, Dad?"

"Break a leg."

Dad musses my hair and then joins Mom in the audience. I bring the phone to my ear.

"Hello?"

"Hey!"

It's Penny!

"So, I thought I'd call to see how BandMasterz is going. Your dad gave me your number. Hope that's okay."

"Of course it is! We're about to go on, actually," I tell her. In truth, my stomach is flip-flopping like a fish on a boat deck, whether from nerves or excitement about talking to Penny, I don't know.

"That's so awesome! Keep me on. I want to hear you play."

"Okay. Hold on."

I set my cell down on the corner of the stage, propping it against a support pole. I look again at the audience, where Dad has found a spot next to Mom. When he sees me, he salutes. I salute back.

Fred steps up to the platform and taps on the mic.

"That was Stratosphere! Nice job, guys," he says. The audience claps. Then he continues. "So, today we have a total of six awesome bands with some of the best young musicians around. For some, this is their second or even third performance. For others, this is their first. But they've all been working really hard to get ready for this. Now it's my pleasure to announce our next band. We've got Khiem

Duong on drums, William Hall on guitar, Dana Rodriguez on vocals and keyboard, and Ryan Rojas on bass! I give you Tyger, Tyger!"

The crowd goes wild, screaming and clapping. The sound fills me with energy, heat surging through every vein from my brain down to my fingertips. I take a second and let Brett and Penny roll through my mind. Today is for them, and for me, and for anyone out there who needs it.

Khiem makes eye contact with the rest of us and gives just the slightest tip of his head, our signal that we're about to begin.

And then I see it—a silver Honda pulls into the parking lot, stopping behind the crowd of people. The back door opens, and someone gets out and starts pushing her way through the screaming audience. She gets as far as the fifth row and waves her arm in the air—a cell phone clutched in her hand.

It's Penny.

"Hang on a sec," I tell Khiem, then I snatch up my phone. "Penny? What are you doing here? I thought you weren't going to come?"

I'm looking right at her, and she's beaming at me with those amazingly blue eyes. And even from here, I can see the lime green guitar pick hanging on the chain around her neck.

"I just had to come," she laughs. "I convinced Dad we could spare twenty minutes, but we're heading to the airport right after your set. We'll be cutting it close, but we'll make it."

"Ryan, c'mon!" says Dana.

"I'm coming," I answer back. Then, into the phone, I say, "When I'm done, promise me you'll wait long enough for me to kiss you goodbye."

There's a slight pause, then Penny says, "I swear."

I see Penny tuck away her phone and grab a seat next to my family. In the next second, Khiem counts us off. I grip my Pick of Destiny and the first notes of Queen's 'Under Pressure' explode from the speakers. The nerves I felt before transform into a sort of power that pumps through me. I look out across the audience where Penny, my family, and almost everyone are whooping and cheering as loudly as they would if they were in a real concert. Seeing them gives me the courage I never thought I'd find.

A warm breeze picks up as I play the song, and I look at Penny. Maybe we'll find a way to visit each other next summer, or maybe today is the last time I'll ever see her. I don't know. All that matters is that right now, in this moment, I'm playing for her, for Brett, for all of us. It's the most awesome feeling I've ever felt before, and I know without a doubt this performance will be nothing short of memorable.

THE END

ACKNOWLEDGMENTS

ON FEBRUARY 23, 2011, my neighbor rented a gun at a local gun club and shot himself in the head.

He and I were more than acquaintances, though not close enough to call ourselves friends. My family ate dinner at his house once, we occasionally chatted over the wall separating our driveways, and my husband helped him in dealing with his disgruntled ex. Brian was gentle and soft-spoken, always kind to my kids, and openly professed his faith in God. He had never married but shared his home with many in need. I liked Brian. We all did.

When he came to our house one afternoon with news that he was moving out of the country, my husband thought the announcement a bit extraordinary. But Brian explained that he had gotten a job in South America. Who were we to question him? He asked if we wanted any of his belongings—tools, books, clothes, anything. My husband politely declined. We had more than enough stuff of our own. But he wished Brian well and closed the door.

It was the last time anyone in our family saw him.

A few days later, we saw a sheriff's car parked in front of Brian's house. Something wasn't right. Later, we ventured over to ask one of his roommates what had happened. Needless to say, we were more than stunned when we learned that Brian had taken his own life. We were devastated. My kids took it very hard. Until she moved out of state, my oldest daughter visited Brian's grave each year on the anniversary of his death. We never have fully come to grips with the *why*.

What has disturbed me the most over the years since Brian's death was the nagging feeling that we should have known better. My family is not completely ignorant about depression and the signs of suicidal behavior. Brian had expressed dissatisfaction with his life on numerous occasions. He was depressed, and then he became resolved. He gave away his things. All warning signs we should not have ignored. But even while those signs were flashing red, we failed to see them until it was too late.

More recently, I was struck by the tragedy of actor Robin Williams' suicide in 2014. Who would have suspected someone so famous, who made a living from making other people smile, would do such a thing? And I too frequently hear about young people taking their own lives because of bullying or depression or whatever. One day at school, my son's teacher tearfully announced that his cousin had killed herself the previous night. And over the past year, two of my kids' friends revealed that other friends had done the same.

In America, someone commits suicide every 13 seconds. Each death by suicide is a loss felt by us all. And every life lost to suicide is a life that should have, could have been saved.

Depression and other forms of mental illness that contribute to depression are treatable. Unfortunately, there is a lingering stigma attached to them. Too many people who suffer, suffer in silence. They fail to seek the treatment they need because they are afraid of what others might think of them. Some refuse to even admit they need help because, in their eyes, to do so is to be weak.

I understand the power of stigma. I used to believe depression wasn't real and that those who claimed to be depressed could choose to feel better if they wanted to. But after coming face-to-face with depression and suicidal behavior through close family members, and after losing our neighbor, I don't believe that anymore. I now believe we must, as an entire community, fight to erase the stigma of depression and mental illness so that everyone who needs help can get it.

That is why I support **Bring Change 2 Mind**, a non-profit organization founded by actress Glenn Close. Bring Change 2 Mind's mission is to erase the stigma of mental illness once and for all.

I wish to thank Ms. Close and her organization for all the good they are doing to help people like Brian recognize that they are part of the human family and deserve to be treated fairly.

I also wish to thank my children, Carissa and Marc, for reading early drafts of this book and providing valuable feedback, even though it hit so close to home that it made them cry. Thank you to my husband for believing in me and in this story, for my parents for encouraging my dream, and to my other children—Stuart, Brennah, and Jarett—for enduring the countless hours I spent at my computer.

Thank you to my friends and early SCBWI critique partners, Cheryl Sena and Alex Little, for all your insights; to my graduate professor, Leilani Hall, for sharing your personal story with me and for planting the seed of *Memorable* in my mind; to beautiful, confident Bella, who has no idea that she has been woven into this story but without whom Penny could never have existed; to Dorine White, Judi Lauren, Gina Panietteri, Lisa Green, Prathima Radhakrishnan, Bryon Quertermous, and Mary Kole for your feedback and suggestions that helped shape this story over many years. Much appreciation to my beta readers: Renee Schultz, Angelica Seifert, Erin Suk, Prasanthi Kunamaneni and Analyn Boydston. And a deeply felt thanks to Amanda Lindsay for allowing me to take notes during your basketball game.

My apologies to anyone for whom this story is too painful to bear. My heart goes out to you. I hope that by sharing Brett's story, someone someday will get the rescue they need.

If you or someone you know is considering suicide, please get help. Call the National Suicide Prevention Lifeline now: 1-800-273-TALK (8255) or visit them online: http://www.suicidepreventionlifeline.org/
Thank you.

—Laurisa White Reyes

Thank you for reading

MEMORABLE

We invite you to post a review on
Goodreads
& your favorite online book retailer.

For a free e-book, join our mailing list at:
www.SkyrocketPress.com

ABOUT THE AUTHOR

LAURISA WHITE REYES is the author of twenty-three books, including the SCBWI Spark Award-winning novel *THE STORYTELLERS* and the Spark Honor recipient *PETALS*. She is also the Senior Editor at Skyrocket Press and an English instructor at College of the Canyons in Southern California.

www.LaurisaWhiteReyes.com
www.SkyrocketPress.com